Roscommon Downs

Bill Noonan OAM

First published by Busybird Publishing 2021

Copyright © 2021 Bill Noonan, william.noonan@bigpond.com

ISBN
978-1-922465-60-3 (paperback)

This work is copyright. Apart from any use permitted under the *Copyright Act 1968*, no part of this publication may be reproduced, stored in a retrieval system or transmitted in any form or by any means, electronic, mechanical, photocopying, recording or otherwise, without the prior written permission of Bill Noonan.

Cover Image: Pexels
Cover design: Busybird Publishing
Layout and typesetting: Busybird Publishing

Busybird Publishing
2/118 Para Road
Montmorency, Victoria
Australia 3094
www.busybird.com.au

Dedicated to Colleen

Contents

Chapter 1

Plenty of Cheek

'He's a winner, Mum!' Will said as he and Mary O'Rourke walked from the horse holding area to the sales barn. 'Big and strong with plenty of muscle and tons of attitude.'

'I can see he thinks he owns the place, Will.'

'Yep, he's got plenty of cheek alright, and the vet assures me that he's physically sound. His racing record confirms a good competitor who can handle the long distances on the flat, and his breeding suggests that with the proper training he could race as a hurdler and steeplechaser.'

'Well, that's what I want. It's time for me to join my friends and take the step into racehorse ownership.'

In the knowledge that Will had become somewhat of an expert in racehorse breeding and bloodlines, Mary was prepared to buy the black five year old gelding her son had selected in the forthcoming auction. Following hours of research studying the 1985 mid-year sales catalogue, Will had developed a list which they had agreed to pursue.

This had led to many long days traipsing around stables in gumboots, enduring the pungent odour of hay and manure to inspect the various horses on offer. And with the assistance of Eric Conroy, a wiry ex jockey, good friend and local horse trainer, Mary was comfortable with the choice they'd made. She was however aware of Eric's disapproval about the price they were willing to pay.

Drawn to the horse's clear steady gaze and calm demeanour, while he in turn was obviously making his own assessment of potential buyers, Mary made a quiet note not to mention that one of the reasons she was attracted to the horse was because she liked his eyes. Her friends would have a good laugh if this information were to become public knowledge.

Mary had always been keen to retain sole ownership of her prized gelding who would assist her to take her place in the Castle Hill social set. She was aware that some owners, being unable to agree on a horse's training regime or racing program, had fallen out while members of a syndicate. However, given that Will was now twenty, Mary decided that should the bid be successful she would list her son as a joint owner. It was also a small reward for all the research he had done.

When taking her seat in the sales barn waiting for the horse to be paraded, she quietly reminded Will of their budget, knowing full well that the excitement of the auction might influence him to overbid. 'Now, you know our maximum bid.'

'No worries Mum, all under control. I won't break our bank.'

A quick look around the large auditorium satisfied Mary that many of the earlier buyers had left, probably moving to the food trucks and beer tent. However, she would continue in her nervous state until the horse was safely stabled at her farm, Roscommon Downs.

Her attention was drawn to the sales ring as the well-dressed and red-faced auctioneer commenced. 'Ladies and gentlemen, I give you lot eighty-nine,' and in what seemed to Mary a flurry of fast talking, yelling and arm waving, Will managed to buy the horse at a reasonable price and under budget.

'Well, there you go Mum! We have our horse. Let's hope he lives up to the promise he's shown. I'll put him in the float so we can leave and settle him in at home before it gets dark.'

Relieved and happy with the success of the day, Mary while gathering her handbag and catalogue replied, 'Okay, I'll lodge the cheque and we can be on our way.'

*

When Will eased the car and horse float onto the highway, Mary felt a great sense of pride in the ability of her son to get things done. Tall for his age and quietly spoken, he had grown into a well built and handsome young man. With a ready smile and mop of dark wavy hair, the likeness to his father was evident. Likewise, Mary was aware that he had inherited her eyes, regular facial features and capable demeanour.

As she readied herself for the trip home, Mary's thoughts turned to her journey to live in Castle Hill, the circumstances of which she struggled from time to time to comprehend. As too was how she ended up running a large sheep property. Her quiet reflections were interrupted by an excited Will, 'Wasn't that terrific, Mum? We got the horse we wanted at a fair price. I'm sure Eric will be pleased.'

'Yes, I must admit Will, I was a bit confused. I'm pleased you knew what was going on. It's been a long day and I'm now looking forward to a good night's sleep.'

As the kilometres passed, Mary was reminded of her meeting with Roscommon Downs' previous owners, Dan and Monica Flanagan, and all that had followed. Now in her mid-forties, she was grateful for the strong bond she enjoyed with Will. But life had not always been as good, and she often wondered if her ownership of the property was as the result of fate, or somehow preordained by a greater power.

Chapter 2

With the Sisters

Mary O'Rourke never knew her parents.

Abandoned at birth, the newborn baby was left on the front steps of St Cuthbert's Orphanage in St Kilda, a bayside suburb of Melbourne. Pinned to her shawl was a scribbled note revealing her name and date of birth – August 1st, 1941.

Mary's formative years lived, under the discipline of the Sisters of the Cross, an old religious order dedicated to the care of girls, ensured her of a good education and a sheltered upbringing. The orphanage built as an addition to the already existing church and school being constructed in a style to complement the other buildings, featured high ceilings and large windows. Dormitory accommodation was provided, and the girls were moved to more private areas when teenagers.

Slate floors created the need for an urgent priority in winter – the lighting of the pot belly stoves which also served as water heaters. Summer days were especially uncomfortable with no means of cooling the building. Thankfully, the nearby beach was available to assist in coping with extreme temperatures.

Mary's early years were post-war. While food was subject to rationing, the Sisters were excellent managers ensuring the girls were well looked after. Work in cooking and cleaning was expected. The nuns maintained a strict regime of peace and order, yet not all the children acted with respect and petty theft within the orphanage was a constant concern.

Good educators, the nuns and lay teachers encouraged the children to use the small school library. Mary enjoyed reading and learning. And as the years progressed, she was also trained in the basic skills of bookkeeping and secretarial work.

Each child carried the same sadness never knowing the enjoyment of a family's love and care. They lived in the hope that a parent might return or that they would be taken in for adoption. Mary was no exception. She prayed that if there was no hope of ever being claimed by a parent then perhaps a sister or brother might come in search of her. But as time went by, she resigned herself to the fact that this would not occur and knew the need would arise in the future to make ready to leave when eighteen and establish her life the best way she could.

Although shyness had always been a problem, Mary befriended some of the other girls. Agnes Wright, a year younger, often accompanied her whenever able to leave the orphanage without a supervisor. These days were keenly anticipated and allowed them to attend a movie or shopping trip, with outings restricted by how far they could stretch their allowance.

However, they were not restrained from window shopping and spent many hours in the city arcades, just a short tram ride away, admiring dresses and fashion accessories priced well out of their reach.

The busy streets of Melbourne were filled with energy as the city readied itself for a royal visit and to host the Olympic Games. Athletes from competing nations wore colourful clothing and carried a heightened anxiousness as they prepared themselves to compete in the various sports. With the games to be televised for the first time, Mary and Agnes squeezed in amongst the crowded fans who huddled around department store windows watching test events and rehearsals on newly arrived TV sets.

Members of the community queued in the hope of being selected as a support volunteer. Although keen to be involved, the girls were disappointed on their return to the orphanage to be told by the Sisters that they were too young to apply. However, they enjoyed attending some of the lead-up competitions which were held at venues close to the orphanage. Watching the athletes train sparked the girls' interest in world travel and on the return tram ride home to the orphanage they discussed the day's events.

'It must be exciting to go overseas and see the places we've read about don't you think, Mary?'

'Perhaps one day we could go together, Agnes. London would be one of my favourite places to visit. We've all seen pictures of Buckingham Palace. We might even be lucky enough to catch a glimpse of the Queen.'

'What about Hollywood? Just imagine going to MGM Studios where all the film stars hang out.'

Mary nudged her friend with her elbow. 'I bet I know who you would most like to see. You've always been in love with Gregory Peck.'

Agnes laughed, 'You're right Mary. I adore Gregory Peck.'

It was always a joy to have a change away from the disciplined orphanage environment. A favourite day for Mary was a visit to the Sunday markets where she could sort through what was on offer at the jewellery stalls. Occasionally she would identify a piece in a collection. This gave her the chance to haggle the price down and pick up something within her tiny budget. The puppies on sale never missed out on receiving a cuddle from Mary who promised herself that one day she'd be able to buy her own.

But the movies were her first love. Mary loved the design and furnishings of the theatres as each in its own way reflected Hollywood glamour with hidden lighting, statues and plush curtains. After the austerity of the orphanage, it was a pleasure to feel thick carpet underfoot and sink into a welcoming seat. She enjoyed the moment the lights dimmed and following previews of forthcoming attractions, the opportunity to become engrossed in the film.

Unlike most patrons who were keen to exit at the conclusion, Mary waited to read the movie credits and enjoy the music, prior to a short walk along Collins Street to the Wild Cherry Cafe. She liked the friendly atmosphere and the surrounding wood panelled walls which were covered in photographs of her favourite movie stars. The mostly female serving staff, also keen movie goers made her welcome. Aware that she had been to the movies, Mary would be asked, 'What did you see today? Were you on your own or did Agnes have you watching a Gregory Peck movie?'

'On my own today ladies. I had to settle for William Holden. It was a bit of a come down from Gregory Peck.'

A happy discussion followed regarding the picture show. The conversation would then inevitably swing over to football and her favourite team. Never having been interested in the game, Mary decided to adopt the Richmond Club as the one she would follow so she could carry a conversation. The next time she visited the market, she purchased a cheap pair of yellow and black earrings to confirm her support.

Given the friendships she had developed with some of the older members of the staff, Mary occasionally assisted in clearing the tables after the lunchtime rush, while participating in some friendly banter with the owner and workers.

There was never any offence intended and she looked forward to staying back after the work was completed to enjoy an extra cup of tea. Indeed, the café became something of a second home for her. Mary was constantly impressed when watching the kitchen staff simultaneously preparing many different meals. On one occasion she asked the chef, 'How do you keep track of all the meals without burning something?'

'It's the skill a short-order cook develops, Mary,' he replied, then added with a smile, 'We learn where to hide our mistakes.'

*

For most of Mary's life, she felt she had kept out of trouble and always tried to do as expected. The days started early with morning prayers. The breakfast table had to be laid, the dishes cleared, beds made, and dormitories tidied, all before the school day began at 9 am. There were rosters, rules and bells to obey and only once could she recall a summons to the office when she had overslept and refused to get out of bed.

Retaining one's privileges was reliant on good behaviour.

So, imagine Mary's shock when one day she returned to the orphanage following a visit to the city and was immediately ushered into Sister Paula's office.

Confronted by a uniformed police officer, he began to question her movements on the previous Saturday. Embarrassed, flustered and on the verge of tears. Mary recalled her day. 'I saw a movie and then spent the rest of the afternoon at the Wild Cherry. I'm sure that my friends at the café will tell you I was there.'

Jotting down the relevant details in his notepad, the officer replied, 'You are not under suspicion. We're just working through the local area as there has been a spate of robberies at the orphanage and nearby houses.'

Noticing Mary's distress, Sister Paula intervened and motioned her to sit on the couch. Aware of the ticking of the clock, Mary took a moment to become a little more composed. 'I know that things have been stolen from other girls and so I'm always careful to secure my locker. I'd hate to lose any of my jewellery. It's not worth much, just a small collection from the market.'

The policeman asked, 'Do you have a pair of yellow and black earrings, Mary?'

'I do!' she nodded. 'I usually wear them to the footy. My friend, Agnes Wright and I go to a couple of games each season, but we haven't been this year. Do you want me to get them? I keep them safely with my other pieces.'

Protective of her young charge, Sister Paula again interrupted. 'No, that won't be necessary, Mary. Sadly, this sort of activity brings everyone under suspicion.' The Sister then turned to the officer as if to cut him short. 'I hope none of our girls are involved.'

'I'm certain that's not the case, Sister. You can be sure that we'll find whoever's responsible.'

'Well allow me to see you to the front door,' Sister Paula said as she excused Mary from the office.

Wanting to be certain that her earrings were in place, Mary went straight upstairs to check her locker. She knew that although the earrings were only a cheap purchase at the market, she didn't want there to be any doubt as to her innocence. But a search of her jewellery box and the shelves of her locker proved fruitless.

Fighting back tears, she rushed downstairs and explained to Sister Paula that her earrings were missing. 'Someone must have taken them while I was out. I don't want to get into trouble, Sister. Will the policeman believe me?'

'It's good that you've told the truth, Mary. Don't worry. I trust your honesty. So, there's no need for tears. Let's be patient and see what happens.'

What Mary didn't know at the time was that a similar earring had been found in a nearby home where several other items were also stolen. The police as part of their investigation, had approached Sister Paula and given the distinctive black and yellow nature of the earring, the trail had led back to Mary.

The following day, Sister Paula happily explained that the police had caught some women selling goods in a secondhand store among which was a single yellow and black earring. When questioned the women admitted to being involved in a string of robberies as suspected in both the orphanage and the local area.

Placing a reassuring hand on Mary's arm, Sister Paula said, 'Just to be clear, your honesty was never in doubt, Mary. But I hope you have learnt some valuable life lessons.'

'Thank you Sister, I certainly have. To be branded a thief, is the last thing I want. I'll be extra careful to keep my things secure and cautious in the future about who I should trust.'

Chapter 3

An Offer

Despite the sisters being firm in their manner, they regarded the girls as family and were sad to see them leave. It was their usual practice to organise a special day to celebrate a birthday. As Mary's eighteenth birthday neared, Sister Paula arranged a morning tea.

Taking the opportunity to address the assembled staff and girls, she said, 'Well Mary, you're now eighteen and it's time to leave our care. Many girls come to the orphanage. We treasure those who, like you, are polite and hardworking. Our younger students have benefitted from your advice and example. We are proud of you. You'll be missed by everyone.'

While Mary was not keen on being the centre of attention and much preferring a quiet parting, she replied, 'Thank you for your care Sister and your kindness in helping me to make a fresh start. It's going to be hard to leave the orphanage which has been my home. I'm going to miss you all.'

With a tear in her eye, Sister Paula said, 'Girls, let's hear three cheers for Mary and wish her well in her new career.'

The cheering, applause and emotion in the room brought many to tears. As the sisters and girls said their private good-byes, Mary knew she would miss their friendship, guidance and emotional support. But most of all Mary would miss the littlies just starting out for whom she held a special attachment.

Without parents to run and cling to in times of need, life could be especially hard when so young. She gently placed a hand on each of their heads as she bent down to hug every child individually.

*

Notwithstanding that she had enjoyed excursions from the orphanage, Mary usually found the hustle and bustle of Melbourne confronting. But while she was inexperienced in the ways of the city, there was no going back to the orphanage, and what she lacked in experience was more than compensated in a determination to establish a successful future.

Her immediate future at the Rex Hotel located close to the orphanage, included employment and accommodation. Mary was aware of the long-standing arrangement that existed between the sisters and hotel management to assist the girls to make a fresh start. The nuns were also comfortable in the knowledge that the known clientele were country people who considered the medium tariff hotel a home away from home, with many having a permanent booking during the Royal Melbourne Show and the Melbourne Cup Carnival.

Mary had no hesitation in taking this opportunity, as it was a welcoming place where she could renew friendships among the girls who had moved there from the orphanage.

The manager, Molly Smith, while climbing the stairs to show Mary to her room, explained her duties and made it clear that the only thing expected was for members of the staff to perform their work, and act responsibly while living at the hotel. 'We prefer that you don't allow anyone in your room, Mary. Management has had some difficult situations arise due to employees entertaining visitors, particularly after hours. So, we decided on a complete ban.'

'That's fine Mrs Smith; I won't give you any problems,' Mary replied as she entered the bedroom and placed her suitcase down.

Molly pulled aside the curtains to let in the daylight through a small window that overlooked the street. 'I hope you'll be comfortable here, Mary. The bathroom is just down the hallway and you have a tiny sink. The laundry maid will collect and replace your towel and linen each Monday morning.'

'Thank you, Molly.'

Molly wandered back towards the doorway. 'I'll leave you now to get settled.'

Mary waited until the door closed and then tested the mattress on the small brass bed pressed snuggly against the papered wall under the eaves. The springs were a little squeaky, but the mattress was soft and cosy. Although sparsely furnished the room was hers and had everything she needed. A table and chair, a wardrobe with mirrored doors and a small chest of drawers. Mary was delighted and set about unpacking her few possessions. As she hung her clothes in the wardrobe, she resolved to buy herself some flowers to brighten the surroundings a little and make the place her own.

*

The Rex, being located close to the railway station, enabled guests to leave their cars in the hotel garage. While not furnished to the style and level of the large city hotels, the rooms and reception areas were nonetheless comfortable and welcoming. Mary thought this made for a nice change from the austere and practical surroundings of the orphanage and was more than happy to experience the luxury and warmth of carpet beneath her feet. Also now earning a weekly wage and living without cost at the hotel, she would be able to join the other girls on their nights out.

After a busy week, an excited gathering would convene each Saturday evening in the foyer so they could travel together to the Hawthorn Town Hall dance – a firm favourite of Mary. Ballroom dancing to the big band music drew a happy and enthusiastic crowd. The classes conducted for an hour before the main part of the evening commenced, opened new opportunities as Mary was quick to learn the steps making her a keenly sought partner. Her ability was soon recognised as she progressed from student to teacher and performed in the exhibition team.

Thrilled with this turn of events, Mary's confidence grew. Making new friends among her group led to additional outings, and special evenings to recognise each other's birthdays.

Deciding to take up an offer to enter a dance competition with her regular partner Glyn Harris, Mary loved the challenge and the keen anticipation she felt leading up to the event.

'This week it's the Modern Waltz, Mary. We should start out with something that really catches the eye, and I think the new pivots and spins we've been working on will be just the thing.' Glyn suggested. 'There'll be some stiff competition, but if we dance well there's no reason why we can't win.'

Mary felt so pleased with the way she looked after going into the city and buying herself a lovely blue dress with a full gathered skirt. She twirled around in front of the mirror in the powder room when she thought no one was looking and applied a further touch of rouge to her cheeks.

The event was conducted during the interval period with those competing receiving warm applause. As the music began Glyn guided Mary straight into the pivots and spins while others were still taking their positions and slow to make a start. All eyes were on them as Glyn provided a strong lead sweeping his partner around the floor with ease. The rhythm of the big band carried them along, and Mary felt like Cinderella at the ball. She was floating on air exhilarated with their performance. When the dance concluded Glyn spun her out into a curtsy, bowed and gave her a beaming smile. She held his arm tightly as they left the dance floor.

As he produced a large white handkerchief to wipe the perspiration from his brow, he was full of praise for Mary's dancing. 'There you go Mary, you were terrific, not nervous, the best partner I've had.'

'I loved every minute Glyn. You certainly know your way around the dance floor,' Mary said, as they were congratulated and encouraged by their friends who suggested they were robbed because they didn't win a trophy. Mary laughed as it was only their first competition and she hoped that further opportunities would present, and they could try again.

*

After twelve months employment at the Rex Hotel with a strong commitment to her duties, Mary felt well settled, having now achieved a grounding in all aspects of hospitality. Recognised as a future manager, she was on occasions left in charge.

She was also thrilled to be joined at the Rex Hotel by tall and blonde Agnes Wright with her bright personality. While the other girls were good company it would be so good to have her best friend to confide in and share in all the fun. Mary's senior position at the Rex provided her the chance to show Agnes the ropes. 'Just think Aggie, we can see so many more movies now you are earning a wage and we're both free to please ourselves. When you get your first pay packet, on our day off we should go shopping in the city and buy you a new dress for the Town Hall dance.'

As Mary was also responsible for monitoring the behaviour of the staff, sharing her trials and tribulations with Agnes at the morning tea-breaks helped lighten her load. 'I just wish the girls would respect the no visitors in the rooms rule. Molly is strong on discipline. I don't want to see anyone get sacked and told to leave the hotel. Molly has also given me the responsibility to ensure everyone is honest with their timekeeping. I'm concerned some are cheating which is stealing.'

Agnes was clear in her view, 'You can only warn them, Mary. If they get caught, they'll have to cop the consequences.'

*

Molly Smith encouraged Mary to attend night school to improve her education. 'I suggest that you work towards achieving some accountancy qualifications as it's important to understand profit and loss when managing a business. You've really shown that you have a future with our hotel chain, so I would urge you to seriously consider resuming study. The company is prepared to assist with time off and course fees.'

This was an unexpected opportunity as Mary had not contemplated a career in hospitality. Now nearing her twenty-second birthday, she decided to give serious consideration to taking up the study offer. A concern for her was locking into a life in the city; for even though she had never experienced life anywhere other than the city, she disliked the lack of space and often dreamt of what it would be like to wander around in the open without people everywhere. So apart from regular trips to the movies, ballroom dancing and occasionally the Sunday markets, she preferred to stay at the hotel.

Attending to her duties had become second nature. Mary not only assisted with the bookkeeping: she loved arranging the flowers in the lobby, organising the table settings, checking the starched white linen tablecloths and specific floral arrangements for each individual diner. She inspected the silverware and china and took charge of those little details that made all the difference to pleasing the guests. On her day off, she often created personalised hotel bookmarks designed with a signature capital **R** swirled in gold lettering to be placed on the pillows.

*

The Rex Hotel owners knowing that their regular clients were time poor people, followed a policy of a hearty breakfast served quickly and efficiently. Mary, Agnes and other staff were well versed in meeting the demands of a busy room while exchanging no more than courteous small talk while delivering the meals. But one morning as breakfast was finishing with tables being cleared, Mary received an unexpected proposal.

A clean-shaven gentleman, neat and well-dressed who always wore a jacket and tie, introduced his wife, Monica, a nice looking, quietly spoken lady. The couple had already made an impression on Mary before they had officially met.

'Good morning Mary. Thank you for looking after my wife, Monica and I this week. We've really appreciated your care and efficiency.'

As Mary answered she could feel a warmth from the couple who were regular clients at the hotel. While her knowledge was limited, she was aware that they were successful Western District farmers aged in their fifties. 'It has been my pleasure, Mr Flanagan, I hope you are enjoying your stay in Melbourne.'

Dan leaned back in his chair to allow Mary to collect the last of the dishes. 'Monica and I have enjoyed catching up with friends. This is an annual event for us. We look forward to entering and hopefully winning some ribbons with our sheep at the Melbourne Show.'

With time on her side, Mary was happy to engage in conversation while clearing some empty plates onto the trolley. 'I must visit the sheep pavilion when our group goes to the Show on Friday night. Sounds silly I know, but I just adore that country farmyard smell. Most times we usually spend our money enjoying the rides. It's a bit scary but a lot of fun.'

As they chatted, Dan seemed a little more intense after receiving a quick nod from Monica. Leaning toward Mary, his casual demeanour changed to a more businesslike mode. 'Can I say that this might seem an unusual proposition, but Monica and I would like to offer you the opportunity to come to work for us at Roscommon Downs in Victoria's Western Districts.'

Seeing how taken aback Mary looked, Dan paused for a moment to ensure that she was able to process his words before he continued. 'We have a two-thousand-acre sheep farm close to Castle Hill. There are only the two of us and a small staff to look after, as well as some extra work helping with the cooking required when additional people are hired during the annual shearing season. We have a comfortable room in our home available to you.'

Mary was astounded to receive the proposal as she had been trained not to address the hotel clients, having no more relationship with him and his wife than serving them breakfast. Mrs Flanagan left Mary in no doubt she agreed with the offer as she nodded her approval.

'Monica and I have been watching you work each morning and are impressed by your politeness and energy.' Mr Flanagan continued. 'You have also received an excellent reference from Molly Smith. We think you would fit in very well.'

'My apologies Mr Flanagan, I'm a bit shocked at your generous offer, it's very kind of you. I really don't know what to say,' Mary replied as she nervously fiddled with the cups on the tray. 'This is my first permanent employment and I'm feeling quite settled. Mrs Smith has been extremely supportive, and although I do have basic cooking skills, most of my work here has been outside the kitchen.'

'Sorry to just drop the offer on you like that, Mary. This is the only chance we have of catching you each day.'

'Well, I am going to need a few days to think about leaving the secure employment I have here.'

'Not to worry Mary, we're staying in Melbourne until Friday and are hopeful you might agree to take up our offer before we leave. Understand that your wage and conditions will be no less than you currently receive. As we both age, we really need home help to assist our day to day living in what we believe is a beautiful part of Victoria. If you agree to come and spend some time with us, and it doesn't work out, there are other employment opportunities in the area we can assist you to obtain.'

'That's kind of you Mr Flanagan. I'm not sure that I could do all you need. I've never even been to a farm or away from Melbourne. It would be a big decision for me to leave here. Mrs Smith is a good employer.'

'Don't worry about your lack of cooking skills, I'm sure that you can easily pick up what you'll need. Monica and I are happy with old fashioned plain food, and if all else fails I'm sure that you would be able to return to work here. In the meantime, if you can organise some time off, perhaps you might like to join us at the Royal Melbourne Show? We're exhibiting more of our sheep during the next couple of days, hoping that another one might win a ribbon.'

Aware that time spent with the Flanagans would assist with her decision Mary replied, 'I have Thursday mornings off so I can join you then.'

Given her lack of knowledge of Victoria's Western District, Mary decided to visit the local library during her midday break where she was able to read about the area's history and pioneers. Photographs of Castle Hill pictured the town's wide streets set amid rolling tree-covered hills. She noted the community commitment to encourage visitors to the area, and the importance placed on the annual horse racing carnival and agricultural show.

Despite her initial reluctance to take up the Flanagans' offer, it did hold some real attraction as Mary was finding it increasingly uncomfortable to live in Melbourne. She felt that she might be better suited to the pace of life in a country environment.

A trip to the showgrounds allowed her the opportunity to meet with Dan and Monica away from the hotel and to also witness the regard they were held in by other exhibitors. They had obviously been showing sheep for many years, and while Mary had no knowledge of quality and grooming, it was evident to her that the Flanagans were people who cared for their animals.

She also welcomed the opportunity to have a long conversation with Monica, as all her prior discussions had been with Dan. Mary loved the lady's open and friendly warmth toward her, which left no doubt that the decision to invite her to live at Castle Hill had been a joint decision.

As they enjoyed a cup of tea in the Country Women's Association kiosk, Monica was clear in her support, 'I can assure you Mary, that Dan and I have been talking about asking you to join us at our farm for quite a long time. We were planning to approach you when here for last year's agricultural show but thought it best to wait until this year. You should also be aware that there is no one else being considered.'

The assurances she received from Monica really assisted Mary to make her decision. A long conversation with Molly Smith was also important. So, at the end of a working day, Mary knocked on her office door, entered and waited as Molly completed the day's accounting. After a little small talk, Mary blushed as the words tumbled out, 'My apologies Molly but I must talk to you about the Flanagans.'

Sensing that Mary was disturbed brought a look of concern to Molly's face. 'Goodness Mary, they haven't been rude to you, have they? Whatever has happened?'

Rushing to assure Molly that all was well, Mary continued, 'No, no, everything is okay. I'm just a bit unsure about an offer they made. It's a wonderful opportunity of live-in employment.'

Getting up from behind her desk and taking a seat next to Mary, Molly took Mary's hands in her own and replied, 'That's come out of the blue. Although perhaps not. We had a long conversation recently during which Dan and Monica asked about you. I should have twigged they were interested in employing you. Is it at their country property?'

'Yes, in the Western District, It's a big step for me. I love living and working here, and up until a few days ago I was content that my future would be in hospitality. Yet it's a bit odd, because although I've never been away from Melbourne, after meeting the people at the Show, I think I might enjoy living in the country.'

'It certainly is a big step for you Mary, but maybe not as big as you may think. You really have nothing to lose and you'll always be welcome back here if it doesn't work out. I know the

Flanagans well. They've been staying here for many years. My feeling is that they are good people so don't be afraid to make the move.'

Buoyed by her conversation with Molly, particularly with her assurance of a return to the Rex should things not turn out as Mary might hope, she decided to accept the offer. Perhaps a new environment would help her to develop new friendships.

Disappointed, Agnes burst into tears when Mary told her the news. 'You can't just up and leave, Mary. What about all your friends? What about your dancing? And what about me? We'll never see each other again.'

'Oh Agnes, how could I ever forget you? We'll always be friends, you know that. When I get settled you can come and visit me. I suspect there'll be a spare bed available. And I'll be sure to return from time to time to visit you.'

Mary started to have misgivings about the sudden reality of her commitment when she received a hand-written note confirming her wages and employment conditions from Dan Flanagan the following morning at breakfast. 'Thank you once again for your service this week Mary, we leave for home today. I hope you'll accept our offer. We might be a bit different at Roscommon Downs, but we really regard all of our people as family.'

'Well Mr Flanagan, as you can appreciate it's a hard one for me, but I'm prepared to come to Castle Hill and do my best. I'll need to give Mrs Smith proper notice of my intention to leave so she can arrange for a replacement. If that suits, I can commence in four weeks.'

'That's wonderful news, and I feel certain a decision that you won't regret. We'll do all we can to make you welcome.'

Mary rested her head on the pillow that evening feeling excited, nervous and a little apprehensive, particularly given that Agnes was so upset. But weighing up the matter, Agnes was young and would quickly get over her disappointment.

Both her heart and her head were telling Mary that this could be such a life-changing opportunity. She had nothing to lose, along with a good reference from Molly Smith and an assurance of re-employment back at the hotel if needed. It was a leap into the unknown but at the age of twenty-two, she was looking forward to the next chapter in her life.

Chapter 4

The Flanagans

Dan Flanagan was born in 1903 in a bush hospital in Barrow, a small western district town of eighty people, which usually trebled in size during holiday periods. Monica O'Brien was born in the same hospital one year later. It was considered a badge of honour in the small proud community to be able to confirm a strong Barrow heritage. So, with both sets of parents being pioneers of the region, there was no doubt that the families were dinky di locals.

Visitors came to the area to enjoy the peace and quiet and to swim and fish in the cool water of the river which wound in a lazy loop around the town. Knowledge of the best places to fish was a closely guarded secret with polite vagueness offered in response to inquiries.

Entry to the town came after negotiating a winding narrow road which alternated between gravel and bitumen. Barrow people were always cautious travellers during summer months because many accidents occurred due to the clouds of road dust. Indeed, unnecessary travel was avoided.

Shops in Barrow were limited to the delivery of basic services. The Dwyer family operated the general store, newsagency and post office which retained the liquor licence from the long-gone hotel. The arrival of the newspaper truck from the nearby regional city was eagerly anticipated by Dan and other locals anxious not to miss purchasing a copy.

Daily banter was exchanged between early arrivals at the store and Bob Dwyer.

Dan was never one to miss the opportunity to stir Bob into activity, often calling loudly, 'C'mon Bob open the doors; we've been waiting for hours. Did you sleep in again?'

Bob would continue at his own pace while taking time to adjust his well-worn eyeshade and reply, 'We open at eight every day. Couldn't you sleep? Or did your wife kick you out of bed again? Give me a sec to turn on the coffee machine.'

A service station opened for a few hours each day to provide fuel sales and truck and car repairs. Following drive-off petrol thefts, unknown customers were required to pay a cash deposit before the pump was switched on.

A small memorial park in the middle of town, established to honour Barrow servicemen and women, provided a popular gathering place to enjoy the mild weather. During holiday periods a combination of community groups catered a restricted menu in the school hall raising funds in support of local projects.

Apart from farming, the main industry in the district was a small timber mill. The mill had survived many bushfires that regularly swept through the area. Barrow men served a lifetime of work at the mill, often employed alongside other family members to proudly produce quality timber for city building projects.

In his youth, Dan enjoyed standing at the town's shallow river crossing watching the loaded bullock and horse wagons being urged along by a commanding voice and the crack of a whip. The supply of logs became a challenge when heavy rain flooded the crossing. In later years when the animals were replaced by trucks, the roar of diesel engines could be heard bouncing off the nearby hills.

Dotted around the town were pieces of forestry equipment which had either worn out or technology had rendered redundant. An active historical society worked to preserve the items to ensure recognition of the town's rich history. Supportive and vibrant, the community was committed to keeping the sporting clubs viable and often received an award in the tidy town category.

The annual forest festival, a local highlight, was held in conjunction with the art and craft show. Craftsmen who had spent years working with timber looked forward to showing their best work and quality pieces were displayed and keenly sought by collectors. The success of these events ensured an important financial boost.

While often tempted to enter the woodchopping competition, Dan held back, preferring not to risk his toes and retain his ability to accompany Monica to the festival bush dance. 'Better to dance than take the chance,' he explained.

As their family homes were within walking distance, Dan and Monica formed a firm friendship at an early age. They enjoyed attending composite classes at the Barrow Primary School with fourteen other children. The teacher, a good educationalist and practical person, also knew the importance of passing on life skills to the students. Quarterly field trips were eagerly anticipated as was the annual mushroom gathering.

The move to secondary college was initially a great adventure for Dan and Monica, who waited with other Barrow children at the general store to board the school bus. Driven by local stalwart and part time philosopher, Gordon 'Gunna' James, the bus left promptly at eight o'clock for the forty-minute trip to Castle Hill. There was no waiting for latecomers.

As 'Gunna' would say, 'It's a good discipline to be on time. If one's late then all's late.'

The 'Gunna' nickname was thought by some to be particularly unfair to Gordon as his voluntary contribution to the life of the community was generous and varied. Operating the automotive repair shop with limited business was a challenge only made viable by tractor and farm equipment repair. His service in that area was keenly sought as he was a good trouble shooter. He would regularly take on an apprentice mechanic from among the local students with the diversity of his work turning out good tradespeople.

Recognised regularly as the 'Citizen of the Year', he was a knockabout bloke who just felt happy to help. On one occasion Dan asked, 'Hey Mr James, why do people always call you Gunna?'

'Just a bit of fun. Doesn't worry me ... like water off a duck's back. People getting stuck into me are leaving everyone else alone. Now did I tell you the story about? ...' and on Gunna would go to relate an entertaining yarn from his many Barrow experiences. It was never a dull day when Gunna was at the wheel.

While Dan and Monica looked forward to the next step in their education, the move from a small primary school to secondary college created the usual nervousness. Despite making new friends, their link remained strong. Dan's ability to perform well in the school football team resulted in an invitation to train and ultimately play for Castle Hill. Monica joined the netball club, and the consolidated club became their second home as they attended weekly training and partnered each other on social outings.

A challenge for Dan when aged fifteen was a visit by an army recruitment officer who spoke passionately to the Castle Hill school assembly about the importance of war service. The lure of a trip overseas to fight for King and Country seemed an exciting opportunity. Many of his school mates put their age up to join. Despite his eagerness to be involved, after talking it over with his parents, Dan decided to defer and join when he was eighteen. His mother hoped that the war might be over before then.

Watching his mates wave goodbye to their parents at the railway station filled Dan with a few misgivings. He'd made his decision. But had he done the right thing? Anzac Day in later years was always a sad occasion when reminded of his many friends who never returned after the war and those who carried lifelong injuries.

With permanent employment limited in the region, Monica sought and found part-time work in Castle Hill. Flexible and competent, she took short shifts in the town bakery, the racecourse and working dog shows. The annual agricultural show provided a further source of income and the opportunity to meet visitors from horse and pony clubs. An excellent singer, she often performed at weddings and funerals. The money earned was carefully saved.

With plenty of mates at the footy club and a willingness to work hard, Dan was invited to join a local shearing team. Employed as a roustabout, he learnt his shearing skills on the job. This secured him a permanent position which although restricting his ability to attend mid-week football training, allowed him to play on a Saturday and spend weekends with Monica.

Strong and fit, Dan was able to handle tough situations and was encouraged to take up the three rounds challenge when the travelling boxing tent was set up during the agricultural show. Responding to the beating drum and excitement generated by the spruiker, some of his mates stepped up.

Watching them come off second best convinced him that it was okay to talk-the-talk but you needed to be able to walk-the-walk. The town bully set out to enhance his reputation by challenging the biggest man in the troupe, only to be quickly sat on his backside. The laughter lasted longer than the fight.

Never having been a man to let a moment pass, Dan decided early in their relationship that Monica was the woman he would marry. His approach to popping the question was carried out in a most unromantic manner in between dances at the footy club, 'Well Monica, I'm going to ask your father if we can marry.'

'All I can say, Daniel Flanagan, is that as long as my mum doesn't mind, I hope that you and my father will be very happy together.'

Dan looked at Monica and laughed. But seizing the opportunity for some further fun, Monica strolled off to take a seat away from the dance floor. When Dan followed and sat down beside her, he said, 'I was meanin' to ask you first of course, Monica.'

Monica's next response was not what he was expecting. 'You're the third person who's asked me the same question. I'll have to include your proposal in among my options.'

Dan's face flushed with embarrassment. Completely stuck for words, his mouth hung open in shock for several moments.

'Other proposals, Monica?'

Fearing that Dan might have some sort of seizure, Monica decided she best give him some assurance. 'Well, I gotcha there, now didn't I! You should've seen the look on your face.' She erupted into laughter. 'It was priceless.'

'There's never a dull moment with you Monica, I've got to keep my guard up all the time. But now, what about my proposal?'

Rising to her feet, Monica took hold of Dan's hands. 'I've got to say it's high time, Dan Flanagan. I felt you might have asked me long before this and yes I'd be proud to be your wife.'

Dan's face again reddened. 'Apologies Monica. Not what I'd call a text-book proposal. Should have done better. You're very important to me.'

'I would most certainly hope so considering that you just asked me to be your wife.'

Dan recovered his composure, 'Before I ask your father, I want you to know that I've taken a permanent place in Bob Murphy's shearing team. We'll be leaving in a couple of weeks for two months work in New South Wales, and as you know it's a tough time on the land. The work is there so I think best to not miss the opportunity.'

'That's a nice old how do you do I must say. Five minutes after asking me to marry you, you are off with the boys gallivanting around the countryside and expecting me to sit home alone awaiting your return.'

Seemed to Dan that he couldn't get much right. 'But I thought you would be pleased, Monica. We'll both be needing to grab every opportunity and must work hard to put the money aside for our future.'

Monica frowned, but she knew that Dan was right and looking out for their best interests.

'I'm not happy to be away from you,' Dan continued. 'But I reckon if I'm careful with my pay packet and stay out of the pub, I can earn enough to add to the money we've already saved and put a deposit on that property you've always been so keen on.'

Monica's eyes lit up and she threw her arms around Dan. 'You're absolutely right, Dan. That place has been on the market for a while, so the owners might be willing to negotiate a price we can afford.'

As they moved to the dance floor, Dan began to relax. 'I knew you'd support me, Monica. We can work hard to develop and improve that property to really make our home in Castle Hill.'

'Of course, I'll support you. This is where I want to live. Our friends are here. We'll get married in the Anglican Church and can have our wedding reception in the Town Hall. I guess we'll be able to hire the regular band. I'll need to think about the bridesmaids, and you'll need to choose your best man.' Monica could hardly stop talking in her state of excitement.

'Finding a best man will be pretty easy,' Dan replied. 'There's any number at the footy club who'll step up. The bigger challenge will be trying to lever whoever that might be into something that looks like a suit.'

'They'll need to do a bit more than just step up, Dan. I hope you're not going to pick out one of those loud-mouthed mates like Whacka Watson, who'll be wanting to get you drunk on the night before the wedding.'

Dan was quick to assure Monica, 'No need to worry on that score, and I'm happy to leave the rest of the arrangements to you.'

'I would have thought that you're forgetting something of importance though, Dan.'

With a further questioning look, Dan had no idea of what Monica was talking about.

'Well, isn't it quite evident? What about a trip to Melbourne to pick out an engagement ring?'

'P'raps you might like to do that, Monica, while I'm away.'

The look on Monica's face said it all.

'On second thoughts, how about we make a day of it sometime next week?'

'That's most considerate, Daniel Flanagan. I hope you'll have your cheque book with you!' Monica winked.

Chapter 5

On the Move

During her final weeks at the Rex, Mary started to have misgivings. She knelt on the floor of her bedroom, case open in front of her and Agnes perched on the end of the bed. How would she ever be able to fit her life at the Rex into one tiny case? 'I hope I'm making the right decision. I'm comfortable here and will miss you Agnes.'

'I really hate that you are leaving Mary, and can understand you're worried. It's a big step. But the Flanagans are good people and will make you welcome. Besides, Molly's already said you can return.'

'I know that Agnes, but I've been having some sleepless nights. What if Molly retires?'

Agnes smiled reassuringly. It was a smile she'd given Mary countless times over the years. 'Don't worry, it's normal to be concerned. You'll be on the train and settled at Castle Hill before you know it.'

Despite Agnes' assurance, Mary was emotional and nervous as she packed for a fresh start.

*

Finding the train scheduled to leave for Castle Hill at 8:30am had been a challenge. The unfortunate timing plunged Mary into the stations busiest hour with the tension increased by throbbing diesel engines and intermittent blasting of train horns.

Unfamiliar with the layout and caught up amid the hustle and bustle, Mary spent nervous minutes getting her bearings. She could feel the energy and anxiousness among travellers possibly late for work or meeting family and friends. This part of life in the city she would happily leave behind.

The arrival and departure announcements lost in the noise were of no assistance. Mary sought directions from a railway employee and managed to board with a few minutes to spare. Noting another woman about her own age, her auburn hair pulled into a smart bun and casually dressed for travel, Mary took the opportunity to confirm that she was on the correct train. 'Excuse me. Are you travelling to Castle Hill?'

With a friendly smile the woman replied, 'No, I'm travelling to Carravale. But this is the right train. My stop is two stations past Castle Hill.'

Seeking her allocated seat, Mary replied, 'Well that's a relief. I've been up and down escalators for the past twenty minutes and became really confused. It's the first time I've been on a country train.'

'I'm not surprised you got lost. It can be a bun fight out there at this time of day,' the woman responded with a quiet laugh. 'But if you don't mind me asking, what's taking you to Castle Hill?'

'I've been offered employment at Roscommon Downs,' Mary replied and placed her suitcase on the luggage rack. 'I'm looking forward to taking up the opportunity.' Reaching out her hand she introduced herself, 'I'm Mary O'Rourke.'

'Lovely to meet you, Mary. My name's, Rhonda North. Friends call me Rhon. I'm on the way home to assist my parents. My mother's unwell.'

'Pleased to meet you, Rhon. I'm sorry to hear about your mother. Has she been in hospital?'

'Yes, quite ill for months, followed by surgery, but now on the mend.'

As she readied herself for the trains departure, Mary said, 'I wish her well and hope we can keep in touch. I know no one in Castle Hill apart from Dan and Monica Flanagan.'

'I know the Flanagans. My parents run the Carravale farm supply store and Dan and Monica have been customers for many years. I should help you settle into the area. I'll leave you my address and telephone number so we can keep in contact.'

As Rhon pulled a notebook and pen from her handbag, Mary said, 'That's very good of you Rhon. Does Castle Hill have much of a social life?'

Jotting down her details, Rhon confirmed, 'The local dances are a great place to meet people particularly during the horse racing carnivals. But hey, we've a couple of hours travel ahead of us, so why not have a cup of tea and a chat in the dining car? There's plenty to talk about.'

*

As the two wandered through the passenger compartment to the dining car, Mary struggled to retain her balance as the train rocked from side to side. Aware of the ever present clickety clack, she was grateful to be seated at a small table from which the diners were able to see the outskirts of the city rushing by.

They ordered their tea, which was promptly delivered in a silvery pot along with white railway labelled china, and Mary felt quite the lady as she took in the details of her surroundings while Rhonda buttered a scone.

Tables set beside each window were small and intimate in keeping with the lack of space. But the compartment was cosy and neatly carpeted with curtains tied back at either side of the windows.

Mary was thrilled with the turn of events and anticipated that given Rhonda's outgoing and friendly greeting, she would be made welcome among her broad group of friends. And as the conversation got underway, she felt especially pleased about the opportunity to attend town dances and thought that her skills in ballroom dancing might come in handy after all.

While they chatted over tea, Rhon was happy to declare her age. Six years older than Mary, she laughed while relating some life experiences which brought a blush to Mary's cheeks.

'I've had a few relationships but no one special. Yet who knows, the right bloke might be just around the corner. Occasionally I go blonde and that seems to excite some interest.' The sudden jolt of the train caused Rhon to take a firm grip on the edge of the table as the cups clattered in the saucers. She paused to allow the motion of the train to get back on an even keel.

It was then that she adopted a more serious tone, 'When you've settled in, we must properly catch up so I can tell you who to watch out for. Many are not who you think they are at your first meeting.'

Mary was taken aback by this comment from Rhonda who, until now. had been nothing but positive. What had occurred to alter her manner in this way? Everything Mary had heard from the Flanagans about Castle Hill had also been of a positive nature. Was Rhonda referring to the Castle Hill or the Carravale community? As the train started to pick up speed, she had a rush of concern. What hadn't she been told?

Mary's contemplation was broken. 'I hope I haven't put you off heading west, Mary?' Rhonda laughed. 'It's a bit late now … we're full speed ahead.'

The return to their seats provoked a sharp and annoyed rebuke from an obviously angry young woman. Mary was quick to feel ill at ease as the flame haired, leather jacket wearing female pointed an accusing finger at Rhon to confirm her displeasure. 'It would have been nice to invite me to share a cup of tea rather than just leave me for dead.'

Mary could see Rhonda, while upset at the outburst, was prepared to reason with the woman. Holding out a reassuring hand she said, 'I'm sorry Lana, I wasn't sure if you were returning to Carravale on this train or one later in the day. I thought you said last night that you might go shopping.'

Shaking her head, Lana replied, 'Might go shopping, I said. Might, doesn't mean that I'd made up my mind. You could have at least checked before you rushed off without me. I was in such a hurry to get to the station so we could travel together that I jumped into the wrong carriage.' Lana whined. 'If you'd waited for a few minutes before going to the dining car, I'd have come with you.'

Lana, looked Mary up and down, 'I see you have a new friend.'

'I can only apologise again, Lana.' Rhonda said as she made the necessary introductions. 'This is Mary O'Rourke. She's on her way to work at Roscommon Downs. And Mary, this is Lana Kenny. We're former schoolmates and long-time friends in Carravale.'

Rhonda received another correction from Lana who amplified her answer by clapping her hands. 'You best start introducing me as Chivon Murphy. Chiv, if you like. But no more Lana Kenny. That name no longer exists.'

Despite feeling comfortable about her meeting with Rhonda, Mary could see that Chivon was much less welcoming. Rhonda broke the silence with a laugh. 'Now come on Chiv, this isn't two's company, three's a crowd. Mary happened along. We're on the train together. No one's trying to freeze you out. Just settle down and tell Mary why you took the opportunity to change your name while in Melbourne.'

Taking Rhonda's advice, Chivon explained to Mary how having been teased at school she was never happy with her name. 'Kids can be cruel with name calling. They tagged me, 'Lana the banana'. I nearly got expelled for fighting. The bullying was terrible. And it flowed over to my working life on farms and warehouses where everyone got a nickname.'

Sympathetic to Chivon's situation, Mary said, 'I understand how being subjected to that behaviour would've been stressful.'

'Yes, I'd had enough, it was time to make a change,' Chivon responded.

As the movement of the train lulled Chivon into a better mood, a calmness seemed to descend between them. She then went on to add that despite her parents not being keen on her decision, she'd gone ahead and adopted the surname 'Murphy'; to now be known as 'Chivon Murphy'.

Showing Mary her new photo identification card, Chivon said 'I reckon my name now is more Irish, Mary. That's my heritage. Mum chose Lana as she loved Lana Turner, the movie star. That was all very well, but it didn't suit me.'

Mary was quick to reply, 'I can see your reasoning Chivon. No one likes to be teased. I hope it works well for you.'

Chivon laughed as she waved the card around. 'Why do we always end up with such a shocking photo? I know I'm much better looking.' The laughter continued as Chivon secured her new card in her wallet.

Settling back into her seat, Mary made a mental note to be cautious when dealing with Chivon. Having seen the result of bullying at the orphanage, she could understand the decision to change her name. But quick to anger and obviously a possessive person who was determined to hold tightly to Rhonda, her current politeness would not sustain.

With Rhonda and Chivon now chatting about issues in Carravale, Mary decided to read her magazine. But she was finding it difficult to concentrate as her thoughts returned to Rhonda's earlier comments regarding the community of Castle Hill and perhaps Carravale. Unsure of what to expect Mary resolved to be cautious as it was clear the future would have enough challenges without harvesting enemies.

Chapter 6

Warmth and Connection

As the train journeyed deeper into the countryside, Mary felt an unexpected warmth and connection to the land. She could not believe the lushness of the Western District set against the Grampians mountain range. Green rolling hills dotted with houses and corrugated iron haysheds made it easy to understand the affection that Dan and Monica Flanagan had for the area.

Large stands of cypress trees protected the inhabitants from the elements, the vivid foliage a contrast to the brilliantly coloured deciduous trees in the process of losing their leaves. Farmers had cleared the land and used local stone to contain their livestock with fences seeming to disappear into the distance. It was a refreshing change to the streets and backyards she'd viewed on her journey through Melbourne.

Mary was drawn to the individually designed historic railway stations constructed with a variety of materials. Many towns, keen to make the station a welcome entry point, maintained the buildings with fresh paint and well-tended garden beds planted with a mixture of shrubs and flowers.

At each stop travellers gathered their luggage in preparation to leave the train. Mary wondered if they were returning home, holidaymakers or, like herself, about to start an entirely new chapter in their lives.

'Next stop Castle Hill. Time to get your things together,' Rhon alerted Mary.

The Castle Hill railway station, similar in its construction to those that Mary had seen along the way was designed by pioneers and built with brick and natural stone. The typical, lovingly maintained flower garden was a welcoming sight. Bidding farewell to Rhonda and Chivon and holding tightly to her suitcase, Mary apprehensively stepped onto the platform.

Conscious of the chatter of other travellers leaving the train and being met by family or friends, she suddenly felt very much alone. For her the only sign of a friend seemed to be the presence of several sparrows chirping around her feet in greeting.

Dan Flanagan had promised she would be met by his foreman, Jim Wilkinson. 'He won't be hard to pick out at the station. Just look for a tall, strongly built, good-looking man in his thirties, wearing a khaki shirt and a broad brimmed hat. He'll be standing alongside a small farm truck with a black and white kelpie in the back.'

Enjoying the brisk air after the stuffiness of the train, Mary noted a couple of tall men, one of whom could be Jim Wilkinson. But he seemed to be fully occupied right at this moment. She thought it best to wait, as the fellow was locked in a warm embrace with a woman about her own age. Their moment was interrupted by the sound of the whistle causing the woman to quickly jump on board the departing train.

As the platform cleared, he approached Mary. 'My apologies, you must be Mary O'Rourke. A warm hello and welcome to Castle Hill. I've been looking forward to your arrival. I'm Jim Wilkinson, the Roscommon Downs' foreman and this is our best dog, Lilly.' Jim reached out politely to relieve Mary of the case.

'I'm pleased to meet you Jim. No need to apologise. I could see you were farewelling your friend.'

Noting that the dog was holding his paw up, Mary smiled and bent down to shake it. 'Lilly certainly is friendly?'

Jim laughed. 'She's friendly alright, loves a pat, and always ready for a day's work, the busier the better.'

'I love dogs and get the feeling that Lilly and I will be good mates,' Mary said while also offering a word of thanks to Jim for meeting her. 'I've been really concerned with the decision I've taken to come here but must say first impressions are excellent.'

Jim ushered Mary towards his truck already loaded with rolls of wire and fence posts and carefully placed her case in the back. 'Nothing to fear Mary, you'll enjoy your new life at the farm; it's a friendly place to work with all of us being looked after as family.'

He politely opened the passenger door and helped Mary into her seat and as Jim got settled behind the wheel, Mary said, 'I must also say that one of the reasons I accepted the Flanagans' offer was because of their warmth and friendliness. You're probably aware of my background, so to become part of a family would be a wonderful outcome.'

'Dan did explain your circumstances. I know that he and Monica were keen to have you come to the farm and once overheard them say something about bringing you home.'

Leaving the station behind, Mary pondered Jim's last comment as they bounced along in the heavily laden truck. How could the Flanagans be bringing her home? She had never travelled away from Melbourne. Perhaps Jim had misunderstood.

Although they had just met, Mary felt as though she had known Jim for a long time. She guessed he would be five to six years older than herself and their relaxed conversation was warm and comfortable. Mary was drawn to his clear and direct manner and had to agree with Dan Flanagan's assessment of him. Certainly, he was tall and good looking: greying at the temples, his face, hands and arms tanned by years of outdoor work. Should she ask about his friend at the railway station? She would need to be subtle as it wasn't her business. But she really was quite eager to know.

As Jim turned into the town centre, he said, 'I'll give you a short tour to help with your bearings. There's not a great deal to Castle Hill, just three pubs, a few shops, a bush hospital, a police station, an Anglican Church and a couple of schools.'

'That sounds like more than enough,' Mary replied.

Jim laughed. 'You're right! It's all we need. The community is proud of the town, and really embraces the annual 'Tidy Street Competition'. I'll introduce you to some of the locals who've been looking forward to meeting you.'

Holding firmly to the roof handle, Mary asked, 'Have Dan and Monica been talking about me?'

'This is a small town. It's hard to keep secrets. A new young woman always excites some interest. So best to beat the rumour mill which works overtime.'

There was little doubt in Jim's mind that Mary would certainly excite some interest. With her brown hair tied into a ponytail she was what could be described as a 'bit of a stunner'. Monica had also informed him of Mary's ballroom dancing prowess which had endowed her with an athletic grace and confident manner. The occasional waft of perfume required a discipline to watch the road. It certainly wouldn't take long before young blokes were beating a path to her door.

Mary admired the wide main street and broad footpaths lined with large deciduous trees located just minutes from the station. Delighted with the absence of heavy traffic, it was a far cry from her morning's experience. The delicious aroma of freshly baked bread led them to a cup of tea at Manny's bakery set in a cluster of well cared for buildings and shops.

Pulling into the kerb to park the truck, Jim said, 'Now Mary, I want to warn you. Don't believe a word any of the women say. They love to stir me up. I don't want to get you off on the wrong foot.'

'Don't worry Jim, any secrets I hear will be safe with me.'

Unsure of what to expect, Mary entered a busy café with a separate fresh bread, cake and pastry retail area. It was clear the reputation and quality of the baking was well known given the number of customers. Many patrons were startled by Jim's hearty and friendly call to the staff announcing his arrival which drew a middle-aged man and three grey haired ladies from the kitchen.

The banter began immediately as they teased Jim. It was easy to see that he was a regular, well-known and liked customer. Mary smiled as he took great delight in introducing her to the owner Manny, and his staff of bakers and café workers. 'Meet, Mary O' Rourke, who has come to help us run Roscommon Downs. I've told her that this is the place to be for the best cup of tea in town.'

Being welcomed by Manny and the staff, Mary felt a moment of emotion and a nostalgic flash-back to her friends at the Wild Cherry. As the banter continued, she fielded many friendly questions about her background and hope for a new life in Castle Hill. The women were determined to have some fun in promoting a possible future relationship between Jim and Mary.

The youngest member of the staff who was holding an icing pipe said, 'Well Jim, it looks like you've landed on your feet with Mary coming to town. The Flanagans are pretty good matchmakers. It's about time you got on with your life. We'll probably be seeing less of you here and I won't need to ice as many coffee scrolls.'

'Settle down Maureen, you can't be saying those things to Mary, otherwise she'll be jumping on the next train back to the city.'

Mary enjoyed the friendly conversation which flowed over to a small group of elderly gentlemen seated at tables outside the front of the bakery with their dogs dozing alongside their feet. Following Jim's quick introduction to, as he called it, the Castle Hill de facto council, one of the men issued an invitation. 'Make sure you have some extra time when next in town, Mary. We always have a story to tell.'

While Jim returned indoors to wind up his conversation, Mary crossed the road and looked at the mix of properties advertised for sale or rent in the window of the real estate agency. Given the prices asked for houses and land within the township, and the nearby broad acre farm lots, she was pleased that her live-in position saved her from having to take on that expense.

The items in the window of the antiques and collectables store next-door encouraged Mary to enter for a browse at the goods on offer. A mixture of reasonably priced toby jugs, crystal glasses and cutlery caught her eye. Old fashioned light fittings of all shapes and sizes including a large chandelier hung at various lengths from the ceiling. Racks of vinyl records overflowed from indoors into boxes on trestle tables out on the footpath. A quick flick through revealed the big band dance music of Glenn Miller and the Victor Sylvester orchestra.

Mary was attracted to a large range of antique and second-hand jewellery contained in a glass covered cabinet, making a note that she would carefully work her way through the pieces when time allowed. Of interest, were the shelves of books, some of which looked like they hadn't been moved or dusted for many years. A small group of Harold Robbin's novels caught her eye and while checking through the pages of 'The Carpetbaggers', Mary's quiet contemplation was broken.

'Can I help you?' a short woman aged about fifty wearing an old-fashioned dust coat asked from the rear of the shop where she sat cleaning a vase.

'No, not really, I was just looking. You have an impressive range of books.'

'It's a big collection built up over the years, many bought from deceased estates. When you take everything on offer in a house lot, you pick up some good things, but also a lot of rubbish. I spend much of my time sorting through boxes of household effects that people have decided to get rid of, having left it in storage for years.'

'I can understand your problem. And my apologies, I should have introduced myself. I'm Mary O'Rourke, just arrived today in Castle Hill. I've come to take a position with the Flanagans at Roscommon Downs.'

'Nice to meet you, Mary,' the woman said as she dropped her cleaning cloth and extended her hand. 'Everyone knows the Flanagans. I heard on the grapevine that you were coming.'

'Goodness, Jim warned me that my arrival would be no surprise.'

'Not to worry. I'm Dorothy Jones. My husband and I purchased the shop and all it contained twelve months ago. It's been here for many years. You're most welcome to have a good look around, there's plenty to work through. I'm still finding things that I didn't know are here.'

'Pleased to meet you, Dorothy. I promise that I'll return when time permits. I've an interest in old jewellery and have a small collection mainly purchased from Melbourne markets.' Mary surveyed the room, her eyes drawn once again to the chandelier. 'And I suspect the chandelier has an interesting history.'

'It's quite an antique that could tell many stories. Originally brought into the area to grace the home of a wealthy grazier, it witnessed the boom and bust, changing hands a couple of times before it found its way to gather dust here. Hopefully, it will have a fresh start. Who knows it might be yours in years to come!'

'That sounds a bit ambitious,' Mary said as her gaze fell upon a clock just behind Dorothy. 'Heavens, is that the right time? It's almost 3. I best not delay as Jim Wilkinson is waiting to take me to Roscommon Downs. He'll be starting to worry that he's lost me.'

'He won't leave without you, Mary. I suggest as you're new in town, after you finish looking at the shops on this side of the street, the community notice board outside the town hall contains lots of local news. There's plenty to do and most of the locals are friendly.'

Returning to the main street and finding that Jim was obviously still caught in conversation, Mary took the opportunity for a quick browse through two clothing and shoe shops and a double fronted bookshop which stocked both new and used books. An arts and crafts shop also caught her interest, with an invitation to attend evening sessions to work with a range of local artists.

Mary was drawn to the locally made costume jewellery on display, together with some work in leadlight. It was clear that community effort had refurbished a former horse stables area at the rear of the shop into an artists' workplace. A blacksmith anvil and furnace had been constructed, which was being put to good use in making iron gates and fire hearths.

Crossing the street to the yellow brick town hall, Mary read that the foundation stone had been laid in 1920 and the building dedicated to the war servicemen and women from the Castle Hill district. As Dorothy had suggested, the community noticeboard was being put to good use. It contained an open invitation to attend monthly council meetings and the opportunity to join service clubs. The list of movies to be shown in coming weeks included 'West Side Story' and 'Hello Dolly'.

Live music at the Commercial Hotel was advertised. The Castle Hill football and netball clubs had posted their fixtures with an invitation for recruits to join. There was also a notice confirming a modern and old-time dance on the first Saturday of each month.

In a large room alongside the entrance, Mary discovered a non-staffed library that operated on an honour system. Also. a program of workshops run by local facilitators for writers of all standards. The notice prompted a moment of reflection, as she had been keeping a diary, having been encouraged to do so by one of the sisters at the orphanage: 'You never know where life will take you Mary. Each of us has a road to travel and one day you might want to record yours for those who will follow.'

When settled at Roscommon Downs, she would apply to join the writing group with the hope of gaining assistance to progressively document her journey. Her contemplation was interrupted by Jim's voice. 'Thank goodness I found you, Dan and Monica wouldn't have believed it if I'd lost you on your first day.'

'No worries Jim, I decided to have a wander. I could see that you were caught up with the ladies in the bakery. They were having quite a bit of fun at your expense.'

'No harm done Mary, they've been my friends for years, and I see you've found the library.'

Mary nodded. 'I'm a keen reader and look forward to joining. I've also quickly looked through the second-hand bookshop. I know I'll enjoy spending time in the antique shop. There are some really intriguing bits and pieces for sale.'

'It's surprising what people have stored in their houses. Much of the stuff Dorothy collects goes to the rubbish tip, but there are often really valuable items displayed in her store.'

'I have a small collection of jewellery that I bought at Melbourne markets,' Mary replied. 'I enjoy fossicking through the stalls.'

As they wandered back to the truck, Jim said, 'There's plenty of that sort of thing available, but you should be aware that a few of the locals reckon the shop is haunted. Folklore has it that the people who have died come back to keep watch over their goods. The previous owners only stayed for four months – couldn't sleep because of the creaking floorboards. They reckoned there was a violin playing during the night.'

Stopping dead in her tracks and turning to look at Jim, Mary replied, 'Seriously, a violin playing during the night? That sounds scary.'

Jim chuckled. 'Then there was the case of Maureen O'Reilly. Her husband Rob killed her with a single shotgun blast. It happened when he was cleaning the safety catch. Reckoned he didn't know it was loaded. The police charged him, but he went a bit crazy after the funeral and was admitted to fulltime care in the city. Their kids were distraught and told Mrs Jones to clean out the house. So, a few of the things you were checking out today would have come from there. Maureen O'Reilly might have been looking over your shoulder just in case you were thinking about buying her violin.'

'Goodness Jim, what have I got myself into?'

'You should talk to the old blokes outside Manny's; they know all the stories. I reckon they might have heard some music when coming home from the pub. They do play up a bit some nights, so who knows what they might have heard. I'm not sure if Archie Jones was at Manny's today, but he would be good for you to follow up. He was married to Dorothy for a couple of years until they had an angry fall out over money. There's always a bit of tension as he sits and watches people coming and going from the shop.'

As they stepped into the truck, Mary said, 'Now you've got me worried Jim, but I'm still keen to have a serious shopping trip.'

Remembering the notice regarding the writers' workshop at the library, she asked Jim if he had any knowledge of the group's activities.

'No, that's something I know little about. I do remember there was a bit of negative stuff in the local paper when some of the group moved here from Carravale. I recall they had some sort of falling out which caused a split and the main part of the group moved here. I guess someone from Carravale would know the story.'

'I met Rhonda North on the train. I think she'd know for sure.'

'I know Rhon and the North family very well. They've been supplying our farm for many years. Rhon usually knows what's going on around town.' As Jim turned the truck off the main street, his eyes flicked to his watch, 'Best we keep moving, as the Flanagans will be wondering if you missed the train.'

*

As they passed the racing club on the way to the farm, Jim explained it held four meetings a year featuring hurdle and steeplechase races. 'The Castle Hill Cup is keenly anticipated attracting a large crowd and is the highlight of the three-day racing carnival. Most of the community are at the track for the big event.'

Jim seemed determined to tell Mary everything there was to know. 'Also held at the racecourse is the annual agricultural show. People come from all parts to attend during that week. I enter Lilly in the working dog muster. She has a lot of fun rounding sheep into pens, being really what she does at the farm. I'm sure you'd enjoy watching the dogs working. Occasionally it all goes pear shaped when young dogs lose concentration. A good old-fashioned bush dance is part of the fun, a night not to be missed.'

Mary again held on tightly to the roof handle and wondered if all farm trucks were this rough to travel in. 'I suspect that Castle Hill bursts at the seams with all the accommodation booked.'

'It certainly does. The young people love the energy it brings to the town. Also gives them some much needed part-time work. It's not unusual for some visitors who can't find accomodation to bed down in the Roscommon Downs' shearing shed. After a big day at the races, they just roll into their sleeping bags. Dan and Monica always make them welcome.'

'I can see that life in Castle Hill is going to be quite different for a city girl. I've never been to a race meeting. I'm going to need some guidance.'

'That can certainly be arranged. The Flanagans are keen supporters and usually sponsor a marquee at the track.'

Mary was beginning to feel a little weary after such a big day and she hadn't even reached Roscommon Downs. But Jim had certainly taken her under his wing and chatted on. 'I expect that you'll attend some of the social evenings at the football clubrooms which are located just behind the racing club grandstand. I played many games for the footy club. Sadly, now I'm getting on a bit with aching bones, I leave the dancing to the young blokes.'

Now late in the afternoon, Mary, having stored a wealth of information, had many mental notes to transcribe into her diary. Having been with Jim for just a short time she wondered again if he had a permanent relationship. Was it with the woman at the railway station? It was going to be a pleasure to be with him at the farm, and hopefully for many years into the future.

Chapter 7

Roscommon Downs

The long road out of town bordered by scribbly gums and paddocks stretched straight ahead for as far as the eye could see. Even so, Jim suggested it might be wise for Mary to take note of the directions. 'Can't have you getting bushed. One of these days you might be out here on your own.'

Mary laughed. 'Goodness, there's no chance of that happening, I don't have a driver's licence.'

'We may need to do something about that. But let's just get you settled first.'

Bouncing around in her seat due to the continual jolt of the truck, Mary held firmly to the roof handle. 'Can you tell me a little about the property, Jim?'

'It wasn't always called Roscommon Downs. The previous owners, Ron and Beryl Knight, laid some of the ground-work and planted a magnificent stand of trees that have matured to provide shade in the garden and shelter for the sheep.'

'What happened to the Knights?' Mary asked.

As Jim slowed the truck and changed gears, he made a left turn and headed in a new direction along a narrow road bounded on both sides by post and wire fencing. The noise of the engine startled a gang of screeching galahs who suddenly took flight.

'The region was struck by an unusually dry spell,' Jim replied. 'Dams dried up and people went broke. There was no support, so a lot gave up and walked away, including the Knights.'

Mary looked out at the unchanging landscape and imagined the hardships, frustration and tears of seeing the livestock starve. 'Sounds like many sad stories. To be expected I guess, given the devastating circumstances of the depression and loss of life during the war. Were you living here in the forties, Jim?'

'Yes, just turned fourteen and wasn't sure if I was going to get caught up in the whole thing. When it ended, the people of Castle Hill lit a massive bonfire to celebrate. But many were broken having lost sons and daughters. Everyday the train would bring home the injured. Some blokes didn't know where they were.'

'I can only imagine the heartbreak and grief,' Mary said.

Jim nodded. 'At war's end, Dan and Monica were well entrenched having started in the thirties with just a few hundred acres. It was bittersweet, as while the depression brought land prices down, it also brought the property within their reach. Determined to make a go of it they took out a loan while taking on extra work to help meet the payments. As success came their way, any profit was put towards buying neighbouring farms. They now have two thousand acres.'

'They must have been driven to succeed.'

'Monica said there were times when they were close to losing everything. But they pressed on rebuilding tumbled down sheds and replacing fences. Dan was able to shear their small mob of sheep with Monica's assistance. Mustering the animals in wind and rain during winter can be a challenge. Yet they toughed it out and I've been lucky enough to become a part of it.'

Mary could sense the pride Jim felt about working so closely with the Flanagans. She remembered Monica's emphasis on being part of a family and hoped her employment would yield the same result.

'I don't know anything about sheep,' Mary reluctantly admitted.

'Not to worry … you'll soon learn. There's always plenty of help available. The wool clip has come a long way. Dan tells the story that he was a bit embarrassed to sell his first bales as it was nothing better than carpet wool. One buyer suggested it would be best used as home insulation.'

Still holding firmly to the roof handle and hoping the journey would soon end, Mary replied, 'I heard Monica talking to friends at the Royal Melbourne Show about wool quality. I must admit the conversation meant little to me at the time.'

'As I said before, you'll come to understand the importance of the annual shearing and wool sale. It's our life-blood.'

Jim gazed across at Mary who looked a little uncomfortable. 'Sorry about the rough ride, the old truck has a big load on.'

'That's okay! Although I must say I'll be pleased to get to the farm.'

'Well, the good news is that we're almost there,' Jim said as he arrived at a dirt road.

Mary was overjoyed to see an impressive-shingled sign hanging from the front gate, 'Welcome to Roscommon Downs'.

The homestead, situated at the end of a long and sweeping driveway, was bordered by both imported and native trees. A group of silver birch with their stark white trunks were at their brilliant best.

A range of garden beds planted with a mix of shrubs, flowers and vegetables graced a generous portion of the property surrounding the house. Rhododendrons and azaleas flourished in the background of well-manicured lawns. Passionfruit vines climbed the walls of the garden shed and trellised triangles held massed roses, a spectacle of colour and perfume. The paddocks and garden were separated by fencing constructed of sturdy white pickets.

As Jim collected her suitcase from the truck, Mary couldn't resist taking a quick peek down a winding path that led to a pond and garden seat. She quickly retraced her steps when hearing Monica's voice. 'There you are Jim, I thought either you were lost, or Mary missed the train.'

'Nothing like that, Monica, I made the mistake of taking Mary into Manny's. You can imagine how well that went.'

'I can! I suspect the tongues are still wagging about you and Mary. But no harm done as they're our friends and love a bit of stirring.'

Greeting Mary with a hug, she said, 'Welcome to Roscommon Downs, Mary. I hope you enjoyed the trip?'

'Yes, Mrs Flanagan, it was so comfortable on the train, and I'm not sure why, but I instantly felt a warm connection to the Western Districts.'

'I'm pleased that you had good first impressions. It's interesting how we often feel at home in a strange place.'

'Jim has made me welcome. He drove around Castle Hill so I could get my bearings. It's a pretty town.'

Jim started the engine of the truck. 'You must excuse me ladies: I want to unload the posts and wire before it gets dark. It's nearly beer o'clock; can't miss that.'

'There's no doubt about you Jim, you've certainly got your priorities right.' Monica laughed. Then returning to her conversation with Mary. 'I'm pleased that Jim showed you around. Dan and I really love the area. Both our parents and grandparents were born in the district, so it was the logical place for us to settle. Sorry Dan's not here to welcome you. He's taken some sheep into the saleyards.'

'That's fine, Mrs Flanagan. I'm looking forward to saying hello to him.'

As they wandered across the fine gravelled paving towards the verandah, Mary said, 'I was fortunate to make a new friend on the train who was travelling to Carravalle. Her parents own the farm supply business.'

'That would be Rhonda North, I suspect. Her family has a good reputation in the district.'

'Rhonda was travelling with a friend called Lana Kenny. She'd been to Melbourne to change her name to Chivon Murphy.'

'Good grief … why on earth would Lana change her name?'

'Apparently she was teased at school, and at work, so she decided it was time for a fresh start.'

Inviting Mary to sit for a moment in a comfortable wicker chair before entering the house, Monica said, 'That's very odd. I suppose it will all come out in the wash. But it'll be strange trying to get used to calling her Chivon. Anyway, enough of that. We need to settle you into your room and give you a chance to unpack and freshen up. You won't be expected to start work for a few days of course, and from now on please call us Dan and Monica.'

'Thank you, Monica. When unpacked, I'm looking forward to a walk around your beautiful garden.'

With Mary's talk of the garden, it was as though Monica momentarily forgot her promise to show Mary to her room, as she seemed content to continue the conversation. 'Dan and I enjoy gardening. It's been a labour of love and has taken many years to get it to this stage.'

'I can see that!' Mary agreed, as she reached into her purse to withdraw a new notebook and show it to Monica. 'I'm also keen to start earning my keep, and meet the other people working on the farm. So, I bought this in town to jot down names to remember and keep track of my duties.'

'Well, that's a great idea, Mary. But we run lean with Dan and Jim being our only permanent workers. I look after the house where I'll welcome your assistance. We do bring in extra hands during the annual shearing and it's good that you've arrived in time to experience the wool clip which is due to start shortly. It's our main source of income which we work towards all year.'

'Jim talked about it on the way from the station. Sounds exciting, although I guess a lot of hard work. I would've been disappointed to miss it.'

'One you'll enjoy meeting and can jot down in your notebook is Mavis Jones. She's been coming here for many years to cook for the shearers and is the reason why we never have a latecomer or a no show in the shearing team.'

Leaning forward in her chair, Monica then lowered her tone. 'Another person you'll meet is Rosemary Cleary, the daughter of our good friends, Tom and Shirley.'

Mary picked up on the fact that judging by the expression on Monica's face something was amiss. 'Is Rosemary someone I should be worried about?'

'Not exactly, Mary. It's a bit awkward however. You see, Tom and Shirley were for many years regulars here at the farm on Sunday evening card nights. So, when a child, Rosemary would accompany her parents. The card evenings ceased five years ago, but Rosemary, who was then fourteen, has continued to visit whenever it suits her, not only at weekends but also on weekdays. We want her to stop. I know we must tell her one of these days.'

Mary frowned, 'Does she stay overnight?'

'She has in the past and that's becoming more regular. My intuition is that she's angling for a permanent position here. The truth is that Dan and I don't want her anywhere near the place let alone living or working here. We've tried to discourage her, but nothing has worked. We suspect she'll be angry with you taking the role she saw for herself.'

'I best be careful then. I don't want to be involved in any arguments.'

It seemed evident that Monica being in no hurry to show Mary to her room had been eager to start with a clean slate and get this news off her chest. Only then, in the hope that Mary wouldn't take fright and flee, did she finally rise from her chair and pick-up the suitcase. 'Don't stress, Mary, Jim will keep his eye on her to ensure nothing untoward occurs. Now, let's settle you in.'

Chapter 8

The Shearing

When unpacking her suitcase on the day of her arrival, some strong emotions came to the fore as Mary realised this was her first real home after the orphanage and the Rex Hotel. Not wishing to let the moment pass too quickly, she decided to record her feelings in her diary. While doing so, it was difficult to stop from shedding a few tears of happiness.

Mary's room, which afforded a view of the garden, was painted in warm colours and furnished in a comfortable manner. Containing a double bed, wardrobe and couch, Monica had informed her that it was previously used for overnight and weekend accommodation. A book placed on a small desk for guests to record their farm stay experiences held many written comments. They were all favourable insomuch as the visitors had received a beneficial education about farm life, while others enjoyed the Flanagans' hospitality and the peace and quiet.

A card also left in the room informed guests about the history of Roscommon Downs. It was a logical naming for Dan and Monica, as a heritage search revealed a link back to their forebears in Roscommon County, a region of Ireland being renowned for its quality sheep breeding.

The Flanagans had worked with a local builder to remodel the solid timber house. But as opposed to many houses Mary had seen on her journey, they had opted for a pitched roof. The outside walls were painted in warm cream to complement the beauty of the garden. A large open fireplace in the main living room, Mary guessed would be popular during the chill of winter. To emphasise the clean and fresh look, the inside walls and ceiling were painted white.

On one side of the house, floor to ceiling windows received natural light and allowed for an expansive view across the property to gum tree covered hills. Double doors opened onto a wide verandah which served as protection from the rain and provided shade during the hot days of summer.

Being aware of the wear and tear that occurs in a country home had led the Flanagans to furnish in a practical manner. Comfortable chairs were available to support aching bones at the end of a working day. A simple but practical kitchen equipped with a large table and wood fuelled stove was one of the busiest spots in the home.

It was in this room where Mary recalled Monica's advice not to stress over the cooking as they were happy with plain food. That would certainly be the case until the oven was mastered. With no instruction book, Mary suspected there might be a few mishaps as she learnt by trial and error. The conversation during dinners prior to the shearers arriving had turned on a successful start to the season, causing Mary some restless nights in anticipation for the days ahead.

*

Mary could feel the pace of the farm picking up as sheep were yarded by men whistling and yelling instructions to a chorus of barking dogs. On a visit to the shed before the shearing started, she was surprised to see how different it looked in work mode.

Swept clean, empty wool bales hooked onto stands, shearing plants humming as they were tested, fleece sorting table readied, a small table holding a large water container with a few glasses and chairs added as a rest area.

Noting Jim checking the contents of a large toolbox, Mary offered to help.

Looking up, he said 'No worries Mary, we're all sorted and ready to go.'

'You know this is new to me, but if I can assist please let me know.'

'It all works pretty well. The older sheep have been through the shed a few times so they know the drill and Lilly will give the other dogs the lead. She's a well-trained dog, who'll run all day and probably do the work of two men. Don't worry if you see her laying on the floor from time to time, she's just pacing herself.'

'I best not interrupt her then.'

'Yes, let her be, she won't want to be distracted. It's an early start rounding up the sheep to fill the main holding yard behind the shed. Lilly then helps the roustabouts to push sheep up the race into the catching pens. The shearers work four two hour runs with a payment for each one shorn so we must keep the pens full otherwise they get annoyed.'

'Sounds like it's busy, busy. I'm looking forward to watching them.'

'It certainly hums along, Mary. But if you notice the catching pens are short of sheep, don't be afraid to push a few in. They often become jammed in the race, so don't be surprised to see Lilly giving some encouragement by jumping on their backs, that's just her training coming through.'

'It's a whole new world for a girl from the city. I understand now why that pair of boots is in my room.'

'Very important, Mary. Thankfully, there's no sign of rain, so we won't have any problems. Wet sheep annoy the shearers no end. They'll down tools for the day. Gives them arthritis in their hands they reckon.'

Eager to assist as best she could, Mary was aware that she needed to help without getting in the way. It was going to be a steep learning curve, but one that she keenly anticipated.

*

Now only a few weeks into country life, Mary's day began at first light. Opening the curtains fully to expose the garden with its backdrop of trees and fields was a delight.

Dressing quickly, she moved to the kitchen to start breakfast arrangements and found a short woman with greying hair in her fifties, wearing a colourful apron and already hard at work.

Looking up from the mixing bowl as she kneaded some dough, 'Hello, you must be Mary O'Rourke; I've been looking forward to meeting you.'

'And you would be Mrs Jones, the shearers' cook. I thought you'd arrived when I woke to the aroma of freshly baked scones. Your reputation has preceded you.'

'That's me, Mary! But enough of the Mrs Jones. While it's nice for you to be courteous, we don't stand on ceremony around here. My name is Mavis, although everyone knows me as Bunty.'

'Why Bunty?' Mary asked.

'It's a nickname I picked up at school. There were two girls called Mavis in my grade, so the teacher and the other kids decided to call me Bunty. I don't mind as I could have been called much worse. I've been known as Bunty Jones for so long, I think most people have forgotten my name is Mavis.'

'Well, I can't wait to learn more about cooking from you, Bunty. I did have some training at the orphanage, but it was pretty basic.' Moving to the stove, Mary looked at it with a puzzled expression. 'Jim showed me how to boil the kettle for an early tea or coffee, but as for the rest, it's a bit of a mystery. I'd really like to learn how to cook those famous scones that I keep hearing about.'

Mavis pressed each round out and placed them onto a baking tray. 'There'll be plenty of opportunity to learn about all that, Mary. Bob Murphy and his team arrive today. Stay close and you'll be an expert much quicker than you think. You might even become my main opposition in the scone-making competition at the Castle Hill agricultural show.'

'I doubt that that'll happen Bunty, but I really would appreciate your help as I want to do as well as I can. The Flanagans have given me this opportunity, and I'm determined not to let them down. So as soon as I finish my morning's work in the house, I'll give you a hand.'

'No rush Mary, no rush.'

Feeling that she could speak frankly to Bunty, Mary took this opportunity to ask some advice about Rosemary Cleary. 'Monica said she could be difficult to get along with, and as the new person at the farm I've no wish to have any arguments.'

Lowering her voice, Bunty replied, 'Rosemary has been visiting the farm for years and saying that she wants to live and work here. She's never clicked with Dan and Monica and has been particularly difficult since the Flanagans mentioned you were coming. We can't worry about her. She'll just have to sort herself out.'

Mary decided the best path forward would be to fulfill her role and try to forget about Rosemary. 'Thanks Bunty, I'll be careful whenever she's around.'

*

'Hey Bunty, is this your new apprentice?' called a friendly voice as Bunty and Mary entered the shearing shed several hours later. 'Has she been trained to cook and show you what to do? Looks like things are about to improve around here boys.'

'Enough of that Bob. This is Mary O'Rourke, a young lady from the city here to look after Dan and Monica. You rough heads better treat her well or you'll answer to me.'

Three shearers dressed in jeans, black singlets and fleecy chequered shirts with sleeves rolled up to the elbows were busy preparing for the work ahead. Bob had a mop of wild woolly hair and seemed blessed with a permanent grin.

'Settle down Bunty, I'm just having a bit of fun. Welcome Mary, I'm pleased to meet you. We have to keep stirring Bunty up, otherwise she'll think there's something wrong with us.'

Mary noticed that Bob was doing most of the stirring and the others were saying little.

'Fair enough Bob, I should be well used to it, as I copped it from your father when he was running his motley crew. And who are your workmates, did you bring them here from the pub?'

'Steady on Bunty, two good mates of mine and even better shearers, Bluey Brown and George Simpson. You must be having a senior's moment as they were here last year. If you look after us, we've told Jim that we'll be done and dusted in eight to ten days. We all want to play in Saturday's footy match for Castle Hill against Timburra, so once we start there'll be no rest for the wicked and a cite less for the righteous.'

'Are you all still playing in the senior team?' asked Bunty.

Bob again replied, 'Well of course George and I are still in our prime and old Bluey, who clocked over forty last week and looks like he's on his last legs can still hold his place.'

He's being a bit tough on you Bluey,' Bunty said as she placed the morning tea on the table. With a grin Bluey looked up and made no comment as Bob continued, 'We all play to help keep the club going, as many of the young blokes have left town for work or go to uni.'

'Well, I know Jim will keep your pens full and I'll make sure you don't go hungry, so it's up to you blokes how long you're here.'

'P'rhaps we might stay on a bit longer now that Mary's here to help out. What do you say boys?' Bob winked.

Mary could feel her face redden and noticed that George, who looked to be in his mid to late twenties and was quite a handsome man, gazed straight into her eyes with a friendly and an almost apologetic smile. She knew immediately he was concerned that Bob may have embarrassed her.

'My apologies, Mary. These blokes don't say much. But I do mean that in the nicest way,' Bob said.

Mary knew he had meant no harm and was drawn to the warmth between Bunty, Bob and his quiet mates. As she watched the shearers sharpening their handpieces on the grinding wheels and readying their workstations, it was clear they were hardworking men committed to making their way in a tough industry.

Bunty had already warned Mary not to be upset by the friendly banter as in her words, it only occurred between people who like each other.

Placing the cups and teapot into the carry-basket after the tea-break, Bunty confided, 'There you go Mary, just a bit of fun. I was the cook for Bob's father when he was leading the team. That was the team that Dan worked in, and of course when young Bob was old enough, his father taught him the ropes, and now he's in charge. We've all been mates for years. You'll really like Bluey when you get to know him. Bob and George will hustle along while Bluey works quietly at his shearing, stopping for the occasional smoke. He's never far behind the others when the end of day tally of sheep shorn is done.'

'Thanks Bunty, I enjoyed meeting them. They're a friendly group and I must say that George looks like a strong sort of character and I wish he had said something so that I could know him a little better.'

'There's a bit of mystery about George, it's like he always has something going on that only he knows about. You'll see him around from time to time. He's a bloke who can turn his hand to electrical, carpentry and plumbing … our emergency fix-it man. While he normally works in Bob's team on big jobs, he also travels and works on his own.'

Mary nodded, 'I noticed that both him and Bluey didn't have much to say. Are they always like that?'

'Think they were just having trouble getting a word in with Bob around.

He enjoys being the centre of attention and could talk under water that bloke.'

Bunty continued as they re-entered the kitchen and she busily rinsed out the teapot. 'For all of that Mary, it's good for you to have met them as you'll run into them around town and they're regulars at the footy club dances. You'll also see a couple of young roustabouts in the shed tomorrow. Their job is to pick up the shorn fleeces, remove the dags from the edges, and press the wool into bales for transport.'

'I'm looking forward to seeing everyone at work,' Mary replied.

Still having the matter of Jim and the mystery woman at the railway station on her mind, she would have liked to quiz Bunty about whether he had a permanent or casual partner. But mulling it over she decided not to raise the question until she was more firmly part of the family.

*

Feeling more settled, Mary decided that when the shearing was completed, she would spend more time in the town centre.

Since leaving the orphanage she had not had the opportunity to purchase new clothes needed to attend a local dance or social events. Suspecting that smart casual would suffice, she nonetheless wanted to look her best when the time arrived and secretly hoped that she might run into George Simpson.

Mary had managed to exchange a few words with him as the shearing got underway and found herself becoming quite attracted to him.

Being a keen reader, she was also eager to browse through the new and second-hand bookshop, take up membership at the library and make an application to join the writers' group. An hour or two at the antiques and collectables shop was another must.

When mentioning her plans to Jim, he said, 'Well I reckon I should come and keep an eye out for you. We can't have any of those ghosts up and about rattling their chains.'

'Yes Jim, I'll need to keep my wits about me. I'd also like to spend some time with the men who sit at the front of Manny's Bakery.'

'Those old blokes and their dogs are there most days having coffee and a yarn. It's a bit like their social club,' Jim paused. 'But with all these places you want to visit, it makes me think that when the shearing's over, we must organise some driving lessons so you can get your licence. That will give you independence to travel without having to rely on me.'

Mary laughed, 'Now you're really starting to worry me, Jim. It might be wise to begin the first lesson in the middle of our biggest paddock so that I can't run into anything.'

Chapter 9

The Simpsons

George Simpson, the only son of Ted and Wendy Simpson, lived his early life with his parents and two older sisters, Thelma and Joyce in Castle Hill.

Ted was a foreman railway ganger, responsible for the maintenance of the railway line between Castle Hill and the South Australian border. The other permanent ganger Claude South was also born in Castle Hill, carried the nickname Southey, and was considered a bit of a lad around town. Ted's team of gangers were itinerant, and when in town lived in the bungalows attached to the back of the railway house.

Ted spent his days walking the railway lines, repairing rail equipment and attending training courses in Melbourne. Consequently, Uncle Claude – as George, Thelma and Joyce came to call him – often acted as their stand-in father. Wendy Simpson was also regularly absent from the family home, giving assistance to the Castle Hill midwife. Many women preferred a home birth to the medical treatment available at the bush hospital.

When George was twelve, his father was promoted. This increased his responsibility and required extra travel resulting in extended periods away from Castle Hill. Restless at home George decided to accompany his father when he moved between towns and railway camps. Wendy and his sisters remained home in Castle Hill. The gypsy lifestyle suited George, as he enjoyed the opportunity to make new friendships.

Disrupting his school placement did nothing for a good learning environment; however, George worked out early on that he was not going to be a candidate for a university degree. Indeed, given the choice of a day in the classroom or with his father, he would choose the latter every time.

A further source of income came from seasonal work. When in Castle Hill George would spend a physically demanding hour or two after school with Wendy, picking fruit and vegetables. This led to bottling and preserving the fruit with Uncle Claude, who claimed to be an expert. Always critical of the judges at the agricultural show when they marked down his entries, 'They just play favourites,' was his claim.

George got quite a shock to find his mother in tears one day because Claude was transferring to Queensland to take up a railway employment promotion.

'I'll miss him, George. He's part of the family.'

'I understand Mum, but we can write, and visit from time to time.'

George was surprised when Claude suddenly left Castle Hill after a quick hug and a handshake. When other men of long-standing left town, there was a gathering to enjoy a few beers. Disappointed with Claude leaving so quickly, George asked his father why there was no traditional drinks session. 'Didn't he want a party? He had a lot of mates!'

'Dunno, just loaded his car and got going.'

George noted that his mother became a regular letter writer asking him to drop her letters to Claude into the post box. However, there was never any return mail. His mother seemed to lose her spark after Claude left, while his two older sisters, who he regarded as dull and duller, carried on without change.

Disappointed at the turn of events but believing that Claude's leaving was final, George decided to get on with his life and school. Casual work provided useful pocket money.

His willingness to work hard stood him in good stead when he applied through his father for a job with Mick Brown as a shearer's roustabout.

It would be a temporary position to fill the six-week Christmas break from school, a quiet period of the year with cricket, a game he had no interest in, the only sport available. George was comfortable meeting Mick, a big man wearing his usual black singlet at a farm close to Castle Hill.

'I've no experience Mick, but I've seen shearers working and reckon I know what to do.'

'I'll give you a week's trial to see if you can keep up with me and my mate. You'll be no good to me if you can't go the distance. If you want to learn to shear and be part of my team you must be reliable. Do that and I'll show you the ropes.'

Mick liked the young man's get up and go. He knew his father Ted as a man not afraid of bending his back. Taking the option of hard work rather than enjoying six weeks holiday was unusual when fifteen years of age.

At the end of the first day in the shed, George was wondering if he had made the right choice. Working with the other roustabout to pick up hundreds of freshly shorn sheep fleeces, sorting, and throwing them into a wool sack for pressing was a solid day's work.

The other roustabout was an experienced hand, so George was able to follow his example in removing dags from the fleeces. The momentum of the day was unrelenting with the constant hum of the shearing plant, the shuffling movement of the sheep, and the occasional bark of the mustering dogs.

George went into the task with an understanding that he would be a bit stiff and sore at day's end, and he was certainly not disappointed on that score. When he woke and prepared for his seven thirty start on the second day, he knew he would need to toughen up to complete the first of the four two-hour shearing runs.

Mick Brown was pleased to see George walk into the shed early at the start of day two ready to work. Clearly, he had passed the first test that many had failed, and given his commitment to work hard, he could go on from there. Although missing holiday time with his mates, George was confident in his decision. After a couple of weeks Mick made good his promise to work him through the basics of sheep shearing.

'It's all in the way you control the sheep George. Move in close while I shear one,' Mick said as he dragged a big ewe from the catching pen.

'You've seen me sit them on their tail bone to start by shearing the belly. If you hold them there; they won't move.' As Mick expertly took the wool off the belly, rear end and legs, he rolled the sheep onto its side and started to remove the wool with long and deliberate strokes.

'You make it look easy Mick.'

With a grin Mick replied as he rolled the sheep to the other side, 'It's the first five thousand that are the hardest. I learnt by going through the motions rubbing them with a big shoe brush. Just learn how to hold them, that's the key.'

As he completed the job and George threw the fleece onto the sorting table, Mick said, 'Some of the old ewes have been through the process many times. They're aware of what's happening, so they'll usually cooperate.'

'Thanks Mick, I hope before I finish my six weeks, I'm confident enough to shear one.'

'Don't be afraid of dragging one out of the pen, they won't bite, and we all had to start somewhere.'

George's commitment convinced Mick that he should make him an offer to become a member of his shearing team. Punctual and having not missed a day's work, George had continued with plenty of energy but hadn't made a move to shear one. Becoming impatient during the afternoon tea break Mick said, 'Are you going to bite the bullet George?'

'No time like the present,'

'Best leave the old ram, just in case you miss and knock off his pistol,'

'I'll be right Mick; I'll just have a go at an old ewe.'

'Take your time, it's not a race.'

Mick watched George pull the ewe onto the shearing boards, and after setting it firmly in place tug the rope to start the clippers and commence removing the fleece. 'Well done George, no cuts on the sheep to sew up, there's a job on the team if you want it.'

Given his father was away for a couple of nights walking the rail lines, now or never thought George as he arrived home. Raising the subject with his mother as she prepared dinner. 'I might as well Mum, I'm going nowhere with school and I turn sixteen this year. Mick's a fair man who looks after his team. I'm sure it's the right time for me to make the break. He's promised to help me work on my skills. In time I'll move from roustabout to shearer.'

'If that's what you want to do George. Go ahead. It's a tough life you're taking on. Remember to hold onto your money. It's a lifestyle that could see you spending plenty of time in the pub.'

Mick Brown had spent many years on the road servicing farmers who relied on him to shear their sheep to fit in with their timetables. The structured work and travel program allowed him to retain his team of shearers and roustabouts in constant employment.

Working with the shearing team was a complete change of lifestyle for George. During the first few months while the team was shearing around Castle Hill, he was able to live at home by organising a lift with a workmate. However, as the daily travel distance became impractical, he stayed with the team in the accommodation that was available which for George was a bed in Mick's caravan.

As he told his mother, 'It's nothing flash; it serves the purpose of a roof over our heads.'

True to his word Mick gave George all the training required to take his place as a shearer in the team on his eighteenth birthday, locking his new role with the comment, 'I'm pleased for you George. You've done the hard yards. I hope you stay with my team.'

'Thanks Mick. It's hard work, but I can cope if I pace myself and take an occasional day's break.'

Apart from his upgraded status in the team, the change made a significant impact in increasing his income and allowed him to plan for his future. Being able to own a vehicle would increase his independence. The extra money would allow the opportunity to choose his accommodation when on the road. There was the matter of women coming into his life. He was a good looking bloke with no ties, keen to take up any opportunities that came his way.

George's life settled into a pattern of travelling the shearing circuit as part of Mick's team, taking accommodation in the local hotel, a clean up after work and then enjoying whatever social life was available. On one occasion he was talked into trying his hand at bull riding when the rodeo was in town.

Hanging on to a bull's back for eight seconds seemed simple enough. But it ended badly with him face down in the dirt, with the crowd having a good laugh at his expense. It should have occurred to him entering the event was a bad idea when he noted that most of the blokes in the queue were limping. After dusting himself off, his mates suggested he would be a natural at riding the buck-jumping horses. George reckoned it was time to change his mates.

While limited during the week, there always seemed to be some activity around the local pubs, and now he had moved on from sleeping in Mick's caravan, his opportunities for sexual encounters increased. George rated attending bachelor and spinster balls an evening not to be missed. Even as a bloke on the loose, he struggled to understand how people who were normally reserved could drink so much alcohol, resulting in them completely losing their inhibitions. But lose them they did, and he was happy to take the sex on offer.

George's life took a dramatic turn when called up for his national army service. Gone were the freedoms, income and lifestyle he'd enjoyed as part of Mick Brown's shearing team. However, he was happy to do his duty with Mick promising to re-employ him. His first few weeks were structured around discipline, training and movement between camps for reasons which at times escaped him.

The regular army trainers seemed to have a competition to register the loudest voice as his group marched endlessly. George was pleased to have a fitness base as many of his fellow recruits really struggled. Shooting at targets on the rifle range presented no difficulties. Less enjoyable was learning the safe way to throw a hand grenade while keeping a close watch on his fellow recruits.

To maintain his skills George took opportunities on days off to join a local team and shear a quota of sheep. While he was a bloke who always enjoyed a cold beer at the end of the working day, he found many of his fellow recruits quickly fell into the habit of regular heavy drinking sessions. He was reminded of Mick's advice when he was leaving to join the army, 'You'll find that you'll have two choices George: either being a lonely man or ending up a pisspot.'

While George initially thought the advice was a bit extreme, after a few months he could see the drinking environment developing around him, so he worked out a survival procedure built around exercise. Working life in the sheds had built a strong body, and as he was planning on returning after his army discharge, George decided to add weight training, and long-distance running to the army fitness sessions. The promotions he received to the positions of lance corporal and corporal were appreciated, although he didn't welcome the added responsibility for the actions of other recruits.

The completion of his statutory service was enough for George who was happy to be discharged to return to his former life. Some of his fellow recruits decided to sign on for a further three or six-year period and urged George to continue. However, having been based at a half dozen army camps up and down the east coast of Australia during his stint he was keen to return to his life working around Castle Hill.

Now with some trade skills learnt in the army to add to his work as a shearer, he reckoned there would be an opportunity to build a small business servicing local farms. George was also carrying a secret he was afraid might catch up with him if he didn't return to what he perceived to be the safe area of Castle Hill. He was aware that the police were investigating the organised stealing of sheep from properties where he had worked as a freelance shearer during breaks from Mick Brown's team.

It was the lure of easy money that got him involved in stealing a few lambs when they were turned out into a holding paddock. Acting on the promise that only a few would be taken and therefore not quickly missed, George's role was to identify the best opportunities to pick up some easy cash. It was an arrangement fraught with danger for George. He was associating with a couple of strangers he had met in the pub.

As it was put to him, 'It's simple George; we have a trailer and will just take a dozen. No-one is going to miss a few lambs from a big mob of sheep. We take them well away from the area, remove the ear tags and sell them to the local butcher shops. All we want from you is to identify the properties, and the best time to act. It's easy money.'

A straightforward arrangement for George in dealing with thieves that he would see no more than a couple of times. They had identified themselves as Tasy and Jim, with George confident that they were false names. But he was unconcerned about clarifying their identities, the least he knew about them the better. George was unaware that the police had Tasy and Jim under surveillance, tracking their movements across the state.

Also unknown to George, they had taken an opportunity to expand their operation, and steal a truckload of lambs which had led police to try to catch them in the act. The police had noted George drinking with them but had not developed strong evidence that he was involved.

George's major concern was that after a couple of thefts, the local farmers had formed a vigilante group to patrol the properties promising strong retribution. He was shocked when Tasy laughingly told him that they had stolen a truckload of lambs, far exceeding the arrangement of 'just a few'.

Knowing full well they would be caught and prosecuted, escaping to his army service was an opportunity to break the cycle of his involvement. Now he was older it was a time of his life he deeply regretted, but what was done was done, and he would just have to live with it.

Chapter 10

Stalwarts

Mary, having been so taken with George Simpson, some days later sat back in the sunshine on the verandah and relived the moments she had enjoyed during the hustle and bustle of the shearing shed.

The morning and afternoon tea breaks soon brought George and Bluey out of their shell and Bob no longer hogged the spotlight. The men were a font of knowledge as their shearing program took them to many farms in the district and as the days went on, they delighted in sharing information.

George seemed to have a story to suit every situation and with the added embellishment and laughter, it was a little like listening to tall tales and true. His favourite was about a mice plague that he and Bluey worked through in New South Wales. 'They were everywhere, Mary. We drove up to the farm in the dark and it was like driving through a swarm of locusts. I couldn't believe it and didn't want to get out of the car.

We kicked mice out from under our feet while we were shearing. The buggers were getting into our sleeping bags trying to eat the lining. So, we hung the bags up from the shed roof during the day and kept giving them a whack to knock them out. It was a shocker.'

'Sounds as if it was quite an ordeal,' Mary remarked.

Looking up from his paper with a nod in agreement, Bluey said, 'I was working the wool press, Mary. I reckon I pressed more mice than wool. When we finished the job, like George said, we couldn't wait to leave. I was really concerned they'd eat all the wiring in my ute.'

Tea breaks were taken at a table in the shed. But right on midday, the shearing plants would be switched off with Bunty ready to serve lunch around the table in the house. Bob and George carried the after-lunch conversation, while Bluey was happy to quietly read the paper and work on the crossword. Occasionally ribbed by the younger men as to whether he was ever able to complete a puzzle, he was never concerned, and just carried on as he called it, 'keeping the brain ticking over'.

Mary was fascinated to also hear the stories of the two sisters who were working as roustabouts while enjoying a gap year from their university studies. She marvelled at their courage to leave their home and family in England and travel to Australia having trust in their ability to pick up work to fund their expenses. Mary hoped that an opportunity might present in the future to allow her to visit some of the many places where they had journeyed.

Respecting the shearers' commitment to complete the job, Mary couldn't help but notice that while the breaks were enjoyed, when it was time to work, they were efficient and methodical seeming to pace each other with the number of sheep shorn. By Monday of the second week, Mary remarked, 'It looks like you've broken the back of the job, Bob.'

'Nearly finished Mary, just the last couple of pens and we're done and dusted. It's been a straightforward job with no problems keeping the sheep moving through the pens and being filled up each day with Bunty's scones. The boys reckon this is the only job in the area where we put on weight. And thanks for helping as we went. I know Bluey and George enjoyed your company. You're a great addition to Roscommon Downs.'

'That's kind of you to say, Bob.'

'Well life here will take a bit of getting used to after experiencing the pace of the big smoke. It wasn't for me. I've not long returned from Melbourne after a few years playing footy and working as a sales rep in sports merchandise.'

Listening to Bob relay his life experiences had Mary questioning how he'd been able to cram so much into so little time. As he knocked off and tidied up for the afternoon, they took a seat in the shed where he told her that he'd been born and raised in the Carravale area and attended Castle Hill Primary School. He had loved the school holidays when he went with his dad on shearing runs and often worked as a roustabout leading him to master the skill of shearing while still a teenager.

'It wasn't difficult for me. I enjoy working with sheep, and with Dad, a shearer, there were plenty of opportunities to take it on. I was also playing footy in the senior Castle Hill team when I was sixteen which attracted the Melbourne football club talent scouts. Offers came my way and included private school scholarships along with accommodation at the home of a host family.'

Mary, who was a good listener and always showed a genuine interest in hearing other people's stories, said, 'You must have been excited for your future.'

'I was! And keen to travel to take up the offer that would residentially qualify me to play for the club that I'd always supported.'

'Did it work out well for you?'

'Pretty much. I travelled with my family to Melbourne during the Christmas break, toured the club facilities and met the host family. Almost straightaway I was learning the ways of a big city while finishing secondary school. After I graduated, I was at a loose end trying to decide which career direction to take. The coach was keen for players to have an alternative activity apart from football.'

'It must have been challenging, trying to work your way through all the options.'

'I wasn't complaining as I enjoyed the life I was leading. While smart enough to pass exams, I was more comfortable working with my hands rather than pursuing a career through university. After I signed a contract, one of the club's sponsors employed me in a temporary role as a marketing cadet. That helped me financially while I worked out what to do.

Bob appeared to be enjoying nothing better than talking to someone as polite as Mary and he didn't need much urging as he animatedly explained that his life from that point developed a pace of its own. The marketing manager was a livewire networker who he decided to spend as much time with as his football would allow. He attended sportsmen nights all over Victoria, often in the most unlikely places, including regular prison visits.

'It was fun while it lasted, but when I turned twenty-two, the coach I liked playing under moved on. Made me lose interest, get dropped from the senior team and lose my contract. I didn't want to play for another club.'

An expression of disappointment came over Bob's face as he picked up a stick and drew a circle in a small patch of dust.

Mary placed her hand on his shoulder. 'That must have been a disruptive period?'

'It was. I'd had enough, came home, got back to shearing and played footy with me mates at Castle Hill. We've set ourselves to win a flag during the next couple of years.'

As she rose to her feet and prepared to leave, Mary said, 'You've certainly had some great experiences, Bob, and I hope we can keep in touch between shearing seasons.'

'Let's do that Mary,' Bob replied, as he stored the last of his shearing gear away. 'The footy club has a social after each home game. I'll get on Jim's back to bring you along. Wouldn't hurt him to come and catch up with a few of his old mates.'

Mary had really warmed to Bob's friendly, knockabout manner in the short time they'd known each other. Although only a year or so older than her, he had established his own successful shearing business on the back of hard work. She was also aware that anyone who received Bunty's tick of approval must have something going for him. It was time to encourage Jim to re-engage with the footy club.

*

Taking the opportunity for a couple of hours away from the farm, Mary travelled to town with Jim who was planning to pick up some supplies.

Constantly surprised and amused at how Lilly seemed blessed with a sixth sense as she anticipated Jim's every move, Mary said, when meeting him in the garage, 'I just saw Lilly waiting patiently beside the truck. How on earth does she know when you're leaving the farm?'

'I've no idea, Mary. I can never get out the gate without her. I don't mind because she keeps me company and stands guard over the goods in the tray. Mind you, I don't believe she'd bite. But if someone tried to pinch something, there's no doubt she'd give 'em a hell of a fright.'

*

Arriving in Castle Hill and leaving Jim to his shopping, Mary could see the attraction of enjoying Manny's coffee, the warmth of the sun and having a chat with mates.

A dog resting at the feet of his master lifted his head and managed a single lazy wag of his tail as the three men seated out front smiled when she approached. 'Hi, I'm Mary O'Rourke, you might remember me.'

'Yes, I remember you, Mary. I'm Sid McHenry,' answered the older of the men doffing his cap. 'Jim introduced you on your first day in town.'

'That's right! Jim said that you're all good blokes and I should say hello.'

'No doubt about Jim, he's a great judge of character.' Sid replied. 'Would you like to join us for coffee?'

'Yes, I'd like that.' Mary nodded, as she took a seat at the table. 'Are you here most days?'

'Yes and no,' Sid again responded. 'Depends on the weather, doctor's appointments and funerals. Sometimes we adjourn to the bowls' club for a few beers. We're all old blokes, so we take life a day at a time.'

Mary sensed a welcoming friendliness as each of the men was introduced.

'As I said, I'm Sid McHenry, and this old fella is Fred Spooner. Our mate with the beard is Clarry O'Connor. Clarry reckons the beard makes him look sophisticated. We think he needs more mirrors in his house.'

'Not everyone can be as good lookin' as you, Sid,' Clarry laughed. 'Isn't that right, Mary?'

'I don't know what to say to that, Clarry. Perhaps I'll just keep out of it and say how lovely it is to meet you all.'

'No worries, Mary! You might notice that we do a lot of stirring, but are good mates and it's never offensive,' Sid chuckled. 'Speaking of which … we thought Clarry was going to peg out last week as he disappeared for a couple of days. Then we remembered it was his turn to buy the coffee.'

With a smile, Clarry just raised his eyebrows as if to say, 'Here we go again' having been the butt of the joke many times before.

'Like I said, it would be best if I keep out of it,' Mary responded.

'Aw yeah, I forgot to introduce my dog,' Sid said. 'His name is Go-round.' Seeing Mary's puzzled look, he explained. 'I used to work in a job which required me to herd sheep into the sale yards … so the dog would hear 'Go-round' all day long and the name stuck.'

The old kelpie's ears pricked whenever he heard his name mentioned, but he remained resting on the ground alongside

Sid who paused to take a mouthful of his coffee.

'Let me tell you a bit more about my two mates. Fred here retired from the railways a few years ago. He keeps telling us he worked in the goods' sheds stacking bags of sugar and fertilizer. He used to be a heavy smoker which has affected his voice. Now he reckons he sounds like Richard Burton, but he's on his own there.' Sid laughed. 'I'm not sure about Clarry. He'd have you believe he's retired. But you have to strike a blow before you can retire.'

It was easy for Mary to see the affection between the men as no offence was taken.

'Most days we're joined by Archie Jones who was married to the owner of the antique shop across the street. A bit of a messy story there,' Fred suddenly interrupted.

'Jim Wilkinson did tell me a little about the shop's history when I arrived. Something to do with the shop being haunted. But tell me, have you all been mates for a long time?'

'Mates might be stretching it a bit, Mary,' said Sid, eager to cut back in on Fred. 'But we've been together for many years. We meet, talk and have a bit of fun. Archie likes to keep watch on the antique shop. He swears he sees ghosts coming and going. We think he drinks too much coffee, and we're not sure what he's smoking these days. Might be playing tricks with his mind.'

Adopting a more serious tone, Sid explained that everyone in the group had suffered a serious illness requiring surgery and they helped each other through life's challenges.

'It's a limited social life meeting your friends at funerals. But enough about us Mary, tell us your story while Fred organises more coffee, and a round of apple scrolls. You must have one, they're a specialty of Manny's Bakery.'

Mary was pleased with the genuine interest the men showed as she summarised her life. They agreed that she had had a few ups and downs, and that things would really improve as the result of her move to Roscommon Downs.

'And what about your journey to live here Clarry? It sounds like Sid gives you and Fred a hard time.'

'As Sid said we're all good mates. He reckons he's in charge, but we know he's only allowed to speak here. That's why we can never shut him up! When he gets home, his wife Gloria rules the roost. But really our support for each other has been important as we've battled along.'

Pausing to take a loud slurp of his coffee, Clarry went on to say, 'Hopefully you can see your way clear to come back and meet Archie. He has a tale or two to tell when it comes to the antique shop. We agree that it's haunted. A couple of the locals reckon it could be turned into a tourist attraction with midnight tours. That'd frighten a few. Particularly if the organisers could convince Maureen O'Reilly to appear every night.'

'Jim warned me to look out for Maureen. I'm not sure what to think. I don't believe in ghosts, but you can be certain that I won't be going anywhere near the shop after dark,' Mary replied.

Fred, a balding and quietly spoken man looked to be in his late sixties. Clarry who was a little younger sported less wrinkles, spoke quietly about their family and working lives, and what had brought them to live together in Castle Hill.

Mary was touched, as Fred explained they'd been good friends while neighbours in Melbourne. When their respective wives passed away, they teamed up to follow country horse racing.

After attending and enjoying the racing carnival for a couple of years, and having made friends in the community, they decided to sell their homes in Melbourne and live together in Castle Hill. They welcomed visits from their children and grandchildren and were comfortable to see out their days in the area.

Taking up the conversation again, Clarry explained, 'As Sid said, we've had the inevitable health issues, and while Sid has Gloria to look after him, Fred and I rely on each other for support. It works okay for us. It's just a shame that Fred isn't a better cook,' Clarry concluded.

'Take what Clarry's saying with a grain of salt, Mary. He's well fed and doesn't miss a meal. And he's always having a top up sausage roll here at Manny's.'

'Apologies Fred,' Clarry nodded. 'You must come for a meal Mary. It's cordon bleu.'

Adopting a more serious tone, Fred continued. 'Just so you're forewarned and forearmed about Archie. It's a bit sensitive and best you know the circumstances.'

Fred explained that the dispute between Archie and Dorothy Jones was about money. Archie had been a long-term construction worker in Melbourne before retiring after receiving a redundancy payment and superannuation. Because of the pressure of his work driving cranes on high rise buildings, his doctors had advised him to move to a quiet stress-free environment. Dorothy had been keen to buy an antique shop in the country and saw the Castle Hill store advertised.

'Where it goes to from there, Mary, depends on who you talk to. The best held story is that Dorothy had some money she'd saved and was expecting Archie to put in his share. While he was prepared to put in most of his savings, and the redundancy payment, there was no way he'd contribute his superannuation.'

'Thanks for telling me, Fred. I can understand when you say it got a bit messy. Now I know the story, hopefully I won't put my foot in it.'

'People and money, Mary. If there's a dispute you'll generally find money's involved. They had a falling out leading to their divorce. Archie hangs about town living at the pub. Goodness knows what he'll do next. We do our best to keep him company.'

Knowing that Jim would be back shortly to pick her up, Mary decided to wish them well and return on another day to meet Archie. After fending off the usual friendly inquiries about a possible relationship with Jim, she promised Manny and his staff that she would return and catch up on the town gossip.

When travelling home, Mary decided to give herself more time on her next visit given the locals were always up for a chat. She had run out of time to join the library or call into the new and second-hand book shop.

Chapter 11

Revenge Renewal

With the shearing completed, the wool baled and taken by truck to the sales, the sheep drenched and turned out into fresh paddocks, life at the farm was much calmer. Work for Jim returned to repair and maintenance, while Mary's cooking skills were enhanced on the back of Bunty's guidance.

Comfortable in her role, she was shocked when preparing lunch to be confronted in the kitchen by Monica. 'It's been brought to my attention Mary, that you've been involved in a police investigation.'

Feeling a rush of anger, Mary replied, 'That's correct, Monica. But not as a thief. People stole from me and others at the orphanage. Why would you suspect me ... what did you hear?'

'A conversation at the library between members of the writing group. They were talking about you with great authority.'

'Well, it's not right ... definitely not right! I'm shocked that they would say such things about me.'

Barely able to control her emotions, Mary explained the circumstances to Monica. 'We had some bad girls both in and around the orphanage who were happy to steal from everyone until they were caught by the police. One of my earrings was found amongst the goods they were trying to sell at a market stall.'

'Those things weren't said. My apologies, Mary. It just goes to show that you need to hear both sides before jumping to conclusions.'

'That's okay! I'm sorry that I got a bit fired up. But now that I come to think of it, I'm not surprised, as I never really did feel comfortable when attending the writing group. They were an odd lot and I always felt like an outsider.'

'Let's have a cuppa, and you can fill me in, Mary.'

Mary told Monica that despite the level of personal details required to join the group, there was a requirement to first attend a meeting to allow the members to appraise her suitability. She would then be advised if they agreed to her admittance.

Monica said, 'That seems odd given it's a community group.'

'As it turned out, I was accepted and received a warm welcome. I explained that I was planning to workshop the contents of my diary in the hope of producing a memoir. The ten members who ranged in age from forty to seventy, said they would help.'

'I can see why you went ahead and joined.'

'Yes, I did join but was mindful of Rhon's advice about their past activities.'

'What did she say about the group?' Monica asked.

'It seems like they had a history of bad form. Rhon said to be careful about what I told them and not to trust the self-appointed leader, a troublemaker known as Sir-know-it-all. Apparently, he had a reputation for causing all sorts of problems that caused the group to get thrown out of their meeting room at Carravale.'

Monica poured herself a second cup of tea. 'Good heavens! If that's the case, why were they then allowed to set up in Castle Hill?'

'I've no idea!' Mary replied.

Having talked the matter through, Monica was quite distressed by what had occurred.

'Even Jim didn't trust them to treat me well. Between him and Rhon, they're a bit like a big brother and sister the way they look after me.'

Mary assured Monica that she had been well regarded during her earlier visits to the workshopping sessions, receiving constructive feedback and encouragement to support her ambition.

Over a couple of meetings, Mary's life in Melbourne was gently probed in a friendly manner during coffee breaks, with discussion about the Flanagans, ballroom dancing, and growing up in the orphanage. And naturally as she read her work, Mary grew confident enough to relay the circumstances surrounding the theft of the earring, the involvement of the police and its consequent recovery.

'There was never any reason for confusion,' Mary said. 'I spelt out the circumstances very clearly and they have deliberately twisted the facts.'

'What a treacherous and scheming lot of so 'n' so's,' Monica again apologised.

The experience had left Mary distressed, but all that really mattered was that Monica believed her and she remained a trusted employee.

*

Mary looked forward to regular catchups with Rhonda in Castle Hill. It was great to enjoy a little shopping time together and a break from the farm. Having reserved their favourite table at Manny's, she was especially keen to tell Rhon about the writing group. 'I should have taken your advice, but I couldn't believe that people would do such things. Perhaps I've led a sheltered life.'

'They did the same thing to a few of my friends in Carravale. They're no more than a bunch of bullies who don't want new members. Particularly anyone who is able to write better than them,' Rhon exploded.

'Not sure that I can claim any great writing skills, Rhon.'

'I don't believe there's much talent amongst them. One of my friends in Carravale who knows a thing or two about writing told me that half of them serve up meaningless poetry. I reckon we should do something about them, otherwise they'll just keep unfairly excluding community members.'

With a nod in agreement, Mary said, 'I'm just disappointed as to how it turned out. I hear what you say about their poetry. I took the opportunity at the orphanage to study the work of many poets. However much of what the local group presented was lost on me.'

*

When returning to the farm, Mary spent a few days thinking about the group's actions. She could appreciate what Rhon was suggesting, in that they bring some friends together and work up a plan of retribution. Mary didn't need to look far to gather supporters.

Meeting Clarry in Castle Hill, he quickly volunteered. 'They're no more than squatters and should be tossed out. More than likely they turned up one evening and took advantage of there being a lack of staff. The library works on an honour system for the community. Some of us oldies would occasionally use the room for cards and board games.'

'I wasn't aware of that, Clarry, and can see why you're upset with them.'

'Too right I am! The Carravale mob blew into town with no authority and took ownership. Because they kept coming back each week, we got used to them being around. A couple had the gift of the gab seeming to know all about council regulations. Serves us right, we all rolled over and left them the room and now they're attacking you. Well it's not on. We'll fix them up this time.'

'Thanks for that, Clarry. We can always try talking to the council, but the group might be a difficult to move.'

'Before we do that Mary, leave me to have a word with a few important people I know. Fred's a bit of a bush lawyer who understands the rules. We've put up with their rudeness for too long while other groups are being prevented from using the room. I'm sure there might be others who have an axe to grind and I reckon with a bit of luck and a good tail wind we can shift them back to Carravale.'

As Clarry rose to his feet with fists clenched, he concluded, 'Too right, we won't do anything to harm them physically, Mary, but they'll get the message.'

*

Now in their early sixties, Dan and Monica lunched together on the front verandah overlooking the garden. Sinking into comfortable chairs was a small reward for many years of heavy farm work digging postholes, straining fencing wire and tending sheep. Thankfully, in later years they could afford to employ casual workers. Tucking into his regular cold roast lamb and pickle sandwich, Dan remarked, 'Nothing better than Mary's sandwiches. You and Bunty trained her well.'

'You're starting to worry me, Dan. You tell me that nearly every day.'

'Oh well, probably a condition of age. I reckon when I'm having a few beers with the blokes at the pub, we spend the arvo repeating ourselves. But you'd have to admit that bringing Mary here was a good decision. She's been a real bonus! Treats people well and works hard to keep things going.'

'You're right, Dan. She's enabling us to stay here in our home, and that's what we want rather than living in a retirement village. I've heard of some who go a bit ratty in those places and I'm pleased that Mary remained with us after what occurred at the library. It was wrong and people shouldn't be allowed to act like that.'

Pleased the matter had been quietly resolved and the group persuaded that their time at the library had come to an end, the meeting space had since been taken over by the local hunting and shooting association.

Dan had always been strong in his view that there was no place for bullies. 'They had no right to spread rumours. Just a low act to try to damage Mary's reputation. I'm pleased she stayed strong. Old Sid had a laugh as he told me the group got a fright when a very red-faced Clarry gave them an old-fashioned serve and told them to get out of town. Sent them running in a couple of directions. All I can say is good riddance to the lot of them.'

'That would have been fun to watch.' Monica laughed. 'I should've known better than to doubt Mary's honesty. Molly Smith at the Rex doesn't tolerate thieves.'

'Thankfully, we can put it behind us. We were right in our assessment that she'd be a real asset and we both know this is where she belongs. She's become the daughter we were unable to have.'

'Well Dan, life takes its twists and turns. As the saying goes, it is what it is. We've been married for many a long year. While our lives would have benefitted from having children, we've been happy together. Hopefully that continues. I'm not looking to peg out just yet. However, at some stage we'll need to enter some clear directions into our Wills to designate the future ownership of Roscommon Downs.'

Monica rose to clear the lunch plates, and Dan stacked up the cups and saucers. 'My wish is for the farm to continue in its current form.' Dan said. 'I realise that's ambitious, but it would be good to see our work continue. I must admit I'm reaching a point with Rosemary. Since Mary came to the farm, she's been difficult to live with. We made no promises, yet she seems to think we owe her something.'

'I agree. Our plans don't revolve around Rosemary Cleary.' Monica replied.

'I forgot to mention that I spoke to her father at the pub to see if he could sort this out. Tom said, no hope. He's trying to get her to leave home, so they can have some peace and quiet.'

'Well something's got to change, Dan. The business of Rosemary arriving uninvited during Sunday lunch, setting herself a place at the table, and expecting food to be available is just not on.'

'I know you're right,' Dan said. 'I used to look forward to sitting down on Sunday. Now Rosemary turns up and I can't get out of the place quick enough.'

'I've noticed that,' Monica replied with a smile.

*

The following morning saw Dan and Jim hard at work with the farm truck backed up to the loading race. it was steady work moving the sheep from the shed into the truck. It was times like this that Dan was happy to let Jim do the bulk of the work as he reckoned it was a poor job that couldn't stand a foreman.

'That looks like a load to me, Dan. What do you reckon?' Jim asked, as he shoved the last lamb into the truck.

Pushing his battered bush hat back on his head, Dan's concentration seemed to be focused more on the look of the sheep rather than the load. 'They're fat lambs this year. It makes a difference having the good feed. Should top the sale again.'

Knowing the friendly competition that existed between the neighbouring farmers to bring top price, Jim expected this type of comment from Dan. With a broad grin, he asked, knowing full well the answer, 'How many years have you topped the sale?'

Dan just laughed when replying, 'Always.'

Satisfied with their morning's work, the two men were startled to hear loud female voices coming from inside the house. Fearing the worst, they followed the noise to the kitchen, and found Mary and Rosemary in a heated argument. Jim had never seen Mary so angry.

'Easy Mary, best we all take a step back.'

'No way, Jim, I've just been called a thief. No one calls me a thief and gets away with it.'

'Whoa Rosemary … you've got no right to repeat the rubbish being put around by that Carravale mob from the library,' Jim said.

In an aggressive mood, Rosemary was not deterred.

Overhearing the argument, Monica rushed into the kitchen. 'That's disgraceful conduct Rosemary, you should know better. You've no right to question Mary about anything, much less call her a thief. Please leave immediately.'

Fearing she might have burnt her bridges, Rosemary tried to talk her way out of the mess she'd created. 'Well, I heard the story in Castle Hill and thought it was true.'

'I don't care where you heard the story. You obviously didn't hear me. There's no place for you here. Come to terms with it. Stop causing trouble and get off the property,' Monica said loudly, pointing the way out.

Shocked and upset at the outcome of her actions, Rosemary wept as she left the room.

Monica followed her out and watched her leave before returning to the kitchen.

'Gosh, Mary, you certainly know how to stick up for yourself. I couldn't believe the yelling. I thought the kitchen was on fire,' Dan said, seating himself down at the table.

Still shaken, Mary replied, 'I hardly know her. She just burst into the room and started making wild accusations. I wasn't going to cop it.'

Monica gave Mary a reassuring hug. 'We know Rosemary has a bad temper. We've seen it before whenever she lets her guard down.'

'When she claimed that she knew all about my criminal past and was going to report me to the police, that was when I really saw red. I'm sorry if I was a bit rowdy.'

'Well good on you, I think she got the message loud and clear,' Monica replied.

Feeling that all had returned to normal, Jim intervened, 'I must say it was exciting while it lasted. Good to see you can stand on your dig, Mary. You'll have some interesting notes for your diary tonight. Now I must get back to the truck and get the sheep to market.'

As he left the property Jim had a good laugh. Mary had shown she wouldn't be bullied. The good news was that it would be quite some time before Rosemary would ever be brave enough to step through the door of Roscommon Downs again.

Chapter 12

Meeting Ollie

The steady drumming of rain on the roof had added to Mary's sleepless night.

Meeting Jim with a grin on his face at breakfast didn't help the slight churn in her stomach. 'Well today's the day, Mary, your first solo drive around the farm.'

'Don't I know it. I've been awake half the night worrying.'

'I'm sure you'll be fine. I've cooked some bacon and eggs to help get you started.'

'I'm thinking I'll pass thanks, Jim. Perhaps I'll have them later. Just too nervous to eat.'

'Don't worry, I'm sure you'll be fine. Just remember what we've been working on. We'll have you down to meet the licence tester in no time.'

I wish I were as confident as Jim, mused Mary as she slipped behind the wheel of the farm truck. Thankfully, the rain had stopped, leaving behind muddy tracks to negotiate. It had been a straightforward enough course that Jim had set on the first day that she'd started her lessons. His words were now ringing in her ears as she kicked over the motor and slipped into first gear.

'Twice around the farm track solo and you'll be ready to head into town,' Jim shouted giving her the thumbs up.

As the truck slowly responded, she worked through the gears, growing in confidence when gate openings were successfully navigated. Out through the paddocks and up the rise to the high ground, through the copse of trees startling some sheep, across the top for a pause to allow for a couple of deep breaths before proceeding.

Having traversed the downhill section on prior occasions with Jim coaching from the passenger seat, Mary was more than aware of what laid ahead. Remembering that the crown of the track was the place to be, she gripped the steering wheel even more tightly and released the brake. Halfway down the slippery slope, the truck started to lose traction on the wet track, causing it to slide sideways before coming to rest at the bottom.

Shutting down the motor, Mary stepped out of the cabin trembling and somewhat relieved when an ashen-faced Jim arrived.

'Gosh Mary, I was afraid the truck was going to roll-over. You did well and kept your head by steering into the skid.'

'No worries, Jim! Can I now go into town and try for my licence?'

'There's no holding you back. I can't wait to tell Dan and Monica how you controlled the big skid.'

As she drove the truck back into the yard, Mary felt happy to let the story play out. It would remain her secret that the downhill slide was out of her control and hopefully it might be quite some time before the hill would again be navigated on a wet day.

*

From her very first lesson of two months prior, it had quickly become clear to Mary that driving the truck was not a skill she would easily learn. But she'd recognised the need to persist and obtain her driver licence and hoped it wouldn't be too difficult after a couple of months tuition bouncing around across the paddocks.

Despite her initial struggles, Mary had at least got past kangaroo hopping having mastered the clutch and learning to change gears without stalling the engine. A couple of circuits later, she had admitted to Monica what she had feared all along – driving was not something that came naturally.

'Thank goodness I'm learning in the big paddock, otherwise I'd have knocked over some fences, not to mention the sheep. Jim's far more confident than I am about passing the test.'

Monica had smiled. 'It's certainly entertaining to watch. I hope I'm safe sitting here right out of harm's way on the verandah. You just need to stick with it as we all have to learn.'

'I'm really concerned about the state of the truck with me crunching the gears all the time.'

'Don't worry, Mary, it's our oldest vehicle. Jim said to expect there might be some wear and tear. But just think, sooner or later you can buy an automatic car which is much easier to drive. It's always best to start out the hard way as all the farm trucks have manual gears. Just work on understanding your road rules because if you fail that section, the test won't continue.'

*

Mary couldn't believe how nervous she felt while waiting to be tested, and rereading the road rules, she was hopeful that the extra time spent preparing would stand her in good stead.

Having given Dan a solemn promise to be extra careful, he allowed her to use the farm's good ute. 'It's my transport to the pub, Mary,' he cautioned, 'Try not to put any dents in it.'

Mary suspected that passing the test was easier in the country than the city, but she still felt pleasantly surprised when it ended, and she proudly slipped her brand-new driver's licence into her wallet.

When Monica received the good news, she kindly suggested that Mary continue to drive the truck for a short time until she could afford to buy a second-hand car of her own.

'Off to the shops for some retail therapy,' Mary promised herself.

*

Having managed not to hit anything between the farm and town, Mary was now feeling extra pleased with herself as she parked the truck in the large parking area behind the Castle Hill Town Hall. Being mindful to avoid busy traffic periods, she was following Jim's advice to just take baby steps to begin and the rest would soon fall into place.

While carefully locking the truck, Mary was surprised to see George Simpson standing on the footpath outside the second-hand bookshop. Mary smiled and asked, 'Are you waiting for me?'

'Yes, I am,' George replied as he lifted the peak of his cap. 'I knew you were coming to town and you'd be certain to look at the books.'

'Why didn't you come to the farm?'

'I wanted to see you on your own and was wondering if you'd consider having lunch with me sometime?' George's face reddened.

'What … like on a date? You really don't mess around.'

'Yep, a date. Messing around is not my go Mary. I reckon we got on well during the shearing and I think we would be good together.'

'You're a smooth talker, George Simpson. Okay, why not! I'm free on Friday if that suits.'

'Should be fun. I'll pick you up at midday.'

Mary felt a certain lightness and excitement at what lay ahead. She had been disappointed when George left after the shearing without any comment for the future. Probably one jump ahead of herself, she couldn't stop from now wondering – what might the future hold?

*

Bunty had recommended the shop assuring Mary that it held a large stock regularly exchanged by community members. Monica had also suggested that she should look through books previously owned or written by Castle Hill pioneers.

An overhead bell jangled as Mary opened the door and entered. She immediately became aware of the smell associated with old books and dust. Casting around the shelves, she browsed through the many titles on offer which seemed to be crammed together in logical order.

Seeking out the section marked 'Castle Hill historical', she was pleased to find a number in a reasonable condition despite having been passed through many hands. Mary noted that there were books written about transport and horse racing. A small section documented the history of kelpie dogs in the Western District. There were also diaries written by local men who served in Gallipoli which brought back the memory of a visit to the town war memorial on Anzac Day when she was saddened to see names confirming multiple family deaths.

While opening and reading inside tabs, Mary was interested to read the many good wishes conveyed probably during gift giving. Stumbling on an old Coles picture book, she was astounded to discover an inscription inside the front cover, 'This book is presented to Maureen O'Reilly as first prize in the Castle Hill Primary School singing competition.'

How sad, thought Mary, that someone so talented could have her life snuffed out so tragically. Her thoughts were interrupted by a voice asking if she needed assistance. Turning to see a short elderly bald man wearing shirt garters and an eye shade, Mary apologised for looking through the shop unattended as she thought the bell would have announced her presence.

'Ah yes the bell, everyone thinks that; the problem is that I'm a bit deaf, and it's hit or miss as to whether I'll hear it. But for all of that, I'm here now. So, can I help you to find anything in particular?'

'I'm interested to learn about books written by people who pioneered Castle Hill. I've discovered a Coles' picture book that was awarded to Maureen O'Reilly. Is this the same person who was killed by her husband?'

'That's right, a very sad situation. I've another of Maureen's books in the travel section at the back of the store. I'll get it for you.'

The owner returned and handed Mary, 'A backpacker's guide to Europe'.

Realising that she hadn't introduced herself, Mary told the owner her name, and her link to Roscommon Downs.

'Thanks, Mary. Yes, I've heard good things about you from a number of people. I hope you feel comfortable and decide to stay. Goodness knows the town needs young people and some new energy. Please, call me Ollie, that's how everyone knows me.'

Seeing that the backpacker's guide was in near new condition, Mary was surprised to find an inscription inside the front cover. 'Everyone should take the opportunity to travel to Europe. I hope you go some day. Best Wishes, Cedric Newton, Principal, Castle Hill Primary School, Christmas 1955.'

'That's interesting Ollie, the principal and Maureen must have been good friends to be exchanging Christmas gifts.'

'I'm not sure we should read too much into it. Cedric was the principal for the whole time Maureen was a student at the school, and quite a few years both before and afterward. With a limited enrolment, the school operated as a family. And if my memory serves me correctly, Cedric attended Maureen's wedding, given she married while still quite young.'

'I'll buy both books. Someone might have a family forwarding address. I'm sure they'd appreciate receiving them.'

Adjusting his eyeshade, Ollie replied, 'Manny's bakery would be a good place to start. A couple of the workers have been locals for donkeys' years.'

*

When leaving the bookshop, Mary took a few moments to reflect on the situation. While her initial thought was to return the books to the O'Reilly family, she worried that she might be regarded as a snoop digging up old rumours. After mulling it over she decided to follow the path of a search for family members.

No time like the present to approach the staff at Manny's bakery, she thought.

After the usual probing regarding the blossoming of a relationship between her and Jim, Mary showed the three elderly kitchen staff the books in question. She was surprised at the direction the conversation was to take. While she was simply seeking a forwarding address, matters emerged concerning a relationship between Maureen and Cedric.

Doris Matthews, the pastry baker, had the clearest memory. 'There were whispers right back when Maureen was a senior student. As you would expect there were also denials all round, but they didn't go away and continued after Maureen left school.'

Doris paused to roll up her sleeves and tidy the benches around her. 'Cedric didn't help matters much because he regularly disappeared most weekends. He said he was visiting his mother in Melbourne. But after he retired from the school, he vanished completely. You could check at the post office to see if he left a forwarding address. But I'd be surprised if there is one.'

'Well,' Mary replied, 'we can't undo the past. I'm just hoping to get an address to post these books to a member of her family.'

When leaving Manny's, Mary was disappointed that Sid and his mates were absent. She felt certain they would have had some fun talking about her driving lessons. Rather than seek them out, she knew this was a story that could wait for another day.

*

Later that evening talking over her visit to Castle Hill with Jim, Dan and Monica, it became clear to Mary that there was a greater mystery surrounding Maureen O' Reilly's death than had at first been considered.

'It was certainly a bit murky at the time,' Monica said. 'Many were in denial regarding the possibility of a teacher/student relationship.'

'I can imagine it would have been quite a scandal.'

'For sure, Mary,' Monica replied. 'The community started to take sides. It was really no one's business, but you can't stop people talking.'

'What happened in the end? Did the police interview Cedric after Maureen was killed?'

'I really can't say. It bubbled along for a while, then just petered out. I suspect the police took it on face value as Rob had confessed. Maureen was gone so they must have decided to leave it at that.'

Mary wondered why the police had not included Cedric as part of their investigation or taken the opportunity of questioning him under oath at the inquest. Perhaps there was no more than just a friendship built over many years, but any chance of denial had been lost.

Considering the time that had passed since Maureen's tragic death and the fact that Cedric Newton had long left the area and may have passed away, Mary decided to hold onto the books. Meanwhile, should the address come to light, she would then deliver them to the children.

Chapter 13

Swimming the Dam

Jim's loyal service since coming to live and work at the farm never wavered. During his youth, it was not uncommon for him to travel on a shearing run with his father, Bob Wilkinson, and Dan Flanagan. Consequently, from an early age he had adopted Roscommon Downs as a second home.

Given his link to farming, and his parents' encouragement, Jim had boarded at the Rural College and studied agricultural sciences. With an ambition to become a successful racehorse trainer, he took the opportunity to work part time in racing stables. It was no fun to be out of bed at 4 am breathing in fresh manure while mucking out horse boxes, but he was developing hands-on knowledge by working closely with horse trainers, which would be invaluable for a prospective career in the industry. Jim was cautious about accruing debt as it became clear that he would need to buy horses at the annual sales, and then seek to syndicate them to prospective owners.

There was no margin for error given his limited funds. He was aware of horse trainers who ran large stables, often unable to fully complete syndicates and being left as part owners. Receiving monthly training fees was problematic. While there could be rich rewards, there were also potential pitfalls. Living with the stress of a large bank overdraft was a financial burden he was keen to avoid.

Betting to overcome debt was a treadmill with no upside. Jim reckoned it a practice which inevitably led to incurring extra financial difficulties. Another consideration was the fragility of racehorses, often going amiss on the eve of a race for which they were being specifically prepared.

Jim was aware that after he graduated from university, he would need to leave Castle Hill for a lengthy period and work in the city at a horseracing stable. This would be vital to increase his knowledge of horse management and qualify for a licence. A network of people would be required for ongoing financial support, an arrangement not attractive to him.

He'd been happy to accept Dan's offer of employment as farm manager. Able to apply his skills and training, it was a decision that both parties had never regretted. A particular benefit being his ability to use his knowledge to raise the quality of the woolclip through astute ram buying and ewe selling.

Returning to the area after five years at university, he was pleased to find many of his mates were still in town. There was no difficulty in settling back into day-to-day life.

He'd played underage football with Castle Hill, and so readily accepted an invitation to train and successfully play with the senior team. Taller than average and strongly built from years of outdoor work, he was well-equipped to cope with the physical demands of the game.

He loved the coach's pre-game speeches. Although he was concerned on a couple of occasions that medical assistance might be necessary given the coach's agitated state.

The football and netball clubs would combine for a social evening after home matches ensuring there was always plenty of fun to be had. Sundays were quiet days spent recovering from the rigours of the game and excesses of drinking and dancing. While a popular person at the footy club, Jim had been unable to forge a long-term relationship with any of the women in Castle Hill, which mirrored his experience at the Agricultural College.

His only potential long-term partner was Tess Lawrence, a nurse working in South Australia, who came to town from time to time to visit her mother. While there were moments when Jim believed Tess might permanently relocate to Castle Hill to enable a strengthening of the relationship, it did not occur. As the years working for the Flanagans rolled on, Jim came to terms with the fact that he was going to live as a single man.

He was thrilled with Mary's arrival, as she brought new energy and curiosity regarding the operation of the farm. At times he felt feelings for Mary that transcended their friendship. She was an attractive woman but held at arms-length. Why wouldn't he be attracted? How did she feel about him? The last thing he wanted was to make a move and be rebuffed.

Dan Flanagan had asked Jim to take Mary under his wing. A request he was happy to accommodate. To retain his qualifications in animal husbandry, he started to take in horses that needed treatment to bring them back to full health. He was pleased that Mary offered to assist.

'Looks like you've become the local horse whisperer, Jim. People are bringing horses from far and wide for you to patch up.'

'I'm starting to worry about where this is headed, Mary. I don't want to pioneer a de facto veterinary practice, as I'm also being approached to look at a couple of kelpies who were injured on the job. I'm just prepared to help because no one wants to see an animal suffering unnecessarily.'

A racehorse with the stable name, Butch, was among the horses that Jim was tending. The horse had sustained significant bruising having fallen during a steeplechase held in Carravale. It was also clear that the horse was suffering a lack of confidence in his jumping ability and would need some positive rehabilitation if he were to race again.

Jim decided to enlist the support of a semi-retired local jockey, Midge Arthur, to encourage Butch back to the track. He also suggested to Mary that her involvement would provide an insight into horseracing.

'He's going to need a lot of walking and swimming before Midge can gallop him in preparation to jump a few steeples. It'll be a feather in our caps Mary, if we can get him fit to enter a race.'

*

Armed with a couple of lumps of sugar, Mary opened the stable door and entered hoping that Butch wouldn't detect her nervousness. While the horse was a perfect gentleman when Jim was present, she was unsure of how he would react to her. After a moment's hesitation, Butch put his head on Mary's arm nuzzling up in search of a treat. My new best friend, thought Mary, as she searched for more sugar in her pocket.

With Jim being busy with other duties, Mary looked forward to helping prepare Butch to gain the fitness he needed for a return to racing. It would be a new experience made possible by following the program that Jim had developed. It was a quiet time of the year, and with the Flanagans approval, she could easily fit the activity into her working day. A tractable animal, Butch would require many hours of grooming which would also help improve her own confidence.

Walking and leading the horse was very straightforward. After a few circuits of the holding yard Mary opted, somewhat bravely, with a tight hold on the lead rope attached to the bridle, for an out and back stroll. She decided to quietly talk to Butch as they walked through a nearby wooded area. This seemed to calm the big animal as much as it relaxed her.

Mary had never ridden a horse. Country people like Jim had grown up with it. But for Mary there was considerable trial and error in developing her confidence to deal with all circumstances. It was one thing keeping the horse under control while trotting around an enclosed yard. It was an altogether different matter being able to pull him up should he decide to bolt and run at full gallop. She was frightened at the prospect of him leaping over a couple of farm fences along the way.

Following Jim's patient guidance, coupled with the horse's cooperation, Mary managed to learn how to saddle and mount.

'Just tie him to the stable fence, hold firmly to the pommel, left foot into the stirrup and swing your leg over,' Jim had instructed.

Easier said than done, thought Mary. But after a couple of unsuccessful attempts, she proudly sat on the horse albeit hoping that it would wait until she caught her breath. Bunty's advice to utilize a milk crate to give her a leg up had been of valuable assistance.

After a couple of weeks in the saddle quietly walking Butch around the holding yard followed by some excursions jogging along their regular walking track, Mary felt ready to swim the horse in the wide and deep farm dam. Jim had advised her not to panic when entering the dam on the horse's back as it would simply swim across and walk out the other side. All she had to do was to hold tightly to the mane and the reins. Not being a strong swimmer, she put her trust in Jim's words.

'No time like the present, Lilly,' Mary said to her now constant companion.

All went well until Butch stumbled on something as he entered the water causing him to take fright and tip her off, while he continued across the dam.

As a safety measure to ensure she stayed with the horse, Mary had wrapped the reins around her wrist. Reaching the other side after being dragged at times under the water, Mary was pleased that no one apart from Lilly had witnessed her unconventional horse swimming. She felt compelled to tell Lilly, 'Not a word to anyone girl, not a word.'

The quizzical look on Lilly's face suggested that she had seen it all before. Thankfully, Butch decided to be a gentleman and wait quietly for her to regain her composure. A wet, muddy and cold Mary decided that her time would be well spent in locating a safe entry point for future horse swimming.

After a couple of months of treatment and rehabilitation which included Midge galloping Butch at the racecourse, the horse was returned to his owners who decided to train him in further racing preparation. Given his role in the treatment, Jim kept track of Butch's return to racing in the form guide and noted that the horse was entered at the Carravale meeting on the following Saturday.

Inviting Mary to accompany him, Jim said, 'I think we've earned a trip to the races to see how Butch performs in his comeback. It's a flat race to improve his fitness, and if all goes well, he could go on and enter a steeplechase in the future.'

'Thanks for the invitation, Jim. This'll be my first day at a race meeting. But I don't have the proper hat and will have to look for something to wear.'

Jim laughed. 'No need for a fancy outfit, Mary. It's not the Melbourne Cup. Carravale's only a small country course. Nothing like the big courses in the city. But the racing's very keen, particularly during the jumps season when there's a regional series of races which includes Castle Hill. I'll let you know on Friday what time we'll need to leave.'

Chapter 14

Racing and Retribution

At various times since her arrival in Castle Hill, Mary had felt a connection to the area which she found both surprising and confusing. Such a moment occurred as she travelled along a gravel road to reach the Carravale racecourse. Pioneers of the town had selected broad acres set within the bowl of a rugged mountain range. Large gum trees predating the course flourished proudly. Mary loved their individual size and conformation. Their years of standing guard had endowed them with a heritage status. Watching over it all was a community-built grandstand offering welcome weather protection.

Jim, an early bird, always arrived well before the first race. 'Can't help it Mary, I've been early all my life. I hate rushing in at the last minute. Gives me a chance to have a look at the horses before the races commence.'

Being among the first to arrive was of little concern to Mary who opted to take a seat in the grandstand where she could witness the course come to life in preparation for an exciting day ahead.

Clearly a day at the races presented an opportunity to leave the hard work of the farm and other commitments behind for a few hours. And notwithstanding her twenty-two years in the city, increasingly Mary felt an empathy with country people as she enjoyed watching patrons set up picnic tables and chairs.

When visiting the stabling area, she was fascinated with the demeanour of the horses listed to race during the afternoon. While some appeared anxious, pawing the ground as if ready to run, others stood quietly, and a couple looked like they were fast asleep.

Knowing that Butch was entered in race four, Mary took the opportunity to move away from the grandstand and sit near the mounting yard to enjoy the early events and soak up the atmosphere. As the horses were paraded around the ring, some seemed to take an interest in the patrons while others, perhaps more experienced, were blasé.

The colourful designs of the silks worn by the jockeys caught her attention. Certain riders, it seemed obvious, may have been starting their careers while others were veterans of the craft. And although slight of stature, they each had the ability to control a large and excited animal.

Coupled with Jim's love of the sport and Dan and Monica's strong commitment to racing, Mary could foresee plenty of opportunities for her to attend local meetings along with important racing events in Melbourne. Mary also suspected, that with a name like O'Rourke, it was a probable Irish trait that attracted her to the track and would possibly keep her engaged in years to come.

Prior to race four, while watching Butch being saddled, she was interested to hear the conversation about tactics being discussed between Jim and the owners. Jim wanted to ensure that the horse had a strong gallop and was keen to point this out to the owners. 'Butch is your horse, but I feel a responsibility regarding today's outcome. If it's planned to enter him in jumping races, then the leg we've been treating must be sound. I really hope he gets through.'

Formulating a simple plan based on guaranteeing a safe and solid run, the owners left to discuss the race with trainer Eric Conroy, and jockey Midge Arthur.

Passing the carpark when returning to the pre-race parade ring, Mary noted the real disparity in the wealth and organisation of the racing stables. Some of the single horse trailers had seen better days and were parked alongside stable branded modern horse trucks.

'That's the way the industry operates, Mary,' Jim explained. 'Large professional horse training outfits, right down to a battling trainer with just a couple of horses literally stabled in his or her backyard. Success at these country meetings is vital for a small training operation.'

Jim picked up the pace and hurried Mary along. 'Now we have a few minutes before the race, let's go to the bookmakers' area so I can introduce you to the folly of backing racehorses.'

Mary's tummy started to rumble as the aroma of hot dogs wafted through the air when they approached the large three-sided shed conveniently located next to a food and coffee truck. The shed housed six bookmakers and was dominated by a television set loudly broadcasting races from across Australia.

People gathered around intently reading newspapers as Jim proceeded to step her through the betting methods available. 'Single bets, running doubles or multiples. It's just a matter of what you prefer,' he smiled. 'And if you're wondering, the people here aren't catching up with the news, just pondering the form guides.'

Listening carefully but being conservative with her money, Mary decided that betting was a practice to be avoided. 'I'm not sure I'll get involved, Jim. I don't like to risk my money.'

'It's in my blood to have a bet, Mary. Part of my life education has been on racecourses. I study the form guide and have small wagers. There's no harm if I stay within my means.'

A constant tension was evident to Mary as races were broadcast with patrons developing a rhythm of assessing form guides, scanning the odds and placing bets. The bookmakers, forever altering the odds on their boards, were keeping a wary eye on the crowd of punters. Mary could only guess at the amount of money changing hands. It seemed unrelenting, cold and clinical. She was reminded of Dan Flanagan's advice when leaving the farm. 'Backing racehorses is a mug's game, Mary. It's brought many people undone.'

During the drive to the course, Jim had explained that occasionally at city meetings there were organised betting moves just prior to a race. 'If punters are rushing to have a wager, I've been nearly bowled over in the crush of people desperate to put their bets on. Something seems to take over their minds. So, a little caution is worthwhile.'

Butch was entered in a two thousand metre flat race under his registered racing name, 'Chardy Boy'. Watching him being led around the mounting yard with Midge Arthur in the saddle, Mary couldn't help but feel a sense of pride in his condition. The bright glow of his coat reflected the many hours of walking, trotting and swimming. Her sole hope was for Butch to run strongly and finish safely.

As the horses were leaving to enter the track a familiar voice interrupted her train of thought. 'Mary O'Rourke; well, it didn't take Jim long to introduce you to bad habits.'

'Rhon, what a lovely surprise. It's so good to see you,' Mary said giving her friend a hug while noting her smart outfit. 'You'll be pleased to know that even though tempted, I'm holding onto my money. Jim and I worked to bring number seven back to good health, so we couldn't miss his comeback run. That's him carrying the red and gold quarters.' Mary pointed. 'He's not expected to win though as he's a steeplechaser.'

'Well, I can see why you're hanging onto your dough, Mary.'

'Anyway, how have you been, Rhon? Perhaps we can chat after the race.'

'Let's do that Mary, and yes I've been well. There's lots to catch up on, particularly a bit of scandal that's been doing the rounds in Carravale. But I'll leave you to it and re-join some friends in the grandstand. Good luck with your horse.'

As the race got underway, Mary was drawn to the movement and sounds while keeping a close eye on Butch's colours. Listening to the broadcaster's call she felt the excitement of owners and trainers as shouts accompanied the thundering hooves galloping to the finishing post. Butch passed her in a flash down the home straight midway between those running first and last.

Returning to the mounting yard, Mary took a keen interest as Butch's performance was analysed and future races planned. She was pleased to hear Midge's clear and concise report: 'Too slow to win this time round, but now fit to jump.'

Jim was happy with the soundness of the horse after his solid performance. While Butch failed to place in the first three, he was able to maintain a strong gallop to the finishing post. Invited by the owners to run his hands over the horse's legs, Jim could detect no problems to prevent an ongoing racing preparation. However, he counselled the owners to recheck that all was well when Butch cooled down.

As they left the racetrack pleased with the day's outcome, Jim said to Mary, 'We've done some excellent work here. Butch was a crock when he came to us. All the swimming in the dam you did with him made the difference. We can now step back and enjoy his progress. Provided the owners don't become too ambitious and enter races beyond his capacity, Butch will go on and bring them a lot of good days.'

While pleased with her contribution, Mary was quietly hoping that it would be some time before more dam swimming was required.

*

'How've you been, Rhon?' Mary asked as she added a spoonful of sugar to her coffee during a get together at Mannys.

'It's been full-on at our farm business, Mary. And if you really want to know, it was starting to do my head in. That day we met at the races was one of my few days off in yonks.'

'Well, it's great to finally catch up. There's more to life than work and I don't know about you, but I enjoyed my day at the races and am looking forward to returning.'

'It's good fun alright. Me and my girlfriends like nothing better than dressing up, enjoying a few glasses of bubbles and getting a bit tiddly on the side. You should join us sometime.'

'I'll keep it in mind,' Mary said.

'Just the same Mary, we've always gotta be on the lookout for the Carravale gossips who'll bring you undone at any opportunity. Just imagine if they see you gadding about in the bookies' shed with your form guide in hand. The rumours'll start and before you know it, you'll be tagged as some high-flying gambler intent on whittling away the Flanagan savings.'

'Seriously? I can't believe anyone would do that.'

'Just try and stop them, Mary. Let me tell you an interesting tale about a gossip who I fixed up recently. The moral to this story is careful who you mess with or it just might come back to bite you on the bum.'

Leaning in and speaking in a quiet voice, Rhon began to relay a detailed account about a woman who had made the mistake of spreading a story about her to anyone who would listen.

*

The question was: why would Margaret Jennings start to receive letters from Townsville?

Given the small amount of mail that came to the Carravale post office, which operated from a corner of the general store, the letters developed some immediate mystery about them. It was impossible for mail sorter Roslyn Wilson, not to notice the Queensland post box address, and almost as difficult for her not to mention it to her friend Nora Field. 'Promise you won't tell anyone, as postal employees are required to retain confidentiality about what we see and hear.'

It didn't take long for Margaret Jennings to hear that the letters were the subject of conversation in the town. People started to make the link between Margaret's employment as a housekeeper with the previous Western District Anglican Minister, and his subsequent transfer to the Queensland diocese. It certainly seemed reasonable to the Carravale gossip mill that there could be a connection.

As Margaret Jennings was considered the originator of many of the local rumours, it was too good an opportunity to pass up.

'This being the result I had hoped to achieve with my anonymous letter writing exercise,' Rhonda told Mary.

Angry at Margaret who had told everyone with great authority that Rhonda North had left Carravale to deal with an unwanted pregnancy, Rhon had vowed to even the score.

After working hard to finish a marketing and communications degree by correspondence and arranging appointments with prospective employers, Rhon had gone to Melbourne for interviews. For a rumourmonger it was an opportunity too good to miss.

Just some blank sheets of paper coupled with a fictitious address in Townsville, and a few stamps, was enough for Rhon to get the rumour mill running. She had no knowledge of a relationship between the minister and Margaret, but why worry about the facts ruining a good story? Margaret Jennings had given no consideration to the feelings and reputation of Rhonda's parents with her false gossip.

The only concern that Rhon had before she embarked on her activity was the impact it might have on her parents should she be discovered. It was a calculated risk that she was prepared to take.

Her original plan was to send a half dozen letters. In the final analysis just three were needed. 'The gossip spread like wild-fire, Mary. It grew legs of its own. People speculating about my supposed pregnancy and what was being said about Margaret Jennings. I started to become a little concerned regarding what my parents would be thinking. So, I made sure that when Dad met me at the railway station the day I returned, I reassured him that all was well with me.'

'I understand the concern. The gossips don't let up.'

'My father said that there'd been people speaking with great authority about me. He and Mum didn't know what to think when hearing of my supposed pregnancy. However, they knew if there'd been any truth to the matter, I wouldn't have run away without telling them.'

'It's good to have that trust, Rhon.'

'Certainly, Mary! I told Dad I was angry when I became aware of what was being said, as there was no need for it.'

'Some people have little to do.'

'That's exactly right. I had to be careful when Dad mentioned that there was some talk around about Margaret Jennings. I didn't want to put my foot in it. Trying to sound just a little interested I asked Dad what was being said.'

'You would've had to be careful not to smile.'

'Gosh you're right there. My father can usually read me like a book. Thankfully, he was driving so he wasn't looking at me. But he told me there was gossip linking Margaret and our former Anglican Minister based on some letters mailed from Queensland arriving at the post office.'

'The plot thickens.' Mary said, stifling a laugh.

'I couldn't help myself. I said to Dad that I vaguely remember her working for a period as the Minister's housekeeper.'

'You must have been nearly bursting to tell your father the truth.'

'I was, but I had to protect him and Mum. Best to keep this secret between you and me Mary.'

'I'm going to struggle to retain my composure if you ever introduce me to Margaret Jennings.'

'It'll be fun Mary. Happy days.'

*

After leaving Mary to travel home, Rhonda was more than content with her decision to return to Carravale. Her experience of six months living and working in the city had been both challenging and enjoyable. Completely satisfied that she had the skills required to fill a communications and marketing role and following a round of interviews, Rhonda had obtained employment to complete a short-term project.

Since the conclusion of this project, she had been offered a permanent position. However, deciding that her preference was for country living and aware her parents had worked hard to build up the farm supply business, it was time for her to relieve some of their workload. She was also looking forward to catching up with her friends in Carravale and firming up a friendship with Mary O'Rourke in Castle Hill.

Although a few years older than Mary, Rhon was sure that there was the possibility of a trusted friendship, with the opportunity to share some war stories from her six months away. She suspected that notwithstanding Mary's quiet demeanour, she would have had many life experiences, so there was the promise of some interesting and lively conversations.

Chapter 15

A Step in Time

Since arriving at Roscommon Downs during the previous autumn, Mary had restricted her activities to settling in and working with Monica. With winter over it was time to take a much-needed visit to Castle Hill for the purpose of freshening up her wardrobe. Jim's regular weekly trip into town to stock up on farm supplies allowed her to accompany him rather than having to drive the truck herself.

As fashion outlets were few and far between in a small town like Castle Hill, Mary's decision making was made easy as there were not a lot of choices. However, being pleased with her purchases, she said to Jim on their return to the farm, 'Well, I'm all set! What about you, Jim? It's time for you to dust off your dancing shoes.'

'You haven't seen my two left feet,' Jim laughed.

'Come on now. That's not what I've heard from the ladies at Manny's. They reckon you can cut the rug when necessary.'

'Don't fall for the trap of listening to the ladies at Manny's. What were they saying?'

'A couple of things come to mind. Champion partner. The one they chased.'

'Those women are getting worse. You can't believe a word they say.' Jim scoffed. 'Anyway, it won't be hard for you to find a partner given the footy season is over. Without the usual limping after games, plenty of young blokes will be eager to fill your dance card.'

'That's an old expression, Jim. Surely local people don't still use a dance card.'

'It's just my way of speaking, I suppose. But it's good to remember if a dance has been promised, the young blokes here can be volatile. They won't allow their mates to push past their place in the queue.'

Mary didn't know quite what to expect at the upcoming dance the following Saturday evening. However, she was hopeful that George Simpson would be in attendance. They'd been keeping their developing friendship quiet. So, enjoying a couple of dances together would hardly attract any undue attention or speculation. But while Mary knew she was able to step through the footwork, she was unsure if anyone apart from George would ask her to dance.

Jim was happy to accompany Mary knowing that she was getting him out and about and away from his usual lazy Saturday evenings. It was a new experience to be polishing boots, ironing a shirt and smartening himself up. He was pleased to have the opportunity to introduce her to some of his former footy mates and the current younger players who were sure to make her welcome.

Mary's only ballroom dancing experience had been in the big suburban halls in Melbourne, so she was pleased to see a large crowd in attendance and be greeted by the mellow sounds of the Glenn Miller orchestra. This familiar strain immediately transported her back to dancing with her Hawthorn partner, Glyn Harris. And as the night progressed a six-piece band alternated with recorded music.

Displayed on the stage was a program of old time and modern dances. Mary noted the Pride of Erin; the Evening Three Step; and a Slow Foxtrot on the list. Halfway through the evening, the progressive Barn Dance, although not her favourite, ensured that the constant change of partners would enable her to meet some of the local men. Mary was surprised to receive a tap on the shoulder when the barn dance ended, and she turned to see a grinning George Simpson.

'I didn't think you were coming George. I'd given up on you.'

'Just late … the shearing job went on a bit. Cleaned up and got here as fast as I could. I wanted to dance with my favourite girl.'

Mary placed her hands on her hips. 'What do you mean, favourite girl! Are there others?' she asked.

'Whoa there, Mary … you've got me wrong. There's only one girl in my life.'

'Just as well, George Simpson! Now, are we going to stand here all night or are you going to ask me to dance?'

*

As the evening went on, Jim had great fun introducing Mary to many of his mates and their wives or girlfriends, and while he was clearly well known and liked, there seemed to be no one enjoying his special attention. Why hadn't he attracted the attention of any of the young women in attendance? He seemed content to have a yarn with his mates and pick and choose his partners for an occasional dance.

Seeing Jim leaning on the bar chatting to George gave Mary cause for concern. He would have surely seen them dancing and might suspect their link. Yet despite having met George for lunch on numerous occasions in Castle Hill, no one at the farm had quizzed her about their friendship. Mary was happy to keep it that way.

Having promised Jim the final dance, it just happened to be her favourite, the Modern Waltz. Mary enjoyed being held close feeling Jim's strength and control as they moved around the floor. There was no way he had two left feet. Quite the opposite in fact. He was a far more competent dancer than he'd been prepared to admit.

After a quick underarm spin to finish, Mary pressed him on the subject.

Jim conceded, 'Remember I'm a country boy, Mary. In the country we all dance. Mind you some better than others. But it's time to hit the road, I can't have you sleeping in tomorrow and being late serving breakfast to Dan and Monica.'

'No worries Jim, I'm always up and about after a night out. My employment at the Rex hotel was good training for early starts.'

Mary saw a look of disappointment on George's face as he watched from afar while they gathered their coats and scarfs from the cloakroom. Well rugged up against the wind, a quick walk to the carpark had them safely in the truck. Mary wiped the frost from the window as she looked back in the hope of seeing George before departing. But he must have still been inside as there was no sign of him. She hoped he wasn't upset that she had left the dance with Jim.

'Thanks for taking me to the dance, Jim. I had a lot of fun and made some new friends who encouraged me to come again next month. It seems the numbers attending ebb and flow depending on the other activities that are happening in Castle Hill.'

'That's right,' Jim replied. 'Look out for the Gala Ball that's held in conjunction with the Racing Carnival. It's a big night when visitors here to attend the races join in and kick up their heels. In days gone by many girls took the opportunity to make their debut during the ball. That fell away when the teacher who trained the deb set moved to another town.'

'What a disappointment for the girls.'

'Yeah, I guess so! But if you're feeling brave, there's always the Bachelor and Spinsters Ball. It attracts mainly young and not so young people and involves more drinking than dancing. Young blokes come from near and far. Many stay the night in their utes.'

'Sleep in their utes?'

'They daren't drive. Our local policeman, Ray Manners, keeps order. During the Ball he stands at the door with his breathalyser and refuses to allow anyone over the limit to leave the hall. Brutal and effective he calls it. But it can get a bit messy late in the evening.'

'Thanks for the tip Jim; I think that I'll stay at home and wash my hair that night.'

During the journey back to Roscommon Downs, Mary found herself again thinking about Jim and the mystery woman he was with at the railway station on the day she arrived. In her short time at Castle Hill, she had not witnessed any attachments between Jim and the local women. She also felt it odd that he had shown no interest in her. Deciding to take a chance, Mary said, 'There were quite a few women at the dance who seemed like they wanted to get close to you.'

Without taking his eyes off the road, Jim replied, 'I didn't notice, Mary.'

*

The community of Castle Hill always looked forward to the Christmas period. There was an eager anticipation among parents as they waited to welcome children, many of whom had spent the year away at colleges and university. Happy to be home and keen to unwind, they brought additional energy to the town pubs and clubs.

The big crowd in attendance at the December dance had the hall rocking with the local band working to an increased tempo. Although disappointed that George was away working, Mary's regular attendance ensured no shortage of dance partners.

Looking forward to the open house at the Flanagans on Christmas day, while helping set up the outdoor roaster, Jim said, 'It's a big day, Mary. We have a crowd arrive straight after church. People love it.'

'I'll talk to Monica when I arrive back from Melbourne and see how I can assist. I suspect a salad or two won't go astray. I'll chance my arm and see if I can reproduce some of Bunty's scones.'

*

Mary had received permission from Monica for a few days leave to travel to Melbourne for a short break. Apart from wanting to catch up with her friends at the Rex Hotel and the Hawthorn Town Hall, she was keen to visit the orphanage. While in many ways resigned to living her life without knowing her parents, she still retained a hope that further information might be available.

Mary had arranged her accommodation at the Rex and was pleased to be greeted warmly by Molly Smith.

'Lovely to see you, Mary. I had good reports regarding your work with the Flanagans when they stayed during the Royal Melbourne Show. They said you have settled in well and become part of the Roscommon Downs' family.'

'Thanks Molly, while I was nervous about the move, it's worked out well. The pace of life is much slower which suits me. People are friendly and have made me welcome. I'm looking forward to the next phase of my life.'

'From what I hear Mary, you've developed some suitors among the locals. I suspect as the new girl in town you would've attracted some keen attention.'

Smiling in response, Mary replied, 'I must admit it's been great fun to go to the dance, and not be a wallflower.'

'That's the benefit of being able to dance.'

'I'm sure you're right.'

Adopting a more serious tone, Mary said, 'I called into the orphanage on my way here.'

'How did that go?'

'It was a waste of time, Molly. They showed me letters sent

to hospitals to seek birth records which produced nothing. The best guess is that I was a home birth with a midwife assisting.'

'I'm sad to hear that. You must feel terribly disappointed?'

'I was hopeful to learn more, but it's over and time to just get on with my life.'

As Mary collected her room key, Molly answered the phone and handed it to Mary, who was surprised to hear the voice of the sister in charge at the orphanage.

'My apologies Mary, I forgot to mention there's a record in the daily call diary. A Rosemary Cleary rang a few days ago on behalf of Dan and Monica Flanagan. Said she's in charge of employment and wanted to check if there was anything untoward regarding your life here or at the Rex Hotel.'

Mary couldn't believe what she'd just heard. Although normally slow to anger, she could feel her face flushing and a rage building inside her. 'Rosemary has no right to do that. She's not employed at the farm. That's disgraceful behaviour.'

'I'm sorry to upset you, Mary. I gave her no information. She really pressed me saying that she wanted to check your honesty and integrity. When I questioned her authority, she rudely hung up.'

Fighting to control herself, Mary felt it best to call Dan and Monica.

Monica's reaction was loud and direct. 'That's wrong Mary, very wrong. I'll sort her out.'

'I'm disappointed, Monica. I've done nothing to harm her.'

'Don't worry. Rosemary Cleary will never be welcome here again.'

*

A better outcome for Mary was her visit to the Hawthorn Town Hall. She'd written to one of her former workmates at the Rex Hotel to advise of her visit, and many of her friends turned up to greet her at the dance.

During a break in the dancing, Mary found herself the centre of attention answering many questions about her new life at Castle Hill. Her former dance partner, Glyn Harris, a man of considerable ego who believed he was the best partner Mary would ever have, was keenly interested as to whether he'd been replaced. 'You must tell me, am I still your number one dance partner?'

'Absolutely Glyn … you're irreplaceable. If you ever come to Castle Hill, you'll be the star at the Saturday night dance. No one has your style and panache.'

'Panache? I'll accept the compliment. Now let's not linger, we have much dancing to do.'

During interval, her girlfriends were more interested in Mary's possible new love life: questions that Mary quietly side-stepped in a bid to maintain her privacy.

*

If the truth had been told, Mary would've admitted to her relationship with George Simpson, but preferred a little more certainty. She accepted that his work was to take him away from Castle Hill from time to time, and on occasions for lengthy periods.

Aware that Jim was not fussed with George, Mary had confided in Bunty who suggested, 'Outdoors work has been kind to him. He's not as handsome as your favourite movie stars, but at least the women at the bakery reckon he's a good sort.'

'Nothing more to say, Bunty.'

Although a few years older than Mary, George was an easy person to be with, being quick with a quip or a joke. His work as a shearer and handyman had exposed him to many funny situations that he enjoyed relating. Importantly during their private moments at his home, he had committed to Mary.

'I'm locked in, Mary. I want our relationship to be long term.'

'That's what I want. But I must be able to trust you when you're away.'

'Please do. I'll only be away for as long as is needed.'

*

Mary had great fun chatting to friends on the Christmas Eve train and was surprised and delighted to be met by George at the station. He held her close and said, 'I wanted to be the first to wish you Merry Christmas. I was worried you might miss Christmas Day.'

'George … that's such a lovely thing to say. Thank you for meeting me. There was no chance of me not returning in time. Dan and Monica would have never forgiven me. But most of all I wanted to be with you.'

Christmas turned out to be the relaxing and friendly day as promised. It seemed to Mary that half of the Castle Hill population dropped into the farm at various times throughout the celebration to be warmly greeted by the Flanagans.

George was especially warm delighting Mary with a gift of a gold bracelet. As he pressed the catch closed on her wrist, he kissed her and said, 'A special gift for the special person in my life.'

Mary struggled with her emotions. 'It's really beautiful George, I'll treasure it forever.'

Despite the heat, Jim continued cooking lamb to complement Mary's salads and bread, with the Flanagans providing cold beer and soft drink.

Mary had arrived back in Castle Hill with gifts to put under the tree for Dan, Monica and Jim, who gently admonished her for spending her hard-earned money.

During a quiet moment Monica advised Mary that Rosemary Cleary had been informed of the Flanagans' disappointment with her misrepresentations. There would be no more chances.

'I'm sorry she put you through that, Mary. It must have been embarrassing.'

'Not to worry, Monica. I'm over it now. I must admit it's the angriest I've felt in a long time. I don't believe I did anything to harm her. She must have been very bitter about my arrival.'

'Rest assured, she won't be back. The fault was totally with her. Dan was especially disappointed as he and her father go back a long way. But as I said before, her time here is over.'

Chapter 16

A Thief in the Night

Mary was growing restless. Although well settled at Roscommon Downs, the next stage of her life needed clarity.

Rhonda had developed into a trusted friend with whom she could have a frank discussion, and as they sat enjoying their coffee at Manny's during a Friday catch up, Mary said, 'We're going to have to lift our game, Rhon. Otherwise, I'll be known as the old maid of Castle Hill. And your 'love-them and leave-them' approach seems to be working well as there doesn't appear to be anyone on your radar.'

'Honestly Mary, I can't be bothered wasting my time with a lot of duds. Perhaps I've set my standards too high. But it's my life and I won't waste it by committing to just anyone.'

Mary drained the last of her coffee and sighed. 'I must say I'm a bit disappointed. It's not as if we've been hiding ourselves away.'

'You can say that again,' Rhon agreed. 'You must have danced with a dozen different partners on Saturday night. I was worn out just watching you. But as for me, at least I haven't got Chiv to contend with anymore.'

'What happened to her?' Mary asked.

'I was fed up with her jealous tantrums. Whenever I started to develop a new friendship, she'd be a spoiler. I'd had enough and told her to leave me alone.'

'Gosh that must have been a moment. How did she react?'

'She wasn't happy that's for sure. But I was going nowhere with her around. Hopefully, I can now move on.' Rhon took a moment to withdraw a compact from her purse and reapply her lipstick. 'What's happening with George Simpson? I thought you two were getting along.'

'George is likeable enough. My only concern is that I'm not convinced he's finished wandering. I need to be sure he's ready to put down some roots. He says he's committed to me but then without a word he disappears every so often and I lose track of him.'

'That doesn't sound good, Mary. But at least he seems to have red blood running through his veins. Not like the other so-called men in town.'

Mary looked round the bakery to make certain that no one could overhear their discussion before telling Rhon what she really thought. 'I just wish George would make his mind up and stick around Castle Hill for a while. At times I feel like I'm in a relationship with a stranger. I realise there are some jobs that might require him to travel, but it wouldn't hurt him to phone or write.'

'Seriously Mary, you'd be waiting a long time for a bloke around these parts to write a letter. Then again, if he's interested, he'll be back for sure.'

'Well, it's not good enough, and when next I see him I'm planning to tell him so.'

It all seemed a bit hit or miss for Mary, so rather than wait around in some sort of breathless anticipation, she got on with her life. Castle Hill dances were to be enjoyed either with or without George Simpson. There was plenty to keep her occupied looking after the Flanagans and Jim always welcomed her assistance in caring for his horses. Also, maintaining the Roscommon Downs home and garden was a big enough undertaking to take her mind away from worrying about George's whereabouts.

*

When George Simpson did eventually return to Castle Hill, Mary was happy to hear the local rumour mill suggest he was home to stay. With his elderly parents now comfortably living in a nursing home, and his sisters no longer in the area, George moved into the family home. He made it known that he was available to take on farm maintenance tasks, along with his willingness to do some shearing.

While his return was welcome, Mary decided that she would remind him of life's courtesies on the first occasion he came to the farm. So, one day finding George kneeling with his hands under muddy water repairing a pump, she didn't mince words when it came to letting him know that she wasn't happy. 'What happened George? Couldn't you find a post office or a phone box?'

With his head down, George sheepishly replied, 'Apologies Mary, I was out at the back of beyond. I guess I could have tried harder.'

'I'm sure you could have. All of the pubs have a phone.'

'Right again, Mary. Hope you can forgive me. I've really missed you and if I didn't have muddy hands, I'd be giving you a hug.'

'Best keep your hands to yourself, George Simpson. You might be a chance when you finish the job.'

Later as they sat chatting over lunch, Mary decided that she had let George off too easily and needed to establish some ground rules. If their relationship was to have a future, George would have to be far more reliable. Deciding to adopt a Roscommon Downs' procedure of off-farm records, she suggested, 'We need a diary so that when you go away for a few days, I can check to confirm your whereabouts.'

'Okay, let's do that, Mary. I want to make our relationship work.'

With arrangements made to catch up later in the week, Mary stood on the verandah watching George drive away. She was pleased about the agreement as it firmed up their relationship. Yet George's lifestyle and come-what-may attitude remained a concern. Other couples of their age normally could be heard discussing home building and joint bank accounts. George took no interest in the future and seemed content to live in his parents' home which needed significant repairs.

Prepared to live with her misgivings, Mary decided to rekindle their friendship. She was pleased that George seemed determined to make up for lost time. Retaining work around Castle Hill enabled him to make regular visits to the farm and time for them to enjoy frequent lunch dates at the pub.

Comfortable together, they spent many hours at George's home and also travelled away from the area to indulge in some romantic escapes. It was as though they were enjoying a pre-marriage honeymoon.

To stifle the gossip, they agreed to publicly admit that their friendship had moved to what was known locally as an 'understanding'.

Mary was thrilled to be able to further pass on this information to Bunty. 'You were right,' she said, 'there was something there. We're going to run with it to see if we should make our partnership permanent.'

'I'm delighted for you Mary, as I'm sure Dan and Monica will be. My advice is to hurry slowly rather than rush into a marriage that might quickly fall over.'

'I hope that's not the case,' Mary assured Bunty. 'George has been away for quite some time and is now settled in Castle Hill. While he hasn't talked about marriage, surely it's on his mind.'

'As I said, we'll be delighted for you. Just remember it's a big step for some men to commit to marriage.'

*

Several weeks later, after bouts of morning sickness, Mary was convinced that she was pregnant. An appointment and examination organised by Rhon with a doctor in Carravale confirmed her condition. While she knew that a visit to the Castle Hill general practitioner would remain confidential, by visiting Carravale, Mary believed she would gain some extra time, enabling her to inform George and her Roscommon Downs' family before the news became general knowledge.

She emerged from the doctor's rooms happy and excited. 'It's wonderful news, Rhon. I'm pregnant. It seems that all's well. If only George had come with me. I hope he'll be pleased.'

Rhon threw her arms around Mary and said, 'I'm really happy for you.'

'Thanks for coming with me, Rhon. I was so nervous and didn't want to meet the doctor on my own.'

'I'm sure you would've done the same for me.'

Overcome with emotion, Mary shed some tears. 'At least I know that George is the father. I can't wait to tell him.'

'The news will test him, Mary. Don't forget his days of being fancy free will end. But you can be sure that you'll get plenty of love and assistance from the Flanagans and Jim Wilkinson.'

'Thanks, Rhon. I best be on my way.'

As Mary walked to the railway station, her mind raced with the events of the morning. Her pregnancy would need to be discussed with Dan and Monica. While confident they'd be supportive, there were her duties to cover. Also to consider were the gossips in Castle Hill. Would they make life difficult for her?'

Jim would look out for her. He'd been urging caution in respect to George, as he reckoned the man was a drifter. Mary hoped that Jim's view was incorrect and that his arms-length friendship with George would improve.

How would George react to her news? Having children had not been discussed, nor had marriage. Despite their irregular relationship she hoped her pregnancy would be the catalyst to have him confirm his love and accept his responsibilities. Sitting on the Carravale station while in wait for the midday train, Mary's original excitement was tempered by the uncertainty of the future.

*

Looking forward to being the first to break the news to George, Mary got quite a shock when she stepped from the train at the Castle Hill station to hear a shout from the local stationmaster. 'Good news Mary, we're all very pleased for you.'

She could not believe her ears when Jim Wilkinson was there to meet and congratulate her. 'Looks like you might need to cut back your heavy lifting and I guess that's the last of the gin and tonics at the end of the working day. Have you spoken to George?'

'Yes, I'm going to need to be careful, and no I've not spoken to George. I was hoping he would meet me at the station. Do you know if he's working in Castle Hill?'

'I've no idea where he is, Mary. I thought he would've given you a lift in his ute.'

'I've not seen him for a day or so. Perhaps he got caught up somewhere.'

As he assisted Mary into the farm truck, Jim couldn't help saying, 'I worry about George, he always seems to go missing when he should be around.'

Although disappointed at her news being spread far and wide, Mary was pleased that the initial reaction from the people that mattered in her life was supportive. She'd been concerned that the pregnancy would have an impact on her capacity to fulfil her duties and Dan and Monica may need to employ extra assistance. In a worst-case scenario, they might terminate her services. Her concerns were totally unfounded as she was warmly welcomed at the farm by Monica.

'Lovely news Mary; Dan and I are so pleased for you. Looks like George will have to get serious with your relationship. It's about time he put down some roots in Castle Hill. Did he react well to the news?'

'I can't answer the question Monica, as I haven't had the chance to talk to him. I was hoping he'd be at the station, but he must be away working. Jim will follow him up. I hope he's as pleased as I am.'

'Don't worry about your work. We're delighted to have a new arrival. Bunty is an old hand with raising children and has already offered to come and help, so we'll all survive. Dan can still boil an egg, although not very well.'

Mary's concern turned to talking the pregnancy through with George. Notwithstanding he was away, news travelled fast. She was keen to seek his agreement to stay at Roscommon Downs during her pregnancy, rather than move to his home in Castle Hill. Given the level of support it seemed logical for her to stay at the farm.

*

Mary had been let down. While her consultation with Dr Harkins remained confidential, his part-time receptionist couldn't help herself. Interested as to why Mary had travelled to Carravale to see the doctor, she checked the folder before filing it away. The news was too good to suppress.

It was not even necessary for her to release the information. It was enough to let a couple of the local gossips know that Mary had been to see Dr Harkins, and then do nothing to stop the rumours.

A few well-placed calls resulted in George becoming aware of the news before Mary's return to Castle Hill. While she had been optimistic that George would take the step to make the relationship permanent, his reaction was completely the opposite. There was no thought that he should prove whether the child was his as he knew he was Mary's only partner.

Unwilling to take on the responsibilities of fatherhood, he decided to leave Castle Hill and move as far away as possible.

For better or worse Mary would just have to rely on the folk at Roscommon Downs. As far as he was concerned, the quicker he could get out of town the better.

Comfortable that he could arrange a new identity and live anonymously interstate, George quietly gathered his gear together, withdrew his money from the local bank and left. Throughout his years of travelling, he had developed plenty of mates who would cover for him and help him disappear.

*

It was Jim Wilkinson who first held the view that George may have left town. Without mentioning his concern, he visited George's home. Finding the house empty, a conversation with the neighbours confirmed that George hadn't been home for a number of days. Follow up conversations with George's drinking mates at the local pub, the local senior constable, Ray Manners, and the staff at Manny's bakery threw no light on his whereabouts.

Jim used the excuse that he had some maintenance work at Roscommon Downs and was keen to get George up to the farm and on the job. His fear that George might have abandoned Mary was confirmed by a casual conversation with Dave Evans, a long-term friend who worked at the local bank. Over a beer at the pub Dave confided, 'I'm looking forward to seeing George's new set of wheels. He came into the bank a few days ago and drew out most of his savings. He said he was travelling to Melbourne to pick the car up and asked me to keep quiet about it. He wanted to surprise everyone when he returned.'

'That's interesting and a bit out of character for George to be buying new wheels. I thought he was in love with his old ute.'

'I guess we'll see what's taken his fancy. He must have really wanted the new vehicle. There's not much left in his account for a rainy day.'

Notwithstanding his knowledge concerning George's absence, Jim felt it best to give him the benefit of the doubt and not trouble Mary unnecessarily. Sooner or later the matter would come into general question and that would be the time to share what he knew. He hoped he was wrong, but he feared his negative view of George was about to be confirmed. Mary deserved better.

Any chance he had to keep his information from her ceased when a day or two later she asked him during breakfast to take her to the Simpson home. Being aware and concerned about Mary's welfare after she had suffered many sleepless nights, Jim tried to defer the travel. 'Why don't we wait until you're a bit stronger? A couple of days won't matter.'

'No, it's been a week since there's been any news of George. He might be ill, perhaps someone in Castle Hill is aware of where he's working, or something bad might have happened to him. I want to know where he is.'

'I'm sorry to be the bearer of bad news, Mary. As I was worried about his absence, I've visited his home, spoke to the neighbours, and other people in town. It looks like he might have permanently left while you were in Carravale.'

'That means he may have left before he received news of our baby.'

'We would be guessing, Mary. While it was general knowledge at the farm, George might have picked up something on the grapevine, or it might have escaped him.'

Feeling nervous and concerned Mary suggested, 'Could there have been an urgent matter that required him to travel? He did mention on one occasion that his sisters moved to Queensland many years ago. George never mentioned other family.'

'I really can't help, Mary. I approached the regional police to see if it's possible to classify him as a missing person. The problem is that we're not family. Ray Manners said he would keep an eye out for George while on his regular rounds and put the message out to see if he's working on any of the local farms. The family home is still there so he might be back at some stage. It's a bit of a mystery.'

'I asked George to keep a diary at his house.'

'Apologies Mary, I used your key. There were no entries, and his clothes were gone.'

'His clothes were gone.' Mary looked broken-hearted. 'I can't believe it. That's so disappointing! George promised me he would maintain the diary. And if you had doubts you should have shared the news with me at the time.'

'I can only apologise again. I wasn't sure and didn't want to upset you.'

Pulling herself together, 'Well, that's it … he's gone! You were right. He's just a drifter.'

*

As the days passed and the realisation that she had been abandoned sunk in, Mary shut herself away in her darkened room and was plunged into a sad and depressed state. It ought to have been a happy period in her life. Instead, she cried in despair feeling sorry for herself.

In their intimacy she believed George was committed to her as they had discussed a life together. She'd hoped that he'd have been excited to know she was pregnant and join her in making plans for the baby's arrival. Why wouldn't he want to plan their future? Was he afraid to make a commitment? Mary was sure the Flanagans, Jim, Bunty and Rhon would assist. But this was not how it was supposed to be.

It took a week for a far stronger and more determined Mary to emerge from her room. The self-pity and tears were gone. She would not allow this to beat her. She would bounce back and raise the baby as a single mother.

Chapter 17

A Wonderful Gift

Morning sickness seemed endless. Bouts of vomiting left Mary lifeless, resulting in long periods of bedrest to recover. She couldn't believe how dreadful she felt. Worried her condition may affect the baby, Bunty's assurances to Mary when she visited the farm were always encouraging. 'Believe me, no one was laid up more than me during the first couple of months,' she said. 'But I had four healthy baby boys and look at them now. Big strong blokes who have no idea what I went through to bring them into the world.'

'I hope you're right Bunty. It's a struggle. I'm supposed to be putting on weight, not losing it.'

'Don't worry, Mary. Just get through the first three months. Stick to the regime of small meals as your doctor advised and you'll be fine.'

Though thankful for the support of everyone at the farm, with Dan and Monica active buyers of baby clothes and furniture, Mary found it a constant source of annoyance not to have George by her side. She tried not to think of him, but each medical appointment she attended was embarrassing as the health centre staff were aware of her circumstances.

Mary appreciated Jim's company at baby birthing classes, knowing full well he could name many places he'd rather be.

He was particularly tested during the delivery breathing class, feeling obligated to take part with the other fathers.

'Thank goodness none of my old mates from the footy club were there tonight,' he later confided. 'They'd have had a good laugh at my puffing and panting. It was harder work than footy training.'

Mary laughed. 'I think you're a natural. You never know where life will take you. One day the training might come in handy.'

'What are you saying, Mary? You better be careful. The gossips will have a field day, and we know how much damage they can cause.'

'Indeed, I do Jim, indeed I do.'

*

Mary's calm demeanour was tested while sitting alone on the front verandah several months later and her water suddenly broke. Her concerned call startled Dan and Jim who had just settled in for an end of the day beer.

Dan was clear in his role. 'My job is to mind the farm.'

'Okay, you call Monica while I shepherd Mary into the ute,' Jim replied.

Mary firmly held the grab handle as Jim drove the ute out of the farm gate on the short journey to the hospital. Although aware of the wonderful support she would receive from her farm family, Mary was nonetheless anxious at what lay ahead. How could George just leave her to it? Yes, Jim had been a great help, but this should be George's moment.

On their arrival, Jim helped Mary to the front door and said, 'Apologies Mary, if you don't mind, despite all the training, I'm going to leave this bit to you. Monica will be here shortly. I hope that's okay with you?'

'Thanks Jim, I understand. I'm sure I'll be okay.'

*

Exhausted after the delivery, Mary said, 'He's a beautiful boy,' as she held her baby close not wanting to give him up. Monica looked on in happiness and Mary asked if Dan had come to the hospital.

'Yes,' Monica replied 'We've been sitting in the waiting room while you were sleeping. We thought we would give you some time to recover.'

'Would you please call him in.'

Mary watched as Monica and Dan held her baby like proud grandparents.

'He's going to bring us much joy, Mary,' Dan said while brushing away a couple of tears. 'There's no need to worry about a thing. We'll support you in every way we can.'

Mary gently touched Dan's hand in thanks. 'I guess we need to let Jim know the good news. But before we do, we must start calling my baby William Daniel O'Rourke, or Will for short. I hope you're happy to be included Dan.'

'Of course, Mary. It's a great honour,' Dan replied, again shedding tears. 'This is all a bit much for an old bloke. It's a wonderful day.'

'It certainly is, Mary,' Monica said. 'Now you and Will must rest. I reckon Dan, Jim and I have a few hours ahead of us wetting the baby's head.'

*

As expected, Dan and Monica were thrilled with the opportunity to fill the grandparent role, promising Mary they would try not to interfere in his upbringing.

As Monica put it, 'You're going to have to forgive us. We won't be able to stop ourselves from buying toys and gifts.'

Mary was unconcerned. She knew they were good people who'd taken her into their family and would do the same for Will. He would not want for love and affection. As she rested in the hospital with Will, Mary could feel a change in her attitude towards George. Whereas she might have once at least tried to understand his reason for abandoning her, that consideration had been replaced with a resolve that he was now well and truly done and dusted.

*

The first months of Will's life were challenging. As Mary explained to Rhon when she visited the farm, 'I've never felt so tired. It's difficult on my own. Everyone's been a great help, but there's only so much they can do.'

Rhon, who never minced words said, 'Pity George didn't stick around to help out.'

'Bloody George! Good riddance, I reckon.'

'I hope I catch up with him, I'll have a few words in his ear.' Rhon scowled. 'Just ran off and left you to it. Have you heard any news of his whereabouts?'

'No, he's disappeared. Probably out the back of beyond shearing and living the good life. But we'll get by. Monica is already making plans for Will's first birthday.'

Aided by her farm family, Mary was able to eventually settle Will into a routine that provided her with the opportunity of some much-needed rest. When Will was old enough to crawl and walk, Dan carried him on his shoulders and took great pleasure in introducing him to the sheep and chickens. Bath time became an important end of the day activity with Mary astonished at the amount of mud that one small boy gathered.

'What happened today?' she would ask. 'Will smells like the chicken coop.'

'Ah well Mary, he went in for the eggs and came out with some added extras.'

'Perhaps we should put him clothes and all into the washing machine,' Mary replied with a smile.

'Just good clean mud Mary, no harm done,' Dan laughed.

Unconcerned Mary would lift Will into a large portable bath on the back verandah. Regular as clockwork Jim arrived to assist with washing, lifting and drying Will which caused Mary to tease him as he seemed to enjoy playing the fathering role.

'Are you sure you haven't done this before, Jim?'

'Steady up, Mary. You'll get me into trouble. Don't forget the gossips. They'll have a field day.'

Bath time followed by Will's evening meal became a warm ritual Mary shared with Jim and occasionally Dan and Monica. Will was never going to want for love and attention. She also noted that Lilly moved her affections to become Will's constant companion.

Constant travel back and forth to Castle Hill was the next necessity and Mary became excited when Dan informed her, 'It's in the garage, Mary. Nothing flash, but it'll get you around. Even better, it's an automatic, so no more crunching gears.'

'What can I say Dan, you spoil me. It'll make life so much easier.'

'Well, I couldn't have you taking him to kinder in the old truck.'

Dan and Monica also volunteered to help with the book reading encouraged by Mary to equip Will for his entry to primary school.

The Castle Hill school community were active supporters of education with many parents keen to assist. Despite their age Dan and Monica were regular participants leading Jim to jokingly suggest they were spending more time at the school than the farm.

Mary was active on the school council, the tuck shop and on sports days. Jim volunteered to be the stand-in father for student excursions. Mary worried about how he would cope, but while it was a new experience, he seemed comfortable and enjoyed the involvement. On occasions the other kids would tease Will about his old dad.

These could be difficult days for Will when reminded of his father. However, during beach excursions he was chuffed with the time and effort Jim gave to help all the kids to learn how to swim and body surf. Their return to the farm required an end-of-the-day report from Jim –

'A challenging day at the beach, Mary. Plenty of sunscreen and hat wearing. We didn't lose anyone. The lead teacher insisted on a count each hour as the kids kept wandering away. I'm pleased it's an annual not monthly event. Thankfully, they were asleep in the bus on the way home.'

School sports days became happy events with Bunty's family joining to cheer Will along. Never quite fast enough at swimming or athletics, he nonetheless did his best winning place-getter ribbons. Will's final day at primary school was marked by parents attending a gathering of the school assembly.

Will was called forward to receive a book inscribed by the principal to acknowledge that he was a hard-working, well-liked student, voted by his classmates as a house leader.

As the assembly broke up, Mary took Jim's arm and Will ran to them in excitement. 'This is your book, Jim,' Will said, as the two embraced.

'No, it's yours Will, you did the work.'

Brushing away her tears, Mary said, 'Let's just agree we make a good team.'

*

Although students were being accepted at the Castle Hill college, Mary preferred to enrol Will in a large co-educational school in Carravale which had agricultural subjects as its primary focus. Servicing a broad part of the Western District, the school was favoured by farming families. Although requiring a daily commute, Will's safety was assured by having older students and a couple of mates from primary school also travelling aboard the school bus.

As his education continued, and although having no set career path, Will felt comfortable that this would become clear as he worked his way along. He was also realistic about his future being locked into Roscommon Downs. Now that Dan and Monica were in retirement, and with Jim alone to cope with the demands of the farm, Will had become Jim's extra hand.

Driving the farm truck, feeding sheep and odd jobs filled the lad's hours both before and after school.

'I don't know what I'd do without you,' Jim would say.

Will was happy to help and from time to time he'd invite school mates to the farm. Riding Jim's lovingly restored motor bike around the paddocks was a lot of fun. With his mother nervously watching from the verandah, he was often close to a fall, but thankfully never coming to grief. As he grew older, he'd come to understand the importance his mother placed on the support of a loving family. She would often refer to her early days at Roscommon Downs and the way in which the Flanagans had brought her into their family.

'It meant so much to me to be asked to leave Melbourne and come to the farm.' Mary explained. 'While I had friends and was settled into my life at the Rex Hotel, the move here gave me the family I'd never had. The nuns were firm but fair and instilled good values in me. I've tried to pass them on to you.'

The love and care Will received resulted in strong family ties. Any benefit of the doubt that he held in George's favour had disappeared when he would occasionally walk to the Simpson home from the school bus stop in the hope that his father may have returned. But the place was always lifeless.

It made Will angry that his mother could be treated in such an off-handed manner. Mary would travel to the Simpson house when Will was not at the bus stop for pick-up. Finding him at the front gate, she could sense his disappointment saying, 'Don't fret for him Will. It's hard for me to say this about your father, but he's just not worth it.'

'Didn't he like me, Mum?'

'Well as you know, he was gone before you were born. Missing you is his loss. Life will catch up with him.'

*

Making her way to the meeting, Mary was apprehensive as it was out of character for the Flanagans to call them all together in such a formal manner. It crossed her mind that they'd decided to sell-up and move to retirement accommodation. This meeting could be to confirm when that might occur so that Jim, Will and herself would have some notice to enable them to make their own arrangements.

Mary had often contemplated this possibility. Having enjoyed many years of country living with a good group of friends in the area, she'd be reluctant to move away. She decided not to jump to conclusions: no matter what occurred, she'd find a way to move on with her life.

Mary was surprised to see Paul Steele, the Flanagans' solicitor – whom she had met at family events – along with Bunty, who was not her usual bubbly self. Taking a seat with Will, she noted that Jim looked also concerned. She decided that whatever the outcome, she'd support him.

Dan Flanagan broke the nervous silence by speaking very deliberately while reading from a sheet of paper. 'My apologies Jim, Mary, Will and Bunty for having the meeting in this formal manner, but Monica and I have made some decisions regarding the future of Roscommon Downs. We thought it for the best to bring you all together as we don't want there to be any confusion. We have asked Paul and Bunty as independent observers to join us, and when I'm finished everyone will receive a document to confirm the situation.'

Dan cleared his throat and shuffled through some further paperwork before he continued. 'Without keeping you in any more suspense, Monica and I have decided with a couple of provisos to leave the farm, and all our assets to Mary.'

Dan's statement was met with shocked silence. It was the last thing Mary expected. She felt overwhelmed by the magnitude and generosity of the decision. As her eyes started to well up, she also felt an uneasiness for Jim. Would he be disappointed?

'Jim, you have been our main backstop here for much of your life, so we're making provision on our passing for you to receive a generous payment and retain a lifetime living wage. You'll have the right to live rent free in your current accommodation until your passing.'

Before anyone had a chance to interrupt, Dan then addressed Bunty. 'Bunty, your loyalty and hard work has been a critical component to the continued success of the farm, so Monica and I have made provision for a payment to you. We know that you'll protest and say you were only doing your job, but we want you to know how much we appreciate your many years of service with us.'

Dan then concluded, 'And that about sums it up from me.'

After a moment or two, Jim managed to say with a shaky voice, 'Thank you Dan and Monica, for allowing me to live out my years at Roscommon Downs. I was afraid that you were going to sell the farm. I've been considering for some time what I'd do if that occurred.'

Dan was quick to reply. 'We were always going to guarantee your future, Jim. You've been more than an employee to us. We hope that you, Mary and Will and whoever else you bring in, keep Roscommon Downs going at the standard we've all set.'

Seeing Mary dabbing at her eyes, Jim rushed to her side, hugged her and said, 'I'm thrilled for you Mary. I'll continue to do as well as I can towards the success of the farm. We can work together to support Will in his education and life.'

Trying hard to stop her tears from turning into a flood, Mary said, 'Thank you, Jim. I could not wish for a better friend or mentor. You have done nothing but help me since my arrival in Castle Hill. I'll never be able to repay you.'

Mary then said, 'Dan and Monica, what can I say? I thought much the same as Jim, that you might have organised today's meeting to advise us that you'd decided to sell the property and move to a retirement village. I'd have understood you taking that step. How wrong was I. I'm lost for words to thank you for this wonderful gift.'

Monica, who had remained silent until this point, said, 'Well Mary, when Dan and I asked you to come and live with us, we agreed at the time that we would treat you as part of our family. You have certainly become the daughter that we hoped for but didn't have. You have worked hard to look after us with nothing being any trouble to you. We've limited time left, and now that we've made this decision we can get on and enjoy our lives. We want to live out our days on the farm.'

Feeling the need to soften the mood, Monica turned to Bunty. 'How could we leave Bunty and her fabulous scones?'

Everyone laughed and Bunty said, 'You've spoilt me today. I love coming for the shearing, it's the highlight of my year. You can count on me, Mary. And Dan and Monica, I'm sure you have many years of life ahead of you.'

As he moved to leave, Paul Steele advised Jim, Mary and Bunty to expect the necessary paperwork. He explained that provision had been made to publicise the Flanagans' decisions which will read as follows. 'Dan and Monica are keen to let their friends in Castle Hill know of their plans. There has been speculation in town that the farm might have been sold or sub-divided, and they want to stop those rumours before they start.'

The solicitor then advised, 'I'll talk this over with the editor of the local paper. None of you should worry about any legal matters. That's for me to finalise.'

Dan intervened, 'I think that's enough for today. Inevitably some people will be unhappy, particularly if they had plans to buy the farm. Others will be jealous and critical. We've considered the ramifications. Anyone who is unhappy will just have to stay that way.'

Mary replied, 'Well Dan, I hope people are happy for me. I suspect there might be surprise and perhaps some criticism. Jim and I will just carry on as normal. I agree there is no point worrying.'

What Mary was unaware of at the time was a completely unexpected turn of events linked to the publicity arising from her future ownership of Roscommon Downs.

Chapter 18

Les O'Rourke

Les O'Rourke was raised in Barradale, a small town in Northern Victoria, by Mrs Margaret Robins. After her husband's death, she decided to serve the community by opening her home to abandoned children. Mrs Robins wasn't sure that the woman who left Les was his real mother.

'It all happened quickly,' she later informed him. 'I heard your mother had remarried and was moving interstate. A couple of strangers arrived at my door with you and the relevant papers to confirm your name and that you were three years old.'

Mrs Robins also said she knew his father had died just after Les was born but she was unaware if Les had any brothers or sisters.

At Christmas and birthday celebrations, Les felt a real sadness that he had no link with his parents. However, he was happy he had a good home with Mrs Robins who was like a mother to him.

Other children had been left with Mrs Robins, creating plenty of activity and noise in the house particularly at mealtimes. Money was tight, but with the help of neighbours and a child support payment, no one went hungry. An important food source came from the vegetable garden with Mrs Robins maintaining a roster to ensure everyone got their hands dirty.

Ducks and chickens ensured a steady supply of eggs which were put to good use in the kitchen. With the rear fence of the property backing onto a forest, caution was necessary when collecting eggs in the warmer months. The occasional surprised shout kept everyone alert to the presence of snakes.

Les caused no trouble for Mrs Robins. He was a good forager when it came to picking fruit and kept watch on the quince trees growing alongside the main railway line to ensure the annual crop was not lost to swarms of birds.

Mrs Robins suggested the use of nets. 'The birds just pick a bit out of each quince and ruin them,' she said. 'If we cover the trees, we won't lose the fruit.'

Les attended the regional composite school, a short bike ride from home. He waited for his mates and they travelled together using off-road tracks. The occasional fall and skin lost from elbows and knees was accepted as part of the fun.

One of the boys, Des Thomas, known as Stumpy who was never lost for a word, reckoned he was Les O'Rourke's best mate and a permanent fixture at his side.

Les would often find it necessary to pull Stumpy up before things got out of hand. 'Hey Stumpy, do you always have to have something to say? How about trying to let things go?'

'They pick on me Les because I'm little. I've got to stick up for m'self.'

'Fair enough Stumpy. But use a bit of judgement. You can't win them all.'

Les was a good student, being encouraged by Mrs Robins to be the best he could be with his studies. In grade six he took on writing and editing the school journal, developing it into a widely read community publication. He enjoyed collating the news and sporting results. Finding he had a flair for drawing he complemented items with small cartoons.

Tall and strongly built with a shock of red hair, he played football with the school team. Knowing that Les was never happy to take a backward step, his teammates were keen to have him around when the going got tough. Stumpy enjoyed playing footy, and when asked on one occasion if he was afraid of being bumped to the ground, he replied, 'No worries there. Haven't got far to fall.'

Unsure of his future career directions when pressed by Mrs Robins, Les would say, 'There's no rush. Things will sort out as I go along.'

Les had already taken a minor step into employment at a transport yard where he helped with the Sunday morning truck washing. His preference was for Stumpy not to be involved. 'You haven't been hit with the energy stick Stumpy. Are you sure you want to be here at work?'

Stumpy would just grunt at Les. 'Don't worry big fella, I'll do me share.'

When allowed to sit behind the wheel, Les visualised the thrill of driving a big truck on the highway. He marvelled at the skill of the mechanics, stripping and repairing the diesel engines, often thinking that might be an interesting career choice. Three hours work returned him useful pocket money to fund school costs and excursions.

During the holidays, Les sought permission to travel in the trucks to Melbourne and on interstate runs. Rod Bond, the company owner, had come into the transport industry through the same pathway. He was happy to accommodate and encourage Les and other local boys to travel with his drivers.

This enabled Les to visit capital cities and meet and mix with hardworking people. Later in life he reckoned that this schooling in the university-of-life, was the most beneficial he'd received. After completing school his writing skills might have led him to study journalism. However, Les decided to continue in the transport industry by accepting an offer of employment from Rod Bond.

'I reckon you could make a go of it,' Rod said. 'While it's a tough industry, there are plenty of career possibilities. Just work hard and take the opportunities as they present. I know you're good mates with Stumpy Thomas, but I won't be making him a job offer. I don't think he's up to it.'

While disappointed for Stumpy, Les was aware he needed to make his own way.

Stumpy was unfazed, saying to Les, 'No worries mate, something'll come up. I'm pretty good with me hands. A couple of our mates are starting a farm fencing business. I've an option to join, maybe take a share.'

'I hope it works out for you, Stumpy. Just make sure you don't get led into something shifty.'

Assisted by the other drivers, Les was able to secure a licence to allow him to drive a small truck with the weekly income helping him to move out of Mrs Robins' home. His workmates had combined to buy a house near Rod Bond's depot and were happy for Les to take a room and share the living costs. While he tried to keep in touch with Mrs Robins, the move to live with his workmates, together with his long hours at work, made contact difficult.

After a couple of years experience, he was able to upgrade his licence and become qualified to drive semi-trailers on interstate transport. Not afraid to speak his mind, he was elected by his workmates to represent them in their wage bargaining and yard disputes. This suited Rod Bond, as he was comfortable with Les who although at times forthright, always acted with common sense and would stand by all deals.

Les was quick to bristle with anger when his integrity was questioned. He'd developed a habit of punching his right hand into the palm of his left hand when making a point. It was a brave and foolish man who continued with the argument to the point where Les felt he was being unreasonably maligned.

Aware of some gaps in his knowledge, this led Les to seek out a link to the drivers-union and arrange a visit by the local organiser.

A few days later, Les was approached at the depot by a short thick set man carrying a small case that had seen plenty of work. 'I understand your workmates have elected you to represent them. Did you call the union office asking for an organiser to visit?' the man asked.

'That's correct, thanks for coming. I'm impressed that you're wearing a tie. We don't see many ties around here.'

'I'm Mark Warren, the Transport Workers Union organiser for the area. And fair enough about the tie. I believe members like to be professionally represented.'

'I'm pleased to meet you, Mark. I'm Les O'Rourke; we haven't seen many union people in the area, so you're very welcome. We don't have many problems that I can't sort out with the boss. However, it's always good to know you blokes are around to back me up.'

'I come through the area on a regular schedule. I'm able to call in as required,' Mark said.

'How about we go to the drivers' room for a coffee, it's nearly drinkable.'

As they sipped their coffee, Les went on to explain the reason for his call. 'My immediate concern is the transport of dangerous goods. It's new work the company has picked up. I need some advice about protective clothing, gloves and safety procedures if there's a spillage. And there are a couple of other matters I'd like clarified.'

'I'm sure I can assist you, Les. I have with me the latest guide for the movement of dangerous goods. There are training courses available. You could suggest to the boss that you attend on behalf of the company.'

'Thanks Mark, I'm sure the guide will be useful.'

'If you can spare me a few minutes Les, there's another matter that I'd welcome the opportunity to discuss with you. Have you time after you finish work today?'

'No worries. I'm always happy to chat. My truck is in for service today. I'll be free after four o' clock.'

With his obvious integrity, and strong support of his workmates, Les was just the sort of union member that Mark was seeking. Disappointed that his union, which he had been a member of for thirty years, had become dominated by politics, he was forming a rank-and-file team to contest the forthcoming union elections.

He believed it time for a fresh team to be elected to take control of the union. In his favour was membership frustration and disappointment in the way the union was being managed. The key to success for Mark was gathering a strong driver's group, who could carry the reform message to the membership.

Later that day, having carefully followed the directions provided by Les to his favourite coffee shop, he was well placed to explain the circumstances of the union and why he was seeking support. As he entered the shop, Les looked up from his newspaper. 'You found the place, Mark. I couldn't have you drinking any more of the work's coffee. It's a shocker.'

'No worries. I've been in transport long enough for my gut to tolerate anything. But down to business, I won't hold you up for long.'

'It's okay, I'm good for time.'

'I hope you can see your way clear to join my team, Les. The industry is rapidly developing with the rush of technology and the union needs to come to terms with it.'

'You're right about the technology. Things seem to change every day.'

'That's right. We've got to get ahead of the game. And there's the matter of protecting the members' funds.'

As he sat quietly and listened to Mark outline the activities of the current management team, Les could see the need to take a role in the reform group. Mark's passion to improve the lot of truck drivers constantly came through. He was clear in his ambition for the union. 'The members must take hold of the organisation and run it as a union. We've got to drop off the politics.'

'You've put forward a strong argument, Mark. Let me think about it for a few days. If that suits, put me on your probable list.'

'I appreciate you listening to me Les. I hope you'll agree to come on board.'

*

While Les was prepared to meet Mark and discuss the conduct of the union, his real focus, apart from continuing his employment, was trying to clarify the history of his parents. He was determined that at some stage of his life he would research his heritage to establish if he had siblings.

During moments of disappointment, Les often thought that Mrs Robins knew more than she'd been prepared to convey. He felt that given her longevity, she would have a strong understanding of his family background which she should release to him and not deliberately withhold.

Les also believed that any publicity or exposure he could generate might assist in bringing about knowledge of his family. Being country based took him out of the reach of Melbourne media. His involvement in a state-wide union election might bring him to people's notice and perhaps promote some connections.

While he had no knowledge or experience of union politics, Les felt that he was a reasonable judge of character. Satisfied with what he'd learned during his short meeting with Mark he conveyed his agreement to be involved by telephone.

'That's great news, Les. I'm really pleased to have you on board.'

'Thanks Mark, you can trust me to give a hundred percent to the campaign and beyond if the team is successful.'

'We'll be having a get together in a week or so. We need photographs for our election material which will be circulated to the union's thirty thousand members across Victoria.'

'Great Mark, I'd best get myself a haircut for the big day.'

*

During their conversations Mark had warned Les that there might be some rough and tumble meetings during the election ballot. 'The incumbents don't like anyone other than their gang having a say at meetings. If they're unsure of who you're supporting, they'll try to intimidate you to be quiet. But I suspect that you don't frighten easily.'

'No Mark, I've spent too many years on the road and footy field to be bothered by a few so-called heavies.'

Les was confident he could handle anything that came his way in that regard. This was an opportunity to grasp with both hands.

*

The meeting of Mark's team for photographs and a strategy talk had Les initially questioning the wisdom of his decision. Having driven for two hours on a Sunday, he was confronted by two short tough looking men blocking the front gate to a home in Melbourne. 'Can we help you mate?'

'I'm Les O' Rourke, here to meet with Mark Warren.'

The shorter of the two men held out a gnarled hand. 'Okay Les, in you go. We can catch up later. The meeting's in the backyard.'

Wally Smith, who was nominating for the position of union president, gave Les a warm welcome to his home. 'Thanks for coming, Les. Mark's just tying up a few loose ends before the meeting gets going. Come and meet some of the other blokes in the team.'

During the next few minutes, Les shook many hands that had done plenty of hard work. He was pleased to see Mark well received by the group. Taking the opportunity of a quiet word to him, Les commented that they were an interesting and likeable mix of blokes with many good storytellers among them. He was heartened by Mark's reply. 'They're all good union members from the broad sweep of the transport industry. They want rank and file members running the union. It's as simple as that.

They'll give you support but will drop off the first time you let them down.'

'I've noticed they call a spade a bloody spade. I reckon I can fit in.'

'There's no worries there Les, you'll be a perfect fit. The key to a successful election ticket is to develop a broad representative balance of members and that's what I hope I've achieved.'

'What's the reason there were a couple of tough buggers out the front?'

'Oh, Tom and Mick reckoned some of our opposition would turn up. They volunteered to man the door. They'd rather have a fight than a feed.'

During a short period of introductions, Les had noted that some members of the team were well known to others. Without any dissent the group were advised by Mark of their positions on his twelve-candidate election ticket. Les was endorsed as a nomination for the committee of management. With the election ticket known, Mark addressed the group from the back verandah.

'Get out and about the transport industry and talk to truck drivers about our team. Talk about us in terms of working truck drivers not the officials running the union. The ballot is decided on first past the post voting, so we don't have a minute to spare to influence the outcome.'

When considering his campaign activities, Les was reluctant to spend any extra time in Melbourne. His options were to visit the Melbourne waterfront or travel to the Western District where he would meet another member of the team, John Black, to improve his knowledge of milk pickup from farms.

Standing with John as they enjoyed a sandwich and cup of tea before the long drive home, Les said 'I've learnt a lot today, I reckon Mark's on the right track. What do you think?'

'I'm a bit like you, Les. It's all new country for me, but somethings got to be done. The current mob are out of control. Mark's pretty gutsy to stand up. He deserves our support.'

'Any chance I can put in a couple of days with you?'

'No worries, mate. I'll organise with the transport manager to take you out in the truck. You'll be an expert in no time.'

'Right John, there's no time like the present. I have Tuesday and Wednesday off next week. How about we make it then?'

*

Easing the large milk tanker out onto the highway, John said, 'Good to be on time, Les. These four o'clock starts on winter mornings are a good test of character.'

'Not to worry, mate, old truckies are always up for a day's work.'

'We'll need to take our time first up.'

'I'm used to driving in the dark. But is it always as foggy as this?'

'Afraid so. It'll get better as the day goes on.'

As he settled back into the passenger seat, Les was pleased that John knew where he was going as he was completely lost. He had quickly warmed to John, linking with a kindred spirit and accepting an invitation to stay at his home.

Enjoying a meal with his wife and children had given Les a good appreciation of John's character and firmed his decision to be involved in the union election. John was strong in his view.

'I'm happy to support any action that's bona fide transport industry related.'

'That's how I see it. Blokes at my depot in Barradale talk about the footy, trucks and roads, never politics. Occasionally someone will start complaining about losing licence points.'

'No different than my yard, Les.'

Always cautious as a passenger, Les was impressed with the way John safely negotiated the dark narrow roads and farm gates.

'How is your relationship with the dairy farmers?'

'All good, Les. I can count on a cup of tea here and there. The results of the local footy are always a topic for Mondays. These people work hard milking both morning and afternoon often in bitterly cold wet weather.'

During a day that passed quite quickly, Les came to understand John's view regarding the work commitment of dairy farmers. He also gained an appreciation of John's value, given his friendly and efficient approach as a representative of his employer. Les noted that there was not a lot that happened in his area that John didn't know about, so conversations flowed freely.

After enjoying a cup of tea at one of the farm pickups, as they walked to the truck, John said, 'Do you have any family in the Western District? The reason I ask is that I had a quick look through the local paper while we enjoyed our cuppa. There was an article regarding a Mary O'Rourke, soon to take over a farm in Castle Hill.'

Les was cautious in his reply. 'I don't think I have any family down this way. My life has been lived in Northern Victoria. Did you say Castle Hill?'

'Yes mate. The farm is called Roscommon Downs. The article said it's been owned for many years by Dan and Monica Flanagan.'

Returning home, Les spent a day or two considering if he would follow up and contact Mary O'Rourke. He had pursued similar leads in the past only to be disappointed. It could also be confronting for people who valued their privacy, and just wanted to be left alone if approached by a stranger.

But he was now forty-six and time was disappearing in his quest to discover any family. He reminded himself that he'd started down this path by agreeing to a role in the union election.

*

Mary didn't know what to think when she received the letter. There was no claim by Les that they might be related. Just a simple request to meet when he was next in Castle Hill. Les had set out his frustration in respect to his parents. He believed that information was being withheld suggesting that Mrs Robins might be more forthcoming in a meeting with Mary. It seemed an unusual request. Why would Mrs Robins be more open with a stranger?

Mary decided to discuss the situation with Monica before responding.

'He's just asking to meet. I guess there's no harm in that.'

'I suppose not Mary. It'd be a bit of a stretch for you to be related to a truckie from Barradale.'

'I like the tone of his letter. If you don't mind, I'll invite him here. Jim and Bunty can be present. There's not much chance of any gold-diggers winning me over with them around.'

Chapter 19

Debutantes

After listening to the same record for a couple of hours at each debutante training session, the tune 'Shine on Harvest Moon' was keeping Mary awake at night.

Finding the album of dance music in the antique shop had been a relief and assisted in stopping a push to use something more modern. There was no way she would sway from a solid strict tempo, telling Rhon during one of their coffee mornings, 'I don't want them to get lost in some rapping nonsense. I'm happy to be called old fashioned.'

Mary was still not sure how Will had managed to talk her into training the deb set for presentation at the racing carnival ball. The big night was two months away and there were a hundred and one reasons why the dancing and evening could go badly. Notwithstanding the excitement among the dancers and her willingness to help, given the day-to-day challenges of managing the farm, she really could have done without the pressure.

Will, on the other hand, was full of confidence saying to Mary as they drove home after one of the sessions, 'Everyone is really looking forward to the ball. We don't get many chances to dress up in Castle Hill.'

'I understand their enthusiasm, Will. I hope everyone is prepared to work hard. Members of the group who pick up the dance steps more easily than others will need to support those who struggle.'

The young people showed their commitment by attending all the training sessions. Many were quick to learn while some were taking extra time to grasp the simple dance sequence. A couple of the mothers volunteered to assist. However, they were more of a hindrance than a help. Many times, Mary felt like shouting, 'I understand you're all trying to help. But please leave the organising and training to me.'

Believing the group would benefit from some intensive coaching, she invited a few of her Hawthorn Town Hall friends to visit for a couple of weekends. Led by Agnes Wright, they affected an immediate improvement by blending into the circle and helping those struggling to catch up.

As they removed their dancing shoes after a training session, Mary thanked Agnes. 'There might be a whole new life you're developing here. You could bring together a travelling dance studio. There must be other schools in need of your expertise.'

'I suppose so Mary, but I reckon this will be a one off for us. We really wanted to come and catch up with you and witness life in Castle Hill. Who knows, the pace of life might rub off and convince some of us to settle away from the rat race in Melbourne.'

'Castle Hill always welcomes new people. You must be entitled to long service leave from the Rex Hotel. Perhaps you could come for a couple of months. There's always a room available at the farm.'

Mary was firm in her view that the boys would wear formal attire consisting of dinner suit, white dress shirt, black bow tie and proper dancing footwear. There would be no half measures. And by a stroke of luck, she located a bin of well used patent leather shoes in the pre-loved shop in Carravale.

The shop owner was happy to part with them at a special cut price. 'I think it's about ten years since I organised enough shoes for the last Castle Hill debutante set. After the Ball, the organising teacher just threw them in the bin, and they've been there ever since. I wish you good luck and good dancing,' the owner said.

'Thank you. I appreciate your good wishes. I suspect I'm going to need them. It might be best if I return the shoes that survive the night for a future occasion.'

Finding dinner suits and shirts presented more of a problem. Agnes Wright came to Mary's aid through an arrangement with a hire company in Melbourne. 'It was unusual for the company to release thirty suits, shirts and ties in this manner. They were very wary of letting them out of town.'

'Pass on my appreciation, Agnes. I'll impress on each of the boys to have a change of clothes before the after party.'

The girls decided to follow tradition and wear white dresses complimented with red and blue sashes, honouring the school colours. When a suggestion was made to encourage the girls to wear long white gloves, Mary wondered if they could be sourced. She hadn't reckoned on the girls' mothers producing the gloves worn on their own debutante night. Many were brought to the dress rehearsals wrapped in tissue paper, having been carefully stored to pass onto their daughters.

Mary had pondered how best to start. Forming the group in a circle she addressed them while trying not to sound like a drill sergeant. 'I want you to walk around the hall while you listen to the music.'

She could see that although one or two had no idea, there was a generally good feel for the music. So, she asked everyone to walk in time with the beat which re-endorsed her suspicion that some were going to need extra training to take their place. Mary was especially pleased to watch Will and his friend, Sarah, who with their obvious feel for the music, moved easily around the floor.

Partnering was a simple procedure for the couples who were friends, but Mary had to match the others the best she could. Will being quick to team up with Sarah Quinn, confirmed a mother's intuition as she had suspected something was afoot. While the dancing was important, it was an opportunity to strengthen their friendship which had been developing pretty much from the first day of Sarah's arrival in Castle Hill.

Sensing some tension among the couples which started to flow over to the training sessions, Mary decided to speak her mind. 'Some of you are playing around and it's time to stop. I'm not partnering you up to get married. I've put you together in a form, so you'll look your best for the ball. Stop whinging about the order of presentation and just concentrate on preparing for the evening. Anything else doesn't matter.'

A stunned silence fell over the group. Continuing her address with an angry tone, Mary made it clear she was receiving some negative vibes and was not about to take any nonsense.

'I'm going to work you through a simple presentation dance that will enable each girl to be presented to the regional mayor. We'll then circle up for a dance called the Pride of Erin. The steps are very straightforward and I'm sure you'll quickly learn them. While the girls are the principle focus, the success of the night very much depends on the boys performing their role. We haven't got a lot of time, so come to rehearsals with your mind on dancing.'

After a few weeks, Mary was pleased with the rapid improvement. A couple of the troublemakers playing up had been brought into line. Even those she thought would never grasp the dances started to lead the way. She was certain that extra informal practice sessions had been occurring possibly in family living rooms. All of which led her to feel comfortable that her troupe would do themselves proud on the night.

This was confirmed a week before the ball when a dress rehearsal was held with all parents, including Patrick and Kathleen Quinn, in attendance. With her time limited given the demands of the rehearsal, Mary promised to catch up with the Quinns. She suggested to Kathleen that although Will and Sarah were young, she suspected they may be planning a future, so it would be nice to spend some time together before her and Patrick returned home.

*

Mary could feel a great sense of pride among the parents, and the excitement that was building among the group. Community members and teachers worked especially hard to decorate the town hall in the school colours. A floral arch was erected for the girls to pass under, and to Mary's delight, Dorothy Jones produced a mirror ball that had been languishing in her antique shop.

'I've no idea how the ball came into my possession Mary, but it will create a great lighting spectacle around the ceiling and walls of the hall.'

Mary was cautiously optimistic for the success of the night, as she watched the early dancing. Many of the parents were quite accomplished and she was reminded of the grace and style required as they glided through the slow foxtrot. For a moment or two, she allowed her mind to drift back to the Hawthorn Town Hall, before the reality of the evening demanded her attention.

As the master of ceremonies cleared the dance floor, the pangs of nervousness associated with her exhibition dancing days returned, to be quickly replaced with the emotion of watching the deb set excitedly assemble in a flurry of dresses and dinner suits. They all looked so well-groomed with not a hair out of place.

The deb set rose to the occasion and gave a faultless display. The hall lights were dimmed, and a spotlight hit the mirrored ball. Another focused on the dancers. It was an exciting spectacle. Parents and friends were enthusiastic with their applause as each girl was presented to the mayor resplendent in his council robes. The gold medallions on his chain of office reflected the shimmering beams of the lighting.

At the conclusion of the formal dance a scramble of parents and friends joined the debutante set on the dance floor for a mass Pride of Erin. It was time to celebrate the special occasion to which they had all contributed. As she watched Will circling the floor, Mary felt a warm glow when reflecting on his growth and their relationship. Her thoughts were broken by the sound of Jim's voice. 'Would you like to join in Mary? If you lead, I promise not to stand on your toes.'

Taking Jim's arm and moving onto the dancefloor, Mary felt an immense happiness with the outcome of her training and preparation. He was very complimentary. 'You've done an excellent job here. I've seldom seen such a happy lot of people in Castle Hill.'

'It was a test at times Jim. but the outcome made it all worthwhile.'

*

Mary could still feel the energy of the previous evening as she drove to Manny's Bakery to meet Patrick and Kathleen for breakfast. While expressing appreciation for Mary's offer of accommodation, Kathleen suggested that Mary would have had enough on her hands organising the deb set without having to worry about them staying at the farm. 'It was a big night, Mary. You must be weary?'

'You're absolutely correct, my feet will take quite a while to recover.'

'You would be pleased with the result. The deb set didn't put a foot wrong,' Kathleen said.

'I certainly am, but I've told Will never again. It was a good experience, but terribly time consuming. It took me away from my work at the farm. Did you enjoy the evening, Patrick?'

'I certainly did. Kath and I were talking about it this morning. We've never seen Sarah look so happy.'

'It's wonderful to see the young people dressed to the nines and enjoying themselves. I guess we'll be seeing a bit more of

Sarah given her part-time work with the Castle Hill vet,' Mary replied.

'Yes, that's a matter we wanted to talk to you about. Sarah's keen to get started. It's an excellent opportunity as the vet takes care of the horses at the races. It's an area she's keen to learn more about to complement her studies,' Patrick said.

'Sounds like a great opportunity.'

'It certainly is Mary, but we worry about our baby daughter.'

Interrupting the conversation, Kathleen said, 'Don't listen to him, Mary. He's the worrier, not me. Sarah is nearly nineteen and it's time for her to get out into the world.'

As they finished their coffee, Kathleen explained the need to visit the shops. 'I have a list of things to take home, Mary.'

'Okay, I'll leave you to your retail therapy and expect you at the farm for lunch tomorrow.'

*

Seated on the verandah enjoying the sun's gentle warmth and watching the wrens chasing the insects above the fishpond, Mary was pleased the garden was looking near its best for the Quinns' visit. She was especially pleased that they had agreed to come to the farm to provide a further opportunity to firm up their friendship.

After the ball, Kathleen had confided in Mary, 'Although we were confident that Sarah would be safe living with her aunt and attending school here, she's our youngest. We did worry about her welfare. We felt much more comfortable when Ruby advised us of Sarah's friendship with Will.'

'That's very kind of you,' Mary had replied. 'It's been a pleasure to watch the friendship grow.'

Mary had laid out the large table with six place settings. With Will and Sarah to attend and Jim also invited, she felt certain a relaxing afternoon was in store.

When everyone arrived and was seated, inevitably the conversation turned to the deb set and the ball. Patrick decided to have a little fun at Will's expense when suggesting that he might have a future in ballroom dancing. Then with a wink he added, 'That of course will depend on you being able to keep our daughter as your partner.'

'Don't get sucked into the conversation, Will,' Sarah laughed. 'Dad's just having some fun.'

'No worries, Mr Quinn. I think I can safely say I won't be making a career out of ballroom dancing,' Will smiled. 'Actually, I was afraid that Mum might burst her boiler on a couple of occasions when my mates started to play up. She totally lost it … but was taking no prisoners I can assure you.'

Mary blushed. 'Will, behave yourself. You know that I'm always calm and composed even at the most trying moments.'

'Could've fooled me, Mum. Sarah and I were shaking in our dancing shoes when you started giving that pep talk.' Will squeezed his girlfriend's hand under the table.

Jim decided to join in the frivolity. 'We all know that your Mum can be a bit of a firecracker once she gets started. It doesn't happen often, but when it does, I tend to run for my life.'

'Whatever are Patrick and Kathleen going to think of me with you lot joking around.'

'Better for them to know the truth, hey Mum' Will poked his mother in the ribs and laughed.

Before long, the small group at the table including Mary, were all enjoying Will's cheeky humour and the happy atmosphere became relaxed and informal.

Following lunch, the discussion took on a more serious note as Kathleen and Patrick spoke of their love for Victoria's Western District and the strong roots their family had in Killarney. Patrick also spoke of his pride in being a descendant of the original Quinns, Michael and Brigid, who arrived in the district in 1922.

'It would have been a challenge taking on farming as their working life had been in factories. But they received great assistance from the already settled Irish community,' Kathleen explained.

'They were certainly tested, but we Irish don't give up easily,' Patrick said.

'I can relate to the struggle as I came here from hotel work,' Mary commented. 'I wasn't sure what I'd struck during my first wet and cold winter.'

Mary offered her guests an after-dinner port and several sips later Kathleen appeared to become a little merry as she looked at Patrick and began to giggle. She then went on to relate the story of their courtship in Killarney. 'At every family gathering, after a few drinks, our children always ensure it becomes the topic of conversation.'

'It's just a bit of fun for them, Mary, we don't mind,' Patrick interrupted. 'Our children are a great joy to us as we can see is your Will.'

Kathleen explained that her family were long-term neighbours of the Quinns in Killarney. Her mother preferred home schooling ensuring her six children were available to assist with milking and maintaining the crops grown to feed their animals.

'Patrick and I just grew up together. We can't remember when the decision was taken to marry. Our children can't come to terms with that. And I can't recall Patrick getting down on one knee. But the real fun they have is about the birthdates.'

'No Mum, not the story about our birthdates,' Sarah insisted. 'It's embarrassing.'

'I'm sure I can cope,' Mary laughed.

'Regular as clockwork, Mum. I heard this story from Sarah's sister,' Will said as he was obviously enjoying the conversation.

'Come on Kath tell the story for God's sake,' Patrick said.

'Very well!' Kathleen agreed, and it seemed that it was now her turn to blush. 'You see Mary, it's like this. Never a St Patrick's day passes without it being mentioned. The reason being that there's a two-year gap between each of the six children. All the births occurring in December with Sarah, the youngest, arriving a week before Christmas.'

'Really Mum!' Sarah raised her eyebrows in disgust and put her hand over her mouth. 'That's far too much information,' she mumbled.

Mary almost spilt her port as she doubled over with laughter. 'Sounds like a hell of a lot of happy St Patrick's days to me, Kath.'

'It's the rhythm method Mary … actually perfect rhythm,' Patrick smiled.

Chapter 20

Barradale and Beyond

Les knew his journey to Castle Hill to meet Mary, who shared the name O'Rourke, might end in disappointment. It was unlikely to be more than a coincidence. But anything was worth a try and he willed himself to remain optimistic.

Many years had passed since he was left with Mrs Robins. Surely there must be someone that either worked with or mixed socially with his mother and father who could provide some answers. Why was he abandoned? Perhaps his parents were running away from an incident that occurred in the town and the local police might be able to assist. Either way, meeting up with Mary, who had also undergone a similar experience, could possibly be his best chance to unlock the past and expose the truth regarding his family.

After he had joined the union movement and relocated to Melbourne, he had lost many of his community contacts. So, he decided to place an article in the *Barradale Times* and organise a drop box at the town hall to enable people to assist him with his search anonymously. Whatever the outcome, this might be his last opportunity and he was going to give it his best shot.

*

Knowing that Les had arranged to come to Roscommon Downs at midday, Mary paced back and forth along the verandah while Bunty sat waiting patiently.

'Thanks for giving up your time, Bunty. I'm unsure about all of this.'

'That's only natural, Mary. But I'm intrigued and looking forward to meeting Les.'

As Bunty spoke, she spotted a stranger walking up the driveway towards the house. She said, 'If this is Les, there's no chance he's related to you, Mary. Not with that shock of red hair.'

'Seems not Bunty. But let's not come to any early conclusions. At least wait until he and I have had a chance to chat.'

Mary noted the man's easy and confident manner as he approached her. 'You must be Les. I'm Mary, welcome to Roscommon Downs.'

Extending his hand and smiling broadly, Les replied, 'Thanks Mary. I decided to walk up from the front gate. It's a bit of a way I can tell you. But I didn't think it proper for me to drive in as if I owned the place.'

Mary felt the warmth and strength of his handshake. 'That's fine Les, but you would have been most welcome to drive in and make yourself at home. Please let me introduce you to Bunty, our shearers' cook.'

'Pleased to meet you, Bunty. I reckon you'd have to be the most important person here.'

Mary could see that Bunty appreciated the compliment as she stepped forward to take his hand. 'You could be right there, Les. I don't get many complaints.'

'The owners, Dan and Monica Flanagan are away, so Bunty is here to help keep the place going,' Mary said. 'You've come such a long way, so let's sit on the verandah where we can enjoy a cup of tea and chat about our families. You might even score one of Bunty's famous scones.'

'I'm looking forward to a scone. Best in the district, I suspect.'

As they sat enjoying their tea and scones, Bunty took her leave to allow the two to discuss their stories. Mary felt a genuine warmth developing between herself and Les which supported her early assessment that he was a well-grounded easy-going man. Given this belief, she was happy and willing to exchange stories in an open and engaged manner. Mary talked through her early days at the orphanage while Les explained his upbringing with Mrs Robins.

Pouring Les a second cup of tea, she said, 'It's a bit of a storybook tale as to how we've both reached this point. Who would have thought with me starting out life at St Kilda and you in Barradale that we would meet here in Castle Hill?'

Taking a sip of his tea and replacing his cup back on the saucer, Les replied, 'I can only agree, Mary. Our stories are hard to believe. But after all you've told me, sadly it doesn't seem likely there's any chance that we're related.'

'I really don't think so, Les,' Mary agreed. 'Not with your red hair.'

'It sets us apart, that's for sure. But aside from all that, I'd love to get to the bottom of my immediate family history as I feel certain you do as well.'

'Yes, I've all but given up hope,' Mary paused while Les buttered another scone. 'But getting back to your own situation, I'm wondering if you've spoken to Margaret Robins recently?'

'No! Mrs Robins, her neighbours and the people who know her, have effectively stopped talking to me. I'm not sure why. And while I can understand that this may sound like an imposition, particularly as we now believe that we are unrelated … I was still hoping you can find a few days to come to Barradale.'

'I must say that since receiving your letter, I've been trying to understand why you seem to think that Mrs Robins will be more open with me, a perfect stranger?'

'I can see your point, Mary, and realise I'm grasping at straws. But it may be that the publicity in the Barradale press release about two abandoned infants bearing the same name could provide some local interest and flush out something of importance. So, I'm hoping that people might feel more comfortable talking to you rather than me.'

Les's eyes darted around the garden as if to allow him a moment to think. 'Mrs Robins is in her eighties and in permanent care. Unfortunately, many of the people who were aware of the circumstances at the time have most likely passed on.'

In anticipation that Les would again ask her to join him in Barradale, Mary had organised Bunty to stay at the farm for a few extra days. And having now given up all hope of finding any family of her own she understood the emptiness Les was carrying. It was an impulsive move on Mary's part to agree to go off with someone she had only just met. But, notwithstanding their limited time together, whatever she could do to help him work through to a successful conclusion she was prepared to embrace completely.

'Okay Les, let's go to Barradale. We can work through this together. But it might be best that you don't build your hopes up. I've run into many dead ends in my own search.'

*

Later when Les had left, Mary discussed her plan with Bunty. 'Do you think it safe for me to go wandering off to some distant country town with a man I have only just met?'

'Normally, my advice would be, no way, Mary. But I think both you and I drew the same conclusion. Les seems genuine and harmless. I would be the first to say don't do this if I hadn't met the man.'

'Oh Bunty, you do make me laugh sometimes. One nice word about your scones and you are completely won over; as you should be, I reckon.'

Neither Jim, nor Will, would have agreed with Mary taking such a drastic decision, she knew that for certain. But sometimes in this life one simply had to trust their instincts. And for some unknown reason, Mary felt an affinity for a person bearing the same name as her own irrespective of whether they were related.

*

Although well able to drive from the farm to Castle Hill and Carravale, Mary lacked the confidence to embark on a five-hundred-kilometre round trip to Barradale alone in the car. Taking the decision to travel by train instead, this allowed her to also take advantage of an overnight stopover in Melbourne, where she was eager to catch up with friends at the Hawthorn Town Hall.

It was always a highlight to enter the Town Hall and be swept up by the music of the big band, the members of which never seemed to age. The place was like a comfortable second home and on this occasion many of her friends were in attendance. They greeted her warmly. But as she searched among the dancers to seek out her regular partner Glyn Harris, she was disappointed to learn that he had not made an appearance for many months.

Calls had been made to both his last known workplace and his home address. As there was no response his friends decided to discontinue their search, lest they were thought to be harassing him. Mary was saddened by the news of Glyn's disappearance, especially since being aware that it was completely out of character for him to leave without telling his friends.

Indeed, he was always punctual, and a person who disliked uncertainty.

Mary explained the purpose of her visit to her friends and emphasized her priority to assist Les in Barradale. She promised that she would then commit to locating Glyn. 'Perhaps he's moved interstate or overseas. I'd be surprised to hear that he's found a new ballroom. Let's just hope that he's safe and well.'

*

The train trip to Barradale journeyed through some of the driest parts of the State. Coming from the green paddocks of the Western District into the north Mary was shocked at the absence of water in the dams and the barren, brown dusty paddocks. The poor condition of the animals was horrifying: the sheep just skin and bones, surviving on no more than stubble in the paddocks.

There was clearly a crisis unfolding, which would require sustained heavy rain to resolve. With none forecast, it was inevitable that many farmers would be forced to walk off their land and lose properties that had been in their families for generations. The real sadness for her was that there was nothing she could do to assist, apart from donating money or sheep feed.

As the train slowed on entering the Barradale railway station, a group of school children who had shared her carriage excitedly gathered their belongings. Two weary teachers urged them to make sure they left nothing behind.

Mary was pleased to receive a warm welcome from Les as he emerged from the throng of parents greeting their children. 'Good to see you Mary. What happened to the rain you were going to bring with you?'

'I can see how badly it's needed, and what I can't understand is how farmers are surviving. It must be very tough for them.'

Helping Mary with her suitcase, Les replied, 'The reality is that quite a few have given up, sold their stock and moved away.'

'Must be heartbreaking trying to hold on.'

'It really is. Hopefully, some might find alternative employment and be able to return when the drought breaks.'

As Les and Mary walked to the car, Mary said, 'I really feel for them and understand how lucky we are at Roscommon Downs to have a supply of water and stock feed. But I haven't come all this way to dwell on the state of the land around Barradale and should ask what's our plan of approach in regard to Margaret Robins and other members of the community?'

'First things first, Mary. I've booked you a room at the hotel. Once you have settled in there it will give you a chance to freshen up.'

While driving a short way to the pub, Les explained that Mrs Robins was currently living at the local nursing home and he had permission from management to enter and meet the residents. 'Margaret's mind is still sharp, and she apparently remembers me. Other people in the facility who are in a similar age group may be able to assist, and a drop box has been installed at the Town Hall and Anglican Church to enable anonymous messaging. There's been nothing come from it yet. But everyone, including the police, know about your visit. The local newspaper even led this week with the headline, 'The O'Rourkes come to town'.'

'Gosh, Les, that sounds like something out of the Wild West.'

'A bit dramatic I guess, Mary. But your visit should catch community attention. The editor will follow up with an interview tomorrow. It's an important opportunity as the paper is published three times a week and popular with the town's fifteen hundred residents.'

Les also explained that he had asked an active member of the community to contact the various service clubs about the visit. There was also the likelihood of attracting the interest of a community newspaper circulating in a nearby major regional city.

It occurred to Mary that there might be value in researching church birth, deaths and marriage records. There could also be knowledge among the church community and if a presentation to the congregation could be arranged, it might open-up some new leads.

Dropping Mary off at the hotel, Les indicated his appreciation of her application to the matter. 'Might be a good idea to have a good night's sleep. It looks like we'll have a fair bit on tomorrow.'

*

The tolling of the church bell summoned worshippers to Sunday services at the Barradale Anglican Church. Non church goers could check their clocks at 10am, relying on the dedicated group of bellringers. Erected in 1910 in the classic design of the time, the church was a solid construction featuring high red brick walls and a front porch leading to two locally made wooden entrance doors. A tall spire could be seen from far and wide above the rooftops of the town.

At the end of the First World War, parishioners had fundraised to install a large leadlight window behind the altar. Built as a memorial depicting the various theatres of war, it recognised the sacrifices of all servicemen and women. Local citizens who lost their lives were remembered on an honour board.

After contacting the local vicar, Les had obtained permission to research the church records. He also suggested that Les and Mary take the opportunity to address the Sunday congregation following the normal morning service.

While enjoying a cup of tea before the service, Les said, 'I can't say that speaking in a church is something I've done a lot of, Mary. I hope the roof has been attached nice and tight. I've written some notes but can't see myself standing up in the pulpit. I'll just stand at the front and speak from there.'

'You'll be fine, Les. Just think of it as one of those meetings you have with truck drivers. You'll have to be careful with your language, but I'll be there to give you support.'

Attending the Sunday service was quite an experience for Les and Mary as the congregation gave full voice to the hymn singing. The nearly one hundred parishioners were very attentive as Les introduced himself and Mary and gave an outline of his situation. Following the formal address there was an opportunity to attend morning tea in the church hall. While very welcoming, no new leads were forthcoming. Equally their research of the church records proved of no value.

Les was naturally despondent as they left the church. 'I fear that I've brought you here for no result, Mary. The people want to assist but I'm afraid any local knowledge about my parents is gone.'

'Let's persevere, Les. We still might uncover something.'

*

The meeting arranged with Mrs Robins at the Barradale Nursing Home quickly raised some questions for Mary. Whether real or manufactured, there seemed to be endless confusion. Were the residents being truthful? Mary listened as Les, at his affable best, spoke to individuals and groups of residents. Her own attempts to gather information being inconclusive.

Mary quickly became concerned as she chatted to one elderly gentleman. 'You've lived here at this home for two years, is that right?'

'Oh yes, two years. I came the same year as Margaret. We came together on the bus.'

'Margaret Robins?' Mary asked.

'Perhaps we came on the train?' the gentleman replied.

Pressing a little harder, Mary said, 'Are you sure you arrived the same year as Margaret. I understood she came a few years before you.'

'Well, I'm happy here. We play gin rummy some days.'

Conversations tapered off with questions being met with broad smiles. Mary noted that the staff decided to have a break during their visit. Call it a woman's intuition but she became quite certain that some members of the elderly community were aware of Les's background.

Why would they not divulge what they knew? Why would men and women in the broad group hide behind the excuse of being old and forgetful, rather than being open and honest?

On their arrival it had been explained that the Nursing Home had belonged to one of the pioneers of the area. At his passing, the estate was left to a trust to manage for the benefit of the elderly. Set on several acres and featuring spacious gardens, securing accommodation in the home, although requiring a large entry fee, was keenly sought. So, it was not unusual for community members to sell their family homes to meet the entry cost.

Mary, while having no understanding of Margaret Robins' financial situation, decided to gently probe Les. Clearly Mrs Robins had led a frugal life given her support for many homeless children, and without an additional generous benefactor she wouldn't have been able to raise the entry fee.

While enjoying a short break in the waiting area, Mary informed Les that as the nursing home brochure set out the entry fee and ongoing charges, Mrs Robins was fortunate to be able to gain a position. 'It's quite an expensive outlay,' Mary pointed out. 'The administrator advises that the final payment can be made following the sale of a family home.'

'I noted that, Mary. There must have been some support to help the old lady in her retirement. I believe Mrs Robins had an arrangement with the local council. To support her welfare activity, she paid a peppercorn rent to live in a council owned house. It never was a lavish lifestyle.'

When re-joining the residents in the day room, a staff member passed Mary a note and said, 'It was here on the sideboard when I returned from my break. I suspect the author wants to remain anonymous.'

Written in simple terms the letter confirmed the early information given to Les by Mrs Robins that Robert O'Rourke was his father and on his passing his mother moved to Queensland to remarry. There were no other children.

The note also advised that his mother, before leaving, had sold the family home and put the money into trust to be kept for Les until he was twenty-one. Clearly, that had not occurred. It was the note-writer's contention, that Mrs Robins, the named executor, had used the money to buy her place in the nursing home.

Handing the letter to Les was a challenge for Mary. The information was going to be difficult to verify and if indeed correct, the money would be impossible to recover. Any move in that direction could result in Mrs Robins being evicted: certainly not an outcome that Les would pursue. Mary suggested to Les that they sit in the garden for a few minutes to allow him to process the information.

After a short spell outdoors, Mary said, 'I'm not sure what to say. It's a bit like the good news and the bad news.'

'It really is, Mary, but at least Mum's money was put to good use. I'm not angry with Margaret as she was a good mother to me. The money's not critical to me. I'm a single man with no ties.'

'At least you can bring this chapter to a close. It's time to get on with the rest of your life.'

*

The following day as they waited for Mary's train to arrive, Les was once again warm in his appreciation for her assistance. 'Well, all I can do is thank you for coming all the way to Barradale. We did our best but have drawn a blank. I'll just have to accept the circumstances.'

'It looks that way and I understand how disappointed you must feel. I agree that we did our best and life does go on. Perhaps we should informally adopt each other as family. You can be the brother I never had.'

'Sister Mary. Yes, it's got a nice ring to it. Whenever I'm in the Western District, I'll be certain to call into Roscommon Downs.'

'Better still, why don't you come for a few weeks when you're taking some leave. We have a spare room. Union blokes have holidays, don't they? A good time would be during the shearing. There's plenty of activity and it'll give you an opportunity to meet all the people in my life.'

'I'll certainly do that, Mary. You never know I might enjoy life in Castle Hill so much I could drop anchor for a bit longer than a few weeks.'

*

On the train back to Melbourne, Mary made a quiet resolution that if the opportunity presented to connect Will to his father, then she would take it no matter the consequences. She had done her best to raise Will, albeit with her son having excellent role models in Jim and Dan. However, she was sure that from time to time, he thought about his father.

In the meantime, there was the matter of Glyn Harris. Mary had been planning to return to Melbourne occasionally to partner him in the exhibition dance team. She missed the excitement and challenges of competitive dancing, and felt there must be a good reason for his absence.

Of greater concern was Dan and Monica's fading health with both now needing constant care and attention. Bunty's support was always forthcoming but restricted by the responsibilities of her own family. It was clear there was a need for Mary to retain some permanent live-in nursing care. There was also the matter of relieving Jim's workload.

Being a proud man, he was stubborn, and didn't want to agree that his work was restricted by a permanent leg injury. Mary knew that her challenge was to find him an assistant whom he liked and could work with. While confident that the person to fill the role of carer for Dan and Monica could be sourced from Castle Hill, the recruitment of Jim's assistant would be somewhat more difficult.

Under no circumstances would the position be advertised. Word of mouth regarding the vacancy would occur and hopefully yield a positive outcome. The best scenario would be to convince Jim of the need to recruit an offsider such as one of his mates to fill the role.

Relaxing into her seat with a few hours of travel ahead, Mary welcomed the opportunity to rest as the rhythm of the train and the warmth of the sun filtering through the window gently lulled her to sleep.

Chapter 21

A Setback

Sad news waited at the Rex Hotel. A visibly upset Molly Smith advised Mary that Dan Flanagan had passed away.

'I'm sorry to be the bearer of bad news, Mary,' she said. 'Your friend Jim called and said he had just missed contacting you in Barradale. He knew you were coming here before returning home.'

Mary couldn't prevent an immediate rush of emotion with tears welling as she struggled to maintain her composure. Her words caught in her throat. 'I'm shocked Molly. I knew he was ill and getting on in years. Did Jim give any more information?'

'No Mary, not much more. As you would appreciate Jim was also upset. Just said to let you know that Dan passed away in his sleep.'

'Thank you, Molly; I best call Monica and return to Roscommon Downs.'

Mary knew her presence was required at home and any thoughts of following up Glyn Harris would need to wait. Monica would be most upset with the loss of her life partner, so a difficult period lay ahead.

*

Being met at the railway station by Jim was an emotional moment – his appearance and bearing that of a man who had lost a very dear family member. Shedding tears, he commented, 'Dan was a good man, Mary. He was as a father to me. Thankfully, he died peacefully. We knew he was quite ill, but the end came quickly.'

'I'm sorry I was away. He was an important person in your life. I understand the depth of your loss which I share. I loved him as I would love my father.'

'Would you mind if we sit here at the station for a few moments? I'm feeling a little shaky.'

'That's fine, Jim. We can take our time.'

After a few moments of quiet reflection, Mary added, 'It's terribly sad not being able to say goodbye. Dan promised at the Rex Hotel to bring me into the family and lived up to that from the first day I arrived.'

'That was his form, Mary. He was a man of his word. Absolutely rock-solid.'

Mary asked, 'How is Monica? Is she coping? I called from the Rex, but she was upset and unable to talk.'

'She's not at all well. Bunty came to give her some company,' Jim's voice was noticeably weak as he wiped his nose. 'I'm okay now, so we should get on our way.'

As they commenced their journey to the farm, Mary steeled herself to cope with Monica's grief. After they had driven a short way, she asked, 'Have you made any funeral arrangements?'

'I've organised the local clergyman and undertaker. We can hold the funeral service in the Castle Hill Anglican Church where Dan and Monica were married.'

'Thanks Jim. You've done well.'

The remainder of the journey continued with them lost in their thoughts about what lay ahead.

*

On their arrival home, Mary's first minutes were spent in a warm embrace with Monica who was obviously shattered by her loss. Quickly joined by Will, many tears were shed. As she dabbed her eyes with a wet hanky, Monica said, 'I can't believe he's gone, Mary. He was the love of my life.'

'I share your grief, Monica. Dan was such a big presence in all our lives,' Mary replied.

After a few more words, Monica excluded herself seeking the solitude of her room, leaving Mary, Will and Jim sitting at the kitchen table. Feeling the need to break the emotion of the moment, Mary said, 'I suspect there'll be a big crowd at the funeral.'

'No doubt about that, Mary. Dan and Monica have many friends. I've organised the church auxiliary to cater for the wake,' Jim replied.

'We'll need to think about who'll speak at the service. I'm pretty sure Monica won't be up to it. Perhaps we could both say a few words and Will could do the service readings.'

'Yes, I'm happy to do that, Mum. I'll just need to rehearse, so I don't choke up.'

'That sounds like a plan, Mary. I can speak about the early days. You follow with your memories. We mustn't worry if we get a bit emotional. The local community know that we're a close family, so they'll expect a few tears.'

Pleased with the arrangements, Jim moved to the stove to boil the kettle, pausing to say, 'And while it's in my mind, Rhon North wants to catch up with you.'

'Thanks Jim, we best support Monica through her difficult time, and then I'll follow up Rhon.'

*

As Jim had predicted the Castle Hill church was filled to overflowing. To accommodate the large gathering the vicar organised the service to be broadcast into the adjacent community hall. In his eulogy he gave an account of Dan's life and his warm friendship with many members of the Castle Hill community confirming he'd been a generous and willing contributor to many organisations. Completing his comments, he commended Monica for her support of Dan during his final days.

Jim struggled with his prepared remarks. Mary noted that to contain his emotions he was carefully avoiding eye contact with Monica. Referring to his early days at Roscommon Downs and being treated as a member of the Flanagan family confirmed his sense of loss. Many were brought to tears as people felt for Jim and remembered their own experiences. To assist in lightening the mood, Jim had sought some stories about Dan from his football and shearing mates.

'Many of you have told me stories about the fun times you had with Dan. I appreciate that you wrote them down for me to deliver today.'

Each story was greeted with laughter and helped bring a softer vibe to the occasion. One story, which was obviously well known to his mates, recounted the day Dan pulled a ram from the catching pen, and in setting it to shear, he got his feet tangled and fell over with the ram falling on top of him. Jim said that no one in the shed could assist Dan while they fell about laughing, as did all the blokes in the pub that evening, when the story was told and retold.

The theme across everything that was said painted Dan as a good bloke, hardworking and loyal. The recounting of the stories was a helpful lead for Mary. After taking a few deep breaths to steady her voice she commenced.

'Monica has asked me to read a few words on her behalf. She wants to thank you all for attending Dan's funeral and for your love and support at this difficult time.'

Mary had privately read Monica's words out loud many times so she would not break down and lose her way. She was worried if she missed a line or allowed emotion to catch in her throat, she would become flustered and dissolve in tears. She wanted to do her best to relay Monica's words of love for Dan and her appreciation for their many years together.

Holding tightly to her notes Mary continued. 'Thank you for coming to farewell Dan. He was the love of my life. Many of you know we were never apart whether during our childhood, at school, in marriage and buying and developing Roscommon Downs. While we mourn his passing, I know Dan would want us to celebrate his life. He was a good man who loved life. I will miss him every day.'

A tearful Monica rewarded Mary with a hug.

In her own words, Mary outlined her journey to Castle Hill at Dan and Monica's invitation. She expressed her eternal gratitude at being brought into the Flanagan family and spoke of the life values Dan had instilled in her.

With Jim's agreement, Mary decided to share with the congregation a pledge made by Jim and herself. 'Jim and I have committed to look after Monica. We will be maintaining the farm in accordance with Dan and Monica's high standards. The open-door policy will continue. Monica wants you all to keep coming to the farm. Your friendship is vital to her.'

Emerging from the church on a grey Castle Hill day, Mary felt the first drops of a passing shower on her face. How fitting for a sad day, she thought as mourners pressed together in solidarity.

In the Irish tradition, a piper led the congregation on foot as it followed the hearse during its short journey to the Castle Hill cemetery. After a few prayers Dan was laid to rest.

Standing at the graveside was a poignant moment for Mary, as she said goodbye to the man who had become a father to her. With an overwhelming sadness, she threw a handful of dirt followed by a rose onto the coffin.

Dan had advised and supported her from her first day at Roscommon Downs. His strength and love had been unwavering after George left. It would have been easy for the Flanagans to dismiss her rather than become supportive grandparents. Clearly that had never been a consideration. Rather, their love for her had grown stronger.

*

The weeks following Dan Flanagan's passing were challenging. Monica spent many days quietly sitting on the verandah and walking in the garden. Jim and Mary dealt with Dan's loss in their own way – Mary immersing herself in the farm's paperwork while Jim shared an occasional beer with his mates at the Arms Hotel in Castle Hill. A meeting with Paul Steele confirmed, as they had anticipated, that Dan's affairs were in order, with documents registered to ultimately pass the farm into Mary's ownership.

Mary was aware that Monica would require long term support. Her life had revolved around living with Dan at Roscommon Downs and she hadn't been a regular visitor to the Castle Hill senior citizens or service clubs. While Mary was working her way through arrangements for the future, a mid-morning approach from Bunty added some new concerns to her planning.

Mary could see that Bunty was flustered and nervous when joining her at the kitchen table. 'Are you okay, Bunty. You look a bit hot and bothered.'

'My apologies Mary, I didn't know how to tell you but I'm going to miss this year's shearing. I need to travel interstate to a family gathering.'

With a smile Mary replied, 'I best get you a cup of tea so you can tell me all about it.'

'I hope you can get through. The kids have been on my back to go. It's a once in a lifetime opportunity to catch up with family members.'

'You must be excited.'

'I am Mary. I haven't seen many of them for years. It'll be quite a reunion and I hope you don't mind that I've organised an excellent replacement. I've trained her in scone cooking and reckon she's ready to fill in.'

'We'll miss you, Bunty. You've been a fixture here for many years and you must promise to return after the reunion. But you have me intrigued, who is your replacement?'

'Rhonda North; she's been here so much lately that she's mastered the kitchen and is ready to take my place. In fact, I believe she's going to speak to you about moving in permanently. I hope that can be arranged as I'm not getting any younger. Apart from helping me at shearing time, she could be good company for Monica. Let's face it; Rhon has really become part of the family.'

Mary had to agree with Bunty's warmly expressed view of Rhonda. As the years had rolled on, they'd become firm friends particularly after Rhon had terminated her friendship with Chivon Murphy. As she had said at the time, 'I did my best to keep the friendship, but it just became impossible for me to put up with her moaning and groaning. Chivon was never happy and made life difficult. I just had to tell her to go away. The last I heard she had gone to Melbourne to live. I hope she finds something or someone to brighten her life.'

Rhon had taken the role of organising the women members of the Castle Hill horse racing club into luncheon and travel groups. She was still a ball of energy notwithstanding, as she called it, her carefree years of ignoring diet and exercise. If there was fun to be had, Mary could always count on Rhon to either organise or find it, with one of her favourite comments being, 'It shows the value of a regular walk to the fridge, Mary. If I wasn't a drinker, I wouldn't get any exercise.'

Mary enjoyed Rhonda's outgoing nature and sense of fun, as her own personality was much quieter and withdrawn. She was delighted to hear that Rhon was keen to move permanently to the farm. Keeping faith with the procedures adopted by the Flanagans, Mary made certain that Monica was comfortable with Rhon coming to stay.

During a follow up meeting with Will and Jim to discuss the matter, Jim really summed up the general feeling. 'Mary that's great news as Rhon will be a real asset. We also know it's a good opportunity for her. A win all round.'

'I must say I'm pleased. From the first day I met Rhon on the train she has been a trusted friend. I love her zest for life. She has really gingered up the women's groups and won't take any nonsense.'

As there was a pause in the conversation, Jim pulled his chair a little closer to the table and ensured the focus was on him. 'While we are all together, I think it a good time to talk about the future of the farm and my problem in keeping up with the work. Over a beer Bob Murphy said he'd be interested in working here. It'd mean giving up leading the shearing team. He reckons he's shorn enough sheep and it's time for him to leave back busting work.'

Mary was pleased to hear Jim's news, as she was increasingly concerned at the strain the work on the farm was placing on him as he was growing older. He would never complain, but his day-to-day tasks always needed to be done and clearly were becoming harder to complete.

With plans made to add extra horses to the stable, Mary was keen for Jim to enjoy the days out at the races. He deserved a reward for his many years of service to the Flanagans.

Following up his suggestion, Mary asked, 'Do we need to make a formal approach to Bob or just let him know he can commence when available.'

'Just a simple matter of me letting him know, Mary. He'll want to give his team notice that he's leaving. One of his shearing mates will take it over.'

'Well, I feel certain you would agree Will?'

'Sure thing, Mum. With the horses racing more regularly, it'll be great for you and Jim to be able to attend more often.'

Jim looked pleased. 'Yes, Will. Having Bob around will be a relief in a way. And you know me, I'm always up for an extra day out at the races.'

'Right then, that's settled,' Mary said. 'We have two new members of our Roscommon Downs' family in Bob Murphy and Rhonda North. I'll contact Paul Steele to put the necessary work contracts in place so we can welcome them here. I'm certain that Dan would be pleased with the steps we've taken today.'

While happy about Rhon joining the team, Mary was secretly delighted that Bob would also become a full-time employee. During the twenty years since their first meeting in the shearing shed, he had developed into a trusted friend and confidant particularly following George's disappearance.

She looked forward to the annual visit with his shearing team and meetings at other times to test advice she'd been given, or to clarify a rumour circulating in the area. If pressed on the subject, Mary would have had to admit feelings for Bob ran a touch deeper than friendship.

Never having married, he was happy to meet Mary at the farm, in Castle Hill, or at Manny's café, notwithstanding being constantly teased by the staff regarding a possible relationship. There were occasions when she felt he might harbour strong feelings for her. Perhaps it was the fear of rejection that held him back. Now that he would be working at the farm, she was looking forward to day-to-day contact, and what that might bring with it.

Chapter 22

A Chain of Events

Jim and Will were aware of Mary's wish for a no fuss family gathering to celebrate her fiftieth birthday. They were also sure that many community members wanted to wish her well, so it was not a day that was going to pass quietly.

Monica was clear in her view, advising Will, 'We need to enjoy our birthdays. Fifty is an important milestone. Let's kick up our heels. How about an open house at the farm? Ask Rhon to get involved and that'll guarantee a day to remember. Don't worry about me. If I feel tired, I'll just get into bed.'

Mary loved to watch Rhon's energy at play when organising a party. Following the bush dance theme, Rhon set out haybales as seating and arranged a buffet supper with a large area reserved for dancing. She was adamant about the size of the floor, telling Mary, 'We need plenty of room to kick up our heels.'

Mary smiled. 'You've certainly guaranteed that'll happen.'

The outcome of the day which flowed into the evening exceeded Mary's expectations. To her surprise the bush dance theme was quickly forgotten as the Castle Hill brass band performed at its best, blowing the cobwebs and spiders out of the shearing shed. Mary was delighted with Bob's energy on the dancefloor. As they sipped a cool drink during one of the breaks, she teased, 'Are you taking some pep pills?'

'No need for pep pills Mary, I'm just enjoying dancing with the prettiest girl in the room.'

'Settle down, smooth talker. Just don't burst your boiler. It's taken us a few years to get together and I don't want you to drop off the perch on me.'

'There's no chance of that happening, Mary. I've still got something in the tank. Come on now, let's get back to the dancefloor.'

As the music recommenced, Mary felt a hand on her arm and Rhon pulled her to one side. 'Who's the big good-looking bloke with the red hair? He's definitely not from around this area.'

'Which good-looking bloke?' Mary asked.

'The one over there talking to Jim.'

'Oh, that's Les, Les O'Rourke. Remember I went to Barradale with him.'

'Yes, you told me about him, but you forgot to mention his good looks. Why is he in Castle Hill?'

'He arrived today to stay for a couple of weeks. Do you want me to introduce you?'

'No, that's okay,' Rhon replied with a cheeky grin. 'I'm able to do my own introductions.'

As Bob grabbed Mary's hand and pulled her onto the dancefloor, Mary called to Rhon, 'Well, you better get on with it. The music won't be going all night.'

During the supper break, following a drum roll, it was nearing time to cut the cake. Will took the microphone to propose a toast to his mother. 'Just a short speech because Mum has warned me to keep it simple. We thank you all for coming to celebrate her birthday. I must apologise for being unable to tell any jokes as she's also threatened to keep me grounded with no TV for a month if I fail to comply. So, there's not much left to say except, happy birthday Mary.'

Mary leaned in toward the microphone. 'Very funny, Will. I think the last time that you were grounded with no TV for a month was when you were in nappies. And believe me that wasn't a pretty sight I can tell you.'

'Here you two … stop blueing and pass me that microphone,' Jim said as he snatched it from Will's hand in a bid to be the next to speak. His stories were the cause of much laughter as he recounted Mary's farming activities, highlighting swimming the dam with the horses and not forgetting to embellish the driving lessons in the truck. Wheel spins and burnouts in the paddocks became pretty much the norm, Jim laughed. 'And then there was the little matter of Mary nearly taking out Monica along with the verandah on one memorable occasion.'

Mary's face was bright red as she tried to defend herself. 'My goodness Jim, you're worse than Will with those tall tales you tell. Please don't take a scrap of notice about what either one of them say,' she laughed.

'Come on Mum, hurry up and cut the cake. We are all starving here!'

Mary placed the knife on the top of cake and sliced it through without touching the bottom. She then took a deep breath and blew out the candles before making a wish.

As fifty helium balloons were released, a raucous singalong of 'Happy Birthday' followed by three cheers and 'For She's a Jolly Good Fellow' made Mary feel like she needed to sit down and rest after all the fanfare.

Councillors and community members weren't allowing the birthday girl to escape quite so easily however, as they came forward to wish her well with a special presentation made in recognition of her continuing charity work. There was, of course, the regular plea to have her contest an elected position on the Castle Hill council.

As the dancing restarted, Mary watched Rhon lead Les onto the dancefloor. Turning to Bob she said, 'I hope Les doesn't have any plans to return to Barradale in too much of a hurry.'

Bob laughed. 'I can see what you were up to, Mary. Old Les doesn't stand a chance.'

As Mary took a seat to enjoy a drink with Bob, she was delighted that Les and Rhon had found each other. Although it was early days, she hoped they would become a couple and a permanent part of her Roscommon Downs family.

*

With the party well behind her, Mary was starting to enjoy race days with Rhon and her friends. It was a thrill to watch her racing silks of primrose and blue adopted from the colours of County Roscommon in Ireland being carried by her horses. With hard work leading to Eric Conroy providing the final polish, their small stable was enjoying some success. Jim's constant attention helped in the rehabilitation of many horses.

Will was pulling his weight with farm work and had become quite an authority regarding pre-owned racehorses with his endless research of catalogues throwing up lists of those worth pursuing. Friday evening dinner was often attended by horse trainer Eric Conroy, with post-mortems held about previous races flowing over to a few drinks, the following day's race meetings and an extensive study of the form guides. As Jim put it, 'There's a winner in every race. We just have to find it.'

An occasional visitor was jockey Midge Arthur, who Mary observed was able to survive on fresh air and a cigarette. Jim and Eric successfully placed the horses in regional meetings which brought prize money and the qualification for a Melbourne race. 'Not sure if it's up to the standard required Mary. But our horse is in the field so we should travel down and take up this opportunity,' Jim suggested.

'Why not, Jim. It will be a nice break away for a couple of days at the very least. I'm sure Bob will be happy to mind the farm.'

Throughout the following days, Mary was surprised and pleased at the level of excitement in Castle Hill as many shops and homes were decorated with primrose and blue ribbons.

Manny's Bakery was no exception being done up to the nines in support of their favourite customers.

During a brief coffee stop, Mary and Jim caught up with their old mates outside.

'The two of yas will be needing to wear your Sund'y best.' Clarry advised. 'You never know who you might be rubbing shoulders with down there in the big smoke.'

'The Sunday best is the least of my worries, Clarry. Mary and I are just keeping our fingers crossed that the horse has a successful run. It seems there'll be plenty of Castle Hill money riding on its back. It promises to be a big day no matter what happens.'

*

Following their normal pattern, Jim arranged to leave early Saturday morning and bring the horse straight to the racecourse common user stables. Mary and Will organised to travel to Melbourne on Friday to allow plenty of time to settle into their hotel and prepare for the Saturday race meeting.

As they waited at the railway station for the midday train, Mary was concerned at the size of the large group of well-wishers and their level of expectation for the following day's race. She turned to Will and said, 'It's just a regional championship. How will the excitement be if it was the Melbourne Cup?'

'That's something to look forward to, Mum.'

Mary was happy that the horse's success had given the community a lift and hoped that not too much of the weekly budget would be wagered on the race.

Due to her excitement, she had difficulty concentrating on her book during the train journey, and recalled Eric Conroy's positive words when loading the horse into the trailer –

'He's a big chance Mary, with solid form and a good preparation. I'm looking forward to the race.'

*

Their arrival in Melbourne brought them into the normal Friday afternoon pressure of the main railway station. But as Mary and Will wheeled the cases out onto busy Spencer Street there came an unexpected moment of shock for Mary.

While waiting to cross the road to catch a tram to the Rex Hotel, she was certain that she saw George Simpson. He was boarding a tram that left before she could point him out. Mary grabbed onto Will's arm and said, 'Did you see him?'

Will looked bewildered. 'See who?' he asked.

'George Simpson. I could swear that I just saw, George Simpson. Well … I think it was George. He was getting on a tram.'

'You saw George Simpson? Are you sure it was George? Did you get a good look at him?' Will asked, startled by the turn of events.

'I'm pretty sure! Although it's been many years since I last saw him, and it happened very quickly. I must say he looked a bit stooped and greyer.'

When the traffic lights turned green and they crossed the road to the tram stop, Will said, 'If it was George, why would he be in Melbourne? Perhaps he's given away the shearing.'

'I've no idea. It's a matter of how to find him. That is if we want to find him.

'Well, I'd like to look him in the eye and ask why he shot through.'

'The problem is Will, we're not family. Perhaps we should wait until this evening when we can discuss the situation with Jim. But we need to accept that people can lose themselves in a big city.'

As Mary expected, Jim was lukewarm on the possibility of finding George. Especially if he had decided to adopt a low profile. A search confirmed that there were many George Simpsons in the phone book. Mary accepted he may be using another name, or perhaps just visiting the city. The possibility of waiting at the tram stop on the following Monday in the hope that George would travel at the same time, was considered. But Jim was quite certain it would be a waste of time.

'Let's face it Mary, George is gone. He's been gone for a very long time. I understand it might be difficult, but didn't you decide all those years ago that it was time to move on. So, why bother trying to find him now?'

However, retaining a deep-seated hope of meeting George, Mary and Will decided that they would arrive early the following Monday and watch the tram stop, before catching the train back to Castle Hill. 'There's just a chance he might arrive perhaps on his way to or from work, or for whatever other reason. It could be an hour well spent.' Mary said. 'There's a few things I want to say to him.'

'Me too.' Will agreed. 'It was a rotten thing he did running out on us. I'd enjoy a few words in his ear. It'd be good for him to see how we've kicked on without him.'

Experiencing a stab of anger, Mary replied, 'Yes, you're right, Will. To see how great our life together has been and understand what he's missed out on will be a sad and sorry sight for him.'

*

George Simpson had been following Mary's racing fortunes. He was happy for her success but had no interest in gambling. Monday newspapers would provide all the information he needed.

After his dash from Castle Hill, he had spent much of his working life shearing in small sheds and supplemented his income picking up various other odd jobs.

Using the name, Dave Roberts, hotels and a caravan provided his accommodation. It didn't trouble George that he had a limited number of friends. Happy to make his way alone, there was no need to get close to people. As best he could he followed Will's early life and current circumstances, but he was reluctant to engage and had no desire to return to Castle Hill.

At some stage confidential arrangements would be needed to sell his late parents' house. The opportunity to take that step had not eventuated. Although many years on, George hoped the neighbours were continuing to cut the grass around the home.

He was keen to see Mary and Will. During all his years away he'd suffered pangs of regret for what might have been. Nights alone in his caravan and hotel rooms reminded him of his cowardice at the time. Aware of the horse's qualification to enter a city race, George decided to attend the meeting believing that given a big crowd at the course, it would be possible for him to see Mary and Will without them being aware.

When Mary, Will and Jim joined trainer Eric Conroy in the saddling enclosure many misgivings flowed through him. Mary was still the woman he felt closest to, but he was unable to reach out to her. Will had grown into a fine-looking young man. He knew that Jim was a decent bloke who had treated him well at Roscommon Downs. The casual and friendly way in which they interacted again reminded him of what might have been.

Moving to a vantage point, George watched as the horse came with a final rush to win the race. As the three hugged and exchanged high fives, he was disappointed at not being able join in the celebrations. It was a bittersweet moment as he observed the presentation in the mounting yard with Will speaking on behalf of his mother. Even from a distance he could see that Mary was bursting with pride.

Given that he'd achieved what he had set out to do, it was time to travel back to his country base. Despite his itinerant life, George had established a reliability to fulfil contracts. If he'd been aware of the unwelcome surprise that awaited him, he might have decided to disappear. George was about to face the consequences of earlier mistakes.

*

As Mary, Jim and Will stood near the winner's stall happily applauding, Mary could not have been more pleased saying to

Jim, 'This is amazing. Our first city winner. Who would have thought this possible?'

'Well, we did a lot of work to get him here, so we need to enjoy the moment. What do you reckon, Will?

'I can't believe it Jim. How good was that? I hope no one noticed me jumping up and down. Old 'Strong and Bold' did us proud. I was thrilled to see our primrose and blue colours flying down the outside.'

'I must admit Will, that I doubted he would bridge the gap and catch the leader. But he was determined to win. We all should enjoy the result. I expect there'll be some excited people back in Castle Hill, and a few beers being drunk in the pubs.'

Mary was particularly pleased for Jim as she watched him clipping on the lead rope. He was working as the horse's strapper after many dedicated hours bringing the horse to racing fitness. She had never seen him so pleased.

'The good news is that given the quality of the race, the racing club has made a trophy available in addition to the prize money. I'll get someone to take the horse to the stables. We need to stay in the mounting yard for the presentation.' Jim said.

If being involved in horse racing in Melbourne was foreign country for Mary, it was nothing compared to the nervousness she felt as they waited for the trophy presentation. 'You speak on our behalf Will. Jim and I will be the silent partners.'

Standing with Jim watching Will make a short acceptance speech that was generous in its praise for Jim and Eric Conroy, Mary was thrilled to see his confident yet quite humble way of presenting himself in front of a large gathering of club members and media. It filled her with immense satisfaction. She could feel Jim's pride in the moment and couldn't help being reminded of her role as a single parent. Jim and the Flanagans had been great stalwarts for her. Their collective hard work and guidance had helped Will mature into a fine young man.

It was times like these that she felt a flash of anger and disappointment regarding George abandoning them. But the negative feelings quickly passed as she enjoyed her first city winner with Jim and Will. Mary suspected that if George was aware of her good fortune, he would be envious wherever and whatever he was doing.

The success of the day confirmed that dinner and a few more drinks would be organised into the evening. It was an easy decision to have a rest day on Sunday. Mary and Will were still keen to pursue a possible sighting of George on Monday morning. As they left the racecourse a joint decision was taken to enjoy the moment. Mary was happy to take the opportunity, suggesting to Will and Jim, 'We can keep the rooms at the Rex. Let's stay and kick up our heels. A few days in the city won't hurt. I could use a bit of retail therapy. We can stay until Wednesday.'

'I agree, Mary. Rhon and Bob have the work covered at home. 'Strong and Bold' will be comfortable with a couple of nights in the stables before I float him home,' Jim replied.

On their return to the Rex hotel, they found the staff enjoying a late afternoon party inside the foyer decorated in blue and yellow streamers and balloons. Warmly welcoming Mary, Jim and Will, Molly explained, 'We all had a small win. It was a great thrill listening to the race. Some of the staff had their first bet. They'll be looking out for its next race.'

'Goodness Molly, I hope we haven't turned them into gamblers. You must tell them that the horse might not win again. I'd be really worried if they started to lose their wages.'

'Don't worry, Mary. It was just a bit of fun. I'm sure it won't get out of hand.'

*

It was a rude awakening, after the tiring drive back to his caravan from Melbourne, when in the middle of Sunday night someone came knocking on the door and a loud voice demanded, 'Open up … police here.'

Unsure if it was a shearing mate having some fun, he shouted in reply, 'George doesn't rise before 6am.'

He was shocked to hear the knocking become louder with the voice now declaring, 'Open the door or we'll break it down.'

Handcuffed and placed under arrest, he spent the remainder of the night in a cold prison cell where he had time to think about the publicity of his misdemeanours and how troubled he would feel to have his secret life exposed.

During his interview at the station, it became clear that the police had been investigating his activities for many months. He couldn't believe how they'd gathered witnesses who conspired against him to confirm the places and dates of his involvement.

By mid-morning, without further sleep, George was standing before a magistrate. He felt like he was experiencing a bad dream as the police prosecutor outlined the reasons for his arrest. After presenting the evidence he summed up the matter in few words. 'Your honour, the defendant is a flight risk, I ask you to disallow bail. He's been living and working under a false name and he has no fixed address. He will likely forfeit bail money and not reappear.'

Of equal concern was the seriousness of the crimes George was facing which could result in him serving a lengthy gaol sentence. He'd been up to his old tricks, identifying a few sheep to be stolen. However, George was shocked to hear that the two co-accused had beaten a farmer. Angry at being robbed, the farmer had been keeping watch over his sheep and caught the thieves in the act.

With bail refused, George was lodged in the cells at the back of the court. The legal aid solicitor was clear in setting out the problems he faced. 'Unless the court can be certain that you'll return to face the charges, you won't receive bail and will stay in gaol until the matter is finalized. These are serious charges. Are you certain there's no one you can approach for support or who'll vouch for you?'

'Not at this stage. I don't have a lot of family or friends,' George replied.

Transferring from the police station to the remand centre brought George's situation home to him. He was ushered with a line of men, some of whom had spent time with him in the cells, into a cubicle in the prison truck. Being offloaded at the remand centre to be processed, completely unnerved him. Handcuffed and taken into the building through the underground carpark, George was certain that a couple of his fellow prisoners were drug affected.

His condition did not improve when locked in a small cell with a short, strongly built stranger, a little older than himself, who seemed to be angry with the world. George's solicitor had warned him not to ask any fellow prisoners why they were being held. 'Sometimes it sends them off on an angry rant, and they become violent towards the person nearest to them.'

Given they were destined to spend the night together, George tried to make conversation. His question, 'Is this your first time here, mate?' was met with silence and an angry glare.

There was no point in asking anyone what the future held for him. The prison officer's sole concern was to process him into the gaol system. His journey to his cell had taken him past the floor which held the inmates charged with serious crimes such as murder and armed robbery. George reckoned he'd been around and seen tough men. The blast of loud heavy metal music, and the sullen stares, ensured he kept up with the group climbing the stairs to his holding area.

Hearing the cell door being locked, hit him hard. Careful to show no emotion or weakness, a restless night followed. The brooding man sharing the cell had no interest in George, preferring to lay on his bunk muttering under his breath. Surrounded by violent men, many of whom had been in gaol numerous times, convinced George that he had to take steps to obtain bail.

His fear of fellow inmates did not diminish when released into the general group for a shower and breakfast. He was careful to avoid eye contact, and only speak when spoken to.

Cautious and determined not to interact, he rejected the option of walking in the exercise yard and retreated to the cell.

He understood the result of a conviction would be a period of imprisonment. If deemed suitable, relocation to a minimum-security prison would shield him from hardcore inmates. However, that was not currently helping him. There was every likelihood the time delay within the courts could mean remaining on remand for many months. Being a newcomer exposed him to standover tactics by criminals to comply with the gaol in-house rules.

His fears ultimately overrode the retention of his secrecy and convinced him to seek Mary's assistance. Taking the opportunity to pass a note during a visit by the public solicitor, he said, 'Mary O'Rourke may assist me. We were friends in Castle Hill. I hope she'll vouch for me.'

It didn't help George having no fixed address. Bail money and a surety were also needed. Having worked under an assumed name for many years and spending freely meant the money earned had left little in reserve. His solicitor would have a hard time convincing a magistrate that Castle Hill could be considered as his permanent place of address when he hadn't lived or worked in the area for more than twenty years.

Notwithstanding the negatives he was facing, he was desperate to obtain release. His application included a pledge that he would return to live at Castle Hill, reporting his presence daily to police until the completion of his court hearing. His two older sisters were unable to assist, as he had lost complete contact with them. He suspected they had passed away.

Being desperate, he hoped Mary would cooperate. And given her standing in the Castle Hill community, surely this would work in his favour. In the interim, he would just have to accept his loss of freedom. Avoiding other inmates as best he could, and carefully adjusting to the routine of the remand centre would be the best way to ensure his safety.

*

After a relaxing weekend and a fruitless wait at the tram stop, Mary and Will were happy to spend Monday shopping. Jim spent the day catching up with some mates. With 'Strong and Bold' in the stables, their thoughts turned to Tuesday with Mary leaning to a day at the movies. As they enjoyed breakfast, she raised the possibility with Will. 'I haven't been to a picture show for years. I'm going to look to see what's on.'

'A picture show, Mum. You've got to be kidding me. No one calls a movie the pictures anymore. Next thing you'll be telling me you're hoping to see a Gregory Peck movie.'

'Okay Will. You choose and it'll be my shout. How's that sound?'

By Tuesday evening as they sat down to dinner, Jim couldn't help stirring Will up about how much he enjoyed the movie. 'Did your mum buy you a packet of 'Jaffas' at intermission?'

'Maltesers, were the go, Jim. But seriously, I'm not even sure what a Jaffa is.'

Their laughter was interrupted by Molly Smith. 'Good evening, Mary. I've had a call from Rhonda North. She's keen to speak to you about a message received at the farm from the public solicitor.'

'Thank you, Molly. I can't imagine what it's about. I'll call straight away from my room.'

As Mary listened closely to the message that she asked Rhonda to read over the phone, Mary struggled to maintain her composure.

Returning to the table, she explained its contents to Will and Jim. 'In essence, it's from a solicitor acting for George. He's in the remand centre charged with a serious crime. I don't know what he's done but it's a plea for help. To assist his application for bail he must have somewhere permanent to stay. The solicitor says that a substantial surety is required that is forfeited if he doesn't appear on his trial date. There is also a requirement to report regularly to police.'

Their collective stunned silence was broken by an angry outburst from Jim. 'Can you believe it, Mary? The bloke leaves you in the lurch. Now he wants to use you, and probably the farm address, to get out on bail. To hell with him, I reckon. Let him stay on remand and take what's coming to him. If I see him at the farm, I won't be responsible for what happens. It won't be pretty.'

'I understand how you feel, Jim. It's hard to feel sorry for George. He's a stranger to us. I've no idea what he's been charged with and have no understanding if I am compelled to reply. Perhaps I should ask Rhon to forward me a copy and we can go from there.'

'I agree with that, Mum. We should talk with Paul Steele. If he has time available he could travel to Melbourne tomorrow, and come with us to meet the public solicitor as soon as possible.'

Mary was pleased to hear the considered and mature approach being taken by Will. It could have easily turned into a difficult and emotional issue. She appreciated Jim's view which was built on love and affection for her. There was little chance that George could ever rehabilitate himself in Jim's eyes. If nothing else came of the matter, Will would have the opportunity to meet his father. It was important not to stand in the way of that occurring.

Chapter 23

A Reckoning

'I bet these walls have heard a few tall tales, Paul,' Will said, while sitting with Mary and Paul Steele in the waiting room of the central courts.

'There's no doubt about that, Will. I reckon I've heard my share. I spent ten years representing people. That was enough. You start to hear the same excuses.'

'What happened to convince you to leave?'

'I'd had enough trying to sort fact from fiction. It was time to move on. Defendants can get confused and forgetful. The challenge in representing them is to be as clear as you can about their circumstances. Believe me some people can tell you a good story. It's quite a shock when you find that what they are prepared to swear on a bible is untrue. I'd done my best, so decided to open a legal practice in Castle Hill. It's a much kinder life.'

Turning to Mary, Paul continued. 'I want to confirm your instructions regarding George. No support for bail, and not welcome at Roscommon Downs.'

'That's correct, Paul. Under no circumstances will my position change,' Mary replied firmly.

Paul Steele had explained to Mary and Will their lack of obligation. However, they decided to be courteous and meet the public solicitor.

The waiting area was a sad and forbidding space that smelt of errant cigarette smoke. Mary wondered how much grief and disruption the people sitting with them were experiencing. She suspected that those who sat clutching court papers and nervously chatting, were facing charges for the first time. Accompanied by family members, they were hoping for a positive outcome.

Others were clearly experienced with the legal system and sat in small groups supporting each other, well understanding the possibility of penalties and gaol time.

Despite being aware of the crimes he was charged with, given their earlier relationship, Mary felt some sympathy for George. However, he'd made a serious mistake, and would face the consequences. She listened carefully as Paul discussed the letter and outlined her position to the public solicitor, leaving no doubt that no support for George would be forthcoming.

During the journey home, Will suggested that he would monitor the daily law lists so they would know when George's matter came before the courts.

'If you don't mind Mum, I'll sit in the back of the courtroom. He won't know me. I can hear the sentence he receives.'

'Just as you wish, Will. I certainly won't be with you.'

While he could completely understand Mary's lack of support for George, Will's feelings were more that of dismay and disappointment. How could it be that the first time he had the opportunity to see his father it would be in a courtroom? What might they say to each other if the opportunity arose? Would their first meeting be in gaol? Would his mother temper her anger such as to allow George to re-enter their lives?

As the train approached Castle Hill, Will decided that he would do no more than follow George's court appearances and allow any other related matters to take their course.

*

George was disappointed but not surprised that Mary had refused to assist him. His solicitor outlined the various pleas that were available and the usual sentence for each of them. His advice to George was, 'Sometimes it's better to plead guilty to a charge which could result in an early hearing and a lesser penalty. My experience is that you will probably receive a sentence of at least six months gaol in a low security facility. There might also be an order to compensate the farmer for his loss.'

The hearing of his charges came soon enough, with more prison van travel and waiting in cells before being ushered into court. George felt a rush of sadness when required to stand with his hands behind his back waiting for a prison officer to lock his wrists together, feeling it unnecessary for him to be treated in this way.

After all, he had not performed a violent act and wasn't present when it occurred. But he was paying the price for the farmer's fractured skull and the theft of sheep. George was hoping that the police would not link him with similar earlier crimes which had occurred in other States; he hoped that many had gone unreported.

It was time to wipe the slate clean by pleading guilty and facing the consequences. He would serve his sentence, sell the family home and make a fresh start well away from Castle Hill.

George was unsure how to react when he saw Will sitting in the back row of the courtroom and wondered if he should acknowledge his presence. He was surprised how much of himself he could see in Will who had avoided eye contact when he'd entered the court and it was now impossible given their seating positions. His feelings for Mary had been rekindled at the races as had pride in Will's bearing. But for all of that, George realised he was no more than a stranger to him.

Questions began to flow and created some optimism that he was going to receive a community work order. While it seemed inevitable, he continued to hold the hope of avoiding a gaol sentence. Perhaps Mary had intervened on his behalf and Will was present in his support.

Those thoughts were quickly swept away as the police prosecutor explained the injuries suffered during the theft. 'Your Honour, the assault was violent resulting in the farmer's skull being fractured which led to an extended period in hospital. He suffered substantial financial loss associated with losing many sheep and the need to employ replacement labour. Although the defendant was not involved in the actual assault, he was a party to the crime and received a financial benefit.'

The prosecutor also highlighted the regularity of sheep stealing in the region. He encouraged the magistrate to take the opportunity to send a message to other would-be thieves.

'These are serious crimes. It needs to be understood that courts will punish offenders accordingly.'

His plea for leniency was not assisted by the farm having been the target for two robberies. After the first robbery, the farmer had been patrolling his paddocks trying to protect his sheep when he was set upon. Following the presentation of the evidence and feeling the attitude within the courtroom, George feared the worst. Gripping the edge of the seat, he fixed his gaze on his legal counsel. After listening to the arguments raised on his behalf, George steeled himself for the outcome.

The magistrate didn't waste time in delivering his findings and sentence. Asking George to stand, he said, 'The court views assault charges very seriously. I accept the defendant was an accessory. However, he was integral to the theft by identifying the best location. A hardworking farmer was bashed and seriously injured. I agree courts need to act strongly to support police in these matters. Future offenders can expect harsh punishment. The court will order compensation for the farmer's financial loss.'

As he listened to the magistrate, George could feel himself wilting as though each word increased a load on his back.

Asked if he had anything to say in his defence, George replied, 'I apologise for what occurred. It was never my intention for anyone to be physically harmed. I've no excuse. I've never been before a court or in gaol. It was a stupid thing to do. It won't happen again.'

The magistrate, after considering the time that George had spent in gaol on remand, determined that he would serve a further twelve months. While being led from the court, George noted that Will had left, and indeed he was on his own.

*

When Will travelled to Melbourne for George's court appearance, there was no chance that Mary would accompany him. The disappointment of being abandoned remained. She was mindful that Will wanted to see his father; however, he promised her that he would do no more than sit in the court and hear the outcome.

Leading up to the hearing date, Will wrestled with a range of emotions, which he struggled to throw off when entering the court. Taking a seat, he challenged himself to sit through the proceedings despite an overwhelming feeling of disappointment that his first association with his father was to be conducted in such circumstances.

Aware of George's history of never taking responsibility, Will reflected that any cash George received had probably been frittered away. His appearance confirmed a tough life had been led. Compared to an earlier photograph of George, his hair was now grey, and his face lined from too many days in the sun. Slightly stooped and walking on permanently tired legs, the man standing before the court had obviously travelled a hard road. The many years of shearing, fencing and an itinerant lifestyle had taken their toll.

Will felt little emotion for the man. Aware that George was trying to make eye contact, he was not surprised to see him unsteady on his feet when the sentence was delivered. He was unsure of what the future held for George regarding where he would serve his gaol time. Would he seek a meeting with him? That was a matter for the future.

*

Will's role at the farm was evolving as Jim sought to lead a more restful life. He enjoyed working and learning from Jim who was always supportive and never critical. Clearly, Rhon and his mother were also looking to the future. He had taken to referring to Rhon as his favourite aunt and loved her vim and vitality. He was pleased and a little bemused that Bob was developing into Mary's regular partner, accompanying her to local and interstate social events.

Bob was no stranger to Will as his annual shearing visits had been part of Will's formative years. Bob's friendly knockabout style would often have them sitting together during work breaks. He was happy to answer Will's questions. So much so that Bob would often be referred to by Jim as a human encyclopedia.

While there was limited acknowledgement of any relationship between Bob and Mary, Will was happy to see his mother enjoying her life. He was determined that the situation with George would not act to harm her in anyway. To reinforce that, Will knew it would be necessary for him to meet George at some stage. But always keeping in mind that he was not part of their lives and certainly not welcome at Roscommon Downs.

There was also the matter of Will's pending wedding to Sarah Quinn which was going to require some careful negotiation. He had successfully obtained her father's agreement but was aware that Kathleen had voiced her concern that Sarah deserved better than a future as a farmer's wife.

Being determined to gain Kathleen's blessing and win her over, Will arranged to meet Sarah at a café in her hometown of Killarney which was some considerable distance away.

As they enjoyed a coffee together, he asked Sarah why her mother was opposed to the marriage.

'I suspect it's because of her hard life on the farm. She believes I should move to Melbourne and seek a career.'

'But we've both been working towards our careers as vets. You have been offered the opportunity to work at the Castle Hill racecourse. It's been our long term plan. I'm a bit confused.'

'Might be best to have some patience. Mum's seen other family marriages breakdown, so she's probably got that in her mind. And then there was my brother Sean's wedding that ended in a punch up at the reception.'

'Gosh that must have been exciting.'

'I'm not sure exciting was the word I'd use. It certainly brought the evening to a close.'

'So, when I come to lunch on Sunday, your advice is to step carefully.'

'Yes, like in a minefield Will.'

*

It was a nervous Will O'Rourke who met Sarah at the Quinn farmgate.

'I'm pleased to see you had a shave and ironed your shirt,' Sarah teased.

'And I had an early night. I'm ready to be on my best behaviour.'

'Mum's been a bit quiet this morning.'

'Is that a good sign?'

As Sarah took Will's hand to lead him into the house, 'I think so.' she replied. She usually chops the head off one of the chooks if she gets really angry.'

As he accepted a glass of ale from Patrick and took his place at the table, Kathleen appeared with a roast chicken fresh from the oven which caused Will to choke on his beer in alarm. Sarah and Patrick laughed out loud.

Kathleen said, 'I bet Sarah told you about me chopping heads off chooks when I get upset.'

'She did, actually.'

'I do nothing of the sort. You shouldn't listen to them. They're just pulling your leg.'

'Thank God for that. I've been worried all night.'

As Will relaxed and enjoyed his meal, he pondered when would be the best time to broach the subject of the wedding. With dessert on the table, he was unable to contain himself any longer. 'I hope Sarah and I have your blessing Kathleen.'

'I'm glad you asked me, Will. I was wondering when you would get around to it. I know you asked Patrick, and Sarah probably told you I was not keen on her having a life on a farm. But I've come around knowing what you both have planned. So yes, you have my blessing.'

The remainder of the afternoon was a happy event marked with tears and hugs. Now the commitment was made, organising a wedding date would need to wait until Sarah returned from overseas.

*

Sarah Quinn was planning her first overseas trip. Funded by her parents, it was a reward for qualifying as a veterinarian. She decided to use her travel opportunity to expand her knowledge in racehorse breeding and treatment. Her commitment to marry Will was strong, as was their intent to establish a vet service attached to the Castle Hill racecourse. The opportunity to visit the horse trainers and stables in England and Ireland was not to be missed. As her father had called it, 'Reward for effort. You've done the hard yards, and your mother and I want to recognise the completion of your studies.'

To financially support herself, Sarah had spent many early mornings working as a track rider at the racing club. She could see a future in determining whether horses were fit to race. Her university mentor who currently filled this role was nearing retirement. She could gain the necessary work experience by accompanying him on race days. Horses had been a constant in her life given her parents ongoing interest in riding clubs, with weekends spent either at local or regional events.

There was not much that Sarah didn't know about horse and pony grooming. Her subsequent track riding added to her broad knowledge of horse conditioning. Many of her school friends had moved on from the lifestyle. However, Sarah was determined not to be side-tracked.

Preparing a travel plan was easy. She worked with Will to scan the farms and stables that allowed visitors. All that remained was to organise accommodation, travel, hire a car and make her way.

Will was keen for Sarah to visit as many stud farms and racing stables as possible. 'It's really important to see how they condition the horses prior to a racing preparation. That will help us in our work here. Remember to take lots of photos and send them back to us. I'm really disappointed that I can't go with you,' he said.

'Well, I'll do my best to keep my blog up to date and promise to text regularly. I'll only be away for five weeks.'

While both families were apprehensive regarding Sarah's proposed travel, they were reasonably confident that all would be well. She was well versed in living alone given her many months spent in Melbourne while attending university. It was however a new experience in working her way through airports and dealing with all the requirements of travel. She struggled with the long hours of international travel, making a silent pledge that she would have company during future trips.

Despite her loneliness, Sarah could not have been more pleased with the outcome of her trip and spent many hours at the end of each day recording her experiences. Being on her own gave her the flexibility to vary her travel arrangements and at the last minute organise a seat on a coach tour or visit a farm alone as part of a pay at the gate group.

She enjoyed joining the queues of tourists and was happy to chat about her travels. Occasionally she attracted unwanted interest from men who in her view ought to have conducted themselves much better. Deciding to adopt a zero-tolerance policy, she would ask in a loud voice, 'Would you say that to your mother?'

Some people had a strong knowledge of horse breeding. Others were regular patrons at race meetings. Many were simply happy to watch the horses being paraded while marvelling at the size and condition of the valuable stallions.

Fulfilling a promise to Mary and Will, Sarah travelled to Roscommon to buy gifts and souvenirs and to send them her photograph taken at the entrance to the town. Her trip now over, she added a few words containing her hope that they might be able to travel there at some time in the future.

Chapter 24

Worthless and Alone

Back in his remand centre cell, George felt worthless and alone. He'd watched as other prisoners received support from family and friends while they were led away. His legal representative, a big man pulling a trolley laden with large folders, gave George some quick advice following his sentencing.

'Your future rests completely with the gaol authorities; they'll decide where you'll serve your sentence. After a short period in medium security, you'll probably transfer to a low security prison possibly in a regional area. I can't assist you past this point. Don't expect parole. Just resign yourself to do your time and start again when released.'

The solicitor's comment provided no comfort for George as he waited to be processed into the gaol system. He'd heard about life in a high security prison from a shearer he'd met on a shearing run. While he felt he could handle most circumstances, he was concerned at the possibility of violent confrontation with other prisoners. Being caught up in a gaol riot was his greatest fear.

George's other concern was encountering his fellow thieves and how they might react. He'd done nothing except plead guilty. They might assume that he'd given evidence against them. His state of mind was not aided by a discussion with his remand cellmate who had also been before a court and received a sentence of three years imprisonment. As this would be his second term in gaol, he paced nervously in the cell while complaining to George, 'I didn't think I'd get three years. I'm certain to be put in medium or high security. I was hoping for fewer years and low security like the first time. I don't have any mates for support. They prey on old blokes like me.'

George didn't have long to wait to learn his fate. Assessed as being a low-risk prisoner, he was advised to make himself ready for transfer to a regional security facility. After gathering his meagre personal items, he joined two other prisoners in a prison van. Leaving the city, the intense sadness he'd felt after receiving his term of imprisonment returned. Through the small prison van window, George could see he was moving through the areas he'd journeyed to on shearing runs.

His life had been a freewheel of no commitments. How shallow it now felt. He cursed himself for leaving Mary in the lurch. It was a cowardly act. His son was a stranger who had attended court to see him ordered to gaol. He listened to his fellow prisoners chatting about their families and hopes for the future. What would be his situation on release?

After two hours of travel the first impressions of the gaol eased his melancholy. Broadly set as a farm, it was a far cry from the austerity of the remand centre. George could see groups of men at work in a large garden that was planted within the quadrangle between what he assumed were accommodation buildings. As he considered the apparent lack of security, one of his fellow prisoners remarked, 'At least we won't have to look at four walls. We'll be able to see and feel the outside world.'

Following a regimented arrival which included a clothing issue, the group had the terms of their detention spelt out by the officer-in-charge. It was a simple set of rules for serving time in a prison without walls. It was made clear that the penalty for attempting to escape was transfer to a harsher prison environment.

The senior prison officer emphasised, 'Just be smart and do your time. If you make a run for it, you'll be caught, and it'll be all downhill.'

Information was provided regarding the opportunities for study, trade courses and community work to assist rehabilitation. George was allocated into a five-person unit which was a welcome contrast to the remand centre. It was a functional room with beds, kitchen, bathroom and a large communal table, in the middle of a building which held similar units. George was comfortable he could live in a dormitory environment, having spent considerable periods of his life in shearers' quarters.

His unit inmates were out working in their daily activities. After receiving an extra briefing from his area supervisor regarding work or study, it was an easy decision to lock in his twelve months. Considering his age and skills, George believed his best path was to work with his hands. There was no value in turning to education. Jobs with prisoner repair crews were also available. A recent bushfire had devastated areas close to the gaol. Building fences and sheds would be a straightforward task.

Satisfied that he knew all the options available, George waited to meet his roommates. A discussion with them would assist him to firm up his work course for the following twelve months. First impressions were favourable with warm handshakes shared. As they sat at the table, George assessed that Brian and Mark were in their thirties and had been employed in white collar jobs. Trevor was a knockabout bloke in his fifties who had clearly spent much of his working life outdoors.

This view was borne out when George was seeking their advice to clarify the activities he was going to pursue. Brian and Mark confirmed they were studying to improve their options for post gaol employment, with Mark indicating that he had only six weeks to serve. He was clear in his resolve to return to his former role in share trading.

'It was guilt by association, George. My partners got involved in some shonky trading. I couldn't prove that I wasn't involved. So, it will be my quest to prove myself innocent of any wrong-doing when I get out.'

'Well good luck with that Mark, I hope you can clear your name. What about you Trevor, what's your area of work here?' George asked.

'Well mate, I'm a long-term truckie who hates being cooped up. I'm part of a prisoner rebuilding group. There's a couple of tradies and a few blokes who worked in building and construction. The recent bushfires were savage on the area. We're assisting farmers get back on their feet. Some poor bastards lost everything. They need help rebuilding houses, fences and yards for whatever stock they've left. We head out each morning with a supervisor. The blokes in the gang are happy to do a day's work. We reckon we're making a real difference.'

'It sounds like my sort of thing. I've a farming background. I think I'll nominate into that area. I've twelve months ahead of me. I stuffed up so I might as well try to do some good for someone.'

Trevor smiled. 'The good news for you George, is that one night a week, Brian puts his chef's hat on and cooks us dinner. The gaol food is pretty-good, but the authorities encourage us to be a bit independent. They want us to bind together and live as a unit. We've been able to get on okay. We've had no blues. You've come in on a good night. Brian's cooking is first class. He enjoys the opportunity to keep his hand in. The even better news is that we're one down so there are only four of us at the table.'

George could see that Brian was pleased to receive Trevor's compliment. He was obviously the quiet man in the group, preferring to speak only when he had something important to say.

'And are we expecting a fifth resident, Trevor?' George asked,
'That's hard to say. People come and go from this place.

There's no rule to it. I've been here six months. We've had an occasional five, sometimes three. The previous bloke was with us for a short time before he got sick. Poor bugger was taken away in an ambulance. We know it wasn't Brian's cooking as we're all still here,' he added with a laugh, 'but of course it's one day at a time.'

George quickly settled into a seven thirty start with breakfast and shower followed by joining the gang in the bus at nine for transport to the job. Rather than returning to the gaol, a sandwich lunch was taken with work finishing at four o'clock. His work with the outside group was giving him a daily reality check on the devastation of bushfires. It was a cruel impact on farmers who lost their fences and stock, convincing him that he wouldn't be a party to such thefts in the future.

While unloading treated pine posts and wire from the prison trailer in preparation to replace a fence, George listened as a farmer complained to the supervisor. 'I was hoping your gang would be here last week. Would you believe there are thieves in the area?'

'Sorry mate there's just so much to do,' the supervisor replied.

'They're just rotten predator bastards. What sort of a mongrel steals from farmers who have lost pretty much everything?'

George decided it might be best not to comment, leaving Trevor to agree while he moved to the worksite. Having spent much of his life working on his own, it was a new experience to find himself as part of a work crew. Trevor and he had mated up and George welcomed the opportunity to have a comfortable conversation. The developing friendship was encouraging him to discuss his family circumstances. After witnessing Trevor having a regular visit from his wife and family, George felt able to discuss his disappointment about his own lack of visitors. 'You're fortunate, Trevor, to have your family coming to visit each month. I don't think I'll have a visitor for the entire twelve months I'm here.'

'You never know George, don't drop your bundle. They might turn up.'

During the lunch break, George had an emotional moment as he considered Trevor's words. As much as he desired a visit it was a forlorn hope to expect Mary to come. However, he hoped that Will might visit, since he had shown some interest after having attended the courtroom.

Assistance in organising an estate agent to sell his home in Castle Hill would be welcomed. It was his only asset and was deteriorating without proper maintenance. The money from the sale would be vital in helping cover his legal and restitution expenses. The balance would provide an opportunity to restart his life. He knew his ability to start the process relied on Will coming and agreeing to assist, which was no certainty.

George decided to try one last attempt to reconcile with Mary and Will by writing a letter of apology. He explained his current circumstances and location. Knowing full well Mary would have no concept of a low security prison, he did his best to allay any fears she might have in visiting. Acknowledging the difficulties surrounding reconciliation, he hoped that there might at least be enough goodwill to have a meeting.

He accepted that their disappointment and anger may prevent them from visiting him in prison. As a fallback he sought permission to visit them at Roscommon Downs after his release. George's letter sparked a conversation with Trevor who noted it was addressed to Mary O'Rourke.

'I wonder if Mary is related to Les O'Rourke who I met in the transport industry. I knew him firstly as a truckie working out of Bendigo. He got elected as a union organiser. Had a good name as a bloke who got things done.'

'Look, I don't think so, Trevor. Mary is a bit short of family history. She spent her early days in an orphanage. She would have loved to have an extended family, but it was not to be. I didn't do anything to help her. I don't think I can recover the ground.'

George's disappointment continued to mount when no reply was received after ten days. While preparing for a day's work he said, 'Well I think I've got to face up to it, Trevor. They've decided that I'm not part of the family and they won't be coming.'

*

There was little sympathy stirred by George's letter. However, a family gathering was arranged at the start of a working day to consider the contents. As they sat at the kitchen table, Jim was clear in his condemnation of George. 'He just left you for dead, Mary. Ran away like a mangy dog. I never much liked the bloke when he was supposedly at his best. He disappears for more than twenty years and gets into trouble. Now he wants you and Will to do things for him while in gaol. To hell with him I reckon.'

Mary quietly responded. 'I respect your view, Jim. He certainly is expecting a lot of us to forgive and forget. Having said that, it's a bit of a running sore for us. We need to take steps to cut him out of our lives, once and for all.'

Getting to his feet and pacing the room, Jim said, 'I can see that situation. I just get angry whenever I think about him. What do you think, Will?'

Cautious to maintain peace, Will added his thoughts. 'I can see both sides of the argument. I respect your view that he ought to leave us alone. However, I also agree with Mum. He says that he'll be in Castle Hill taking steps to sell the family home. If we aren't open with him, he's just as likely to try to ambush us in town. The worst-case scenario Jim, would be him turning up on our doorstep.'

'Well let's be clear about that ending badly for him.'

'I understand that, Jim,' Will replied.

It was evident to Mary that meeting George at the farm was the worst option and would only cause division. There was a need to establish that he was not welcome now, or anytime in the future. Taking control of the meeting, Mary was in no doubt of the best path to follow.

'I suspect there's no option but for me to travel to the gaol. I'll meet George and spell out his situation with us. I can think of plenty of other things that I'd rather do. But we have to get this problem out of our lives.'

'Well Mum, if you go, I'll go with you. We can be brutally honest and impress on George exactly where he stands. In my view, we won't have any input with him regarding the sale of his house. He's written to us. He can just as easily write to one of the Castle Hill real estate agents. He doesn't need us to get things underway.'

Mary had been hoping that Will would volunteer to accompany her. It was a long trip to the gaol in northern Victoria and would require an overnight stay. She would fulfill the promise made at Barradale. While these circumstances were different, Mary knew that Will would benefit from meeting his father. Where he wanted to take the relationship in the future was his own business, and not for her to interfere. She would be quite definite with George that he had no role in her life. Not now or anytime in the future.

Life at the farm was going well. Bob had moved to take over many of Jim's duties to allow him time to invest in his de facto vet service. Will was a good worker and slotting in well. Rhon was helping Mary to take care of the house and the shearing now that Bunty had retired. Under no circumstances would George Simpson be allowed to disrupt the current arrangements at Roscommon Downs.

*

As Will parked the car mid-morning outside the regional gaol, Mary said, 'It doesn't look like a gaol, Will. More like an old country school with a farm attached. I guess if you're going to serve a sentence, this is the place to come.'

'Yes, no walls. It must operate on trust.'

'Don't prisoners run away?' Mary asked.

'Not usually. Mostly just do their time and make a fresh start.'

'I guess that's their choice.'

'Yes, the ball's in George's court.'

Mary was thankful for Will's company. Apart from the physical and mental support he provided, he'd also been prepared to drive, which saved the extra time and effort required to travel by train. After resting overnight at a local motel, they were refreshed and ready to enter the gaol. As far as Mary was concerned, this would be a difficult and final conversation.

The entrance into the official gaol area surprised them, notwithstanding they had prepared themselves for a visit to a low security prison without any real knowledge as to what to expect. A well established and maintained garden was a welcoming entrance. After an induction by a senior corrections officer of their responsibilities while on site, they were escorted to a large open plan meeting space. Will was surprised at the layout, remarking to Mary, 'Looks like one of the big halls at the showgrounds, Mum. I thought we might have to meet George talking on a telephone behind a glass screen.'

'I guess this is what's meant by low security, Will. The prisoners must be sufficiently trusted to meet in this open area sitting at a table. It's less intimidating than what we see in the movies.'

Looking around the room, Mary was struck by the quite relaxed tone of the furnishings and colour scheme. Judging by the demeanour of some of the prisoners, she suspected they were veterans of the corrections system with their visitors well versed in the regime of the gaol. From the snippets of the conversations she could hear, many prisoners were anxious about how their loved ones were coping without their presence at home.

Mary felt particularly sad for the children visiting their fathers in such circumstances. They would be bearing the burden of explaining to their friends why their father missed important family events. Mary suspected that like her, they had learnt to cope and make the best of their lives.

Her contemplation ceased when George sat down at the table. After a moment of awkwardness, it was Will who broke the silence.

'Hello George. I'm your son Will.'

George's face reddened, 'Yes Will, I know who you are. Thanks for coming all this way to be with me. It's sad we're meeting under these circumstances. But at least we're meeting, and I'm pleased about that. And thanks for coming Mary. I appreciate that you feel a lot of anger and disappointment about me. I can't undo the hurt I've done. It's something I have to live with.'

Mary looked directly at George and replied, 'George, let me be clear. I feel nothing for you. You walked out and left me for dead. I only got through because of the love and support of the people at Roscommon Downs. You passed out of my life a long time ago and you won't be coming back. I only came to tell you that you are not welcome at Roscommon Downs, either now, or anytime in the future.'

Mary could see George was taken aback by the firmness of her statement and unable to reply, he continued to sit with his hands pressed firmly on the table. Perhaps he was hoping for a warmer reception. There was no chance of that occurring. As far as she was concerned there would be no reconciliation.

As they sat silently, each contemplating their position, it was Will who spoke. 'Just understand George, my mother has had many struggles since you disappeared. She's in no mood to continue any relationship with you. But at least we've come. I've met you, but I won't be retaining any contact in the future.'

'I can understand how you feel, Will. I want you to know that I've been following your life from a distance, particularly your involvement with horse racing. I travelled to see you and Mary when your horse won that important race recently. I saw you give your mounting yard speech. I didn't have the courage to speak to you after the race. Now we meet with me in gaol.'

Will believed enough had been said and it was time for them to leave. Realising this, George decided to seek Will's support to sell his Castle Hill property. So, as they rose to their feet, he said, 'I'd appreciate your assistance Will, to sell my Castle Hill property. It's my only asset. I hope to use most of the funds to pay my bills to help start my life again. I'll probably head interstate on a shearing run. The sale will also help me make some restitution to the farmer injured during the theft. I just need someone to keep an eye on the sale. It's important that it's sold for a fair price. There's also a car and caravan that was left when I was arrested.'

'Let me think about helping you, George. If I do decide to assist, it would require you to promise you will never return to Castle Hill.'

During the trip home, Mary spoke a little more benevolently about George: chatting about her early days at the farm, she laughed in between explaining her first experience with shearing, sharing the development of their relationship during George's work around the farm, and their subsequent courtship. 'George was really the first man I loved. I'd really miss him when he was away shearing and would look forward to his return. Everything pointed to a life together at the farm. I never thought he'd run away and abandon me to have you on my own.'

'The kids at primary school used to ask me if Jim was my father.' Will said.

'No wonder! He was always there when we needed him. We should call him Saint Jim for coming to the birthing classes. I pity the families we saw back at the gaol living without their father. It makes life so difficult.'

'I understand how grateful you must feel, Mum.'

They fell silent in their contemplation of the day.

Chapter 25

A Passing

George was upset for many days following his meeting with Mary and Will. His withdrawal from any unnecessary conversation and his demeanour prompted Trevor to say, 'You've gone quiet on us mate, didn't your meeting go well?'

'No, no good. I was hoping for another visit, but not to be.'

'That's a bit rough, but there's nothing you can do about it, mate. Just have to cop it sweet.'

While George had expected a negative reception, he'd been hopeful of being able to continue communicating. A contact outside gaol could help him in many ways. But that was obviously not possible. There was no option other than to return to his work and serve his time. He'd held a hope that at least Will and he might reconcile. George could understand Mary's anger, and decided to accept her position which seemed to be final.

He resolved that he would delay the sale of his house and attend to it when released. His continuing anxiety regarding squatters would need to be addressed by writing to the Castle Hill police to request their support. As he and Trevor dug a post hole, he shared his concern. 'I don't want squatters wrecking the place. Hopefully, the police will drive past occasionally and keep their eye on it.'

'Fair enough, George. There's no reason for them not to have been doing that. The coppers won't want squatters moving in.'

George appreciated the opportunity to discuss matters with Trevor, who was really his only friend. As he used a post hole shovel to remove the dirt loosened by Trevor, he said, 'I can understand why Mary and Will don't want anything further to do with me. I'll just have to live with it and see if anything changes in the future.'

'There's really not much else you can do.' Trevor grunted as he drove his crowbar into the hole. 'This bloody shale rock halfway down the hole is beating us. Let's move the post a foot or so.'

George agreed, 'I was going to suggest that a few minutes ago.'

'Yeah, that'd be right. Bloody experts are everywhere. At least there's a good feed coming up tonight.'

'Yes, we'll miss Mark. It'll be good to give him a proper send off. He's been a good mate causing us no dramas. We hope his replacement is of the same ilk.'

As the day's work ended and Trevor started to load the tools into the back of the truck, he said, 'Who we'll get is a fair dinkum lottery, the wrong bloke can make life a bloody misery.'

During the dinner, Mark explained about his life and the pressure he put himself under to maintain a lifestyle completely above his financial capability. While in gaol he had reconnected with his family and was hopeful for his future. However, it didn't take more than a couple of days for George, Trevor and Brian to be hoping to see the back of his replacement Kevin Morris.

He was to be only with them for a few weeks. Imprisoned two years earlier, he had a release date but seemed determined to complain right up until it was time to leave. His former roommates had requested his transfer. Immediately on his arrival it quickly became obvious why he had worn out any goodwill. There was no end to his constant whining about the circumstances of his arrest, the weather, his work area and his workmates in the number plate making area. On and on it went, complaining day and night.

As they prepared for a workday, George felt the need to pull him up. 'Seriously Kevin, I can understand why the previous group wanted to kick you out. You never shut up complaining about how you got here. Face it; it's your own bloody fault. If your fool of a mate hadn't got greedy and started to sell the stolen smokes in the pub, all would have gone along okay.'

'It's easy for you to say, but it doesn't make it right.'

'Why would I be trying to make it right? How can I make it right? Really mate you're becoming a pain, constantly moaning about it. I reckon just knock it off and give us some bloody peace,' George replied.

'I warned him that undercover coppers are everywhere around the docks. It was a dopey thing to do. He'll be told when I'm out next month,' Kevin continued, shaking his head in dismay.

Pulling on his outdoor jacket, George finished the conversation. 'Well in the meantime, you've only got a couple of weeks to go, so how about you just suck it up, and give us some peace.'

Little did they know the problems that awaited them as they bid farewell to Kevin. A day or two later when returning from the outside work detail, George and Trevor were confronted by a big man with red hair and a bushy beard probably in his forties. Using an aggressive manner to try to bully and intimidate as he spoke, while sitting at the table, confirmed that he was used to getting his own way by word or fist.

'They say I've no option but to bunk with you blokes. My name is Basil, but my friends call me Baz or Boof. I can see you have your designated beds. If I don't like mine, I expect to change to one of yours.'

George could see that Trevor had taken an immediate dislike to the new arrival. Trevor was also a man prepared to stand on his dig. Stepping in close to the big man he explained, 'Let's be clear Basil, Baz or Boof. We have our designated beds and irrespective of what you want, we aren't moving. This is the wrong place to think that you can come and start throwing your weight around. You'll soon find that it'll come back to whack you quicksmart.'

To emphasize his point, Basil rose to his feet aggressively. 'Is that right? Then just be clear. If there's any whacking around here, I won't miss you mate.'

George decided to play peacemaker, notwithstanding he was of the view that the newcomer was out of line.

'Now Baz, let's see if we can all take a step back and start again. I'm George, he's Trevor, and you'll soon meet Brian when he returns from his classroom. Trevor and I are members of an outside work gang. We work hard at keeping the peace. We're committed to do our time. Best to try to do it as easily as we can. There's no point in blueing with each other.'

'Yeah, well okay,' Basil replied remaining standing as he considered his next move.

George's words seemed to calm the big man, at least to the extent that he returned to sit at the table and ponder his circumstances. After a few minutes he became very emotional and started hitting the table to emphasise his words. 'It was very wrong what happened. They made me the fall guy. You won't believe me when I say I was wrongly convicted.'

George decided to keep engaging Baz in an endeavour to keep him calm. 'Look mate, we aren't here to judge you. We understand your anger. But there's nothing we can do. You just have to do your time and then sort out the people who did you in.'

As he settled, Baz explained his role as secretary/treasurer of the local darts' club. Total administration had been left to him. The club was always short of funds, most of which was expended on day-to-day costs. The committee decided to introduce an annual invitational tournament. Added to Baz's responsibilities was the organising of the event and raising the prize money.

Basil continued. 'They put me in charge, but it got out of hand. They invited interstate players. Where were they supposed to stay? The coppers got involved when the club learned there were no funds left to cover the advertised prizemoney. They reckoned I'd stolen everything. They'd set me up to fail.'

George could feel some sympathy for Baz's situation. 'Well Baz, just understand we don't judge you. Hopefully, you can sort out your situation through the courts. No matter how they get here, blokes just try to live in peace and cause no trouble. We do our work and wait to get back to our lives.'

Brian's return to the unit also served to calm Baz who seemed to have resigned himself to his circumstances. Over the evening meal he questioned the others as he started to consider his options. 'You blokes are telling me that I can make my own mind up. If that's the case, I should be able to find something that suits me.'

Explaining that his normal trade was in sheet metal work, he reckoned that making number plates would require a minimum of effort. It was a simple choice to commit to the machine shop. In letting the others know of his decision, he said, 'I can camp there and do my time. I won't enjoy it. I'll just do what's necessary. The end will come soon enough. I can't wait to get out. I'll go and sort out the bastards that put me in here.'

*

As he was interviewed in the wrecked mess hall, Trevor, supported by Brian, explained to the homicide squad detective, it was hard to pinpoint just exactly what had set Baz off in an uncontrollable rage. 'He was a loose cannon. Always going crook about something. Would blow up at the drop of a hat. We'd keep out of his way. Wanted to blue about anything and nothing.'

Brian confirmed that they were extra cautious when Baz was waiting with them and the other prisoners for the evening meal service to start. 'After a day's work, he'd be whinging and moaning about the food. Kept saying it was crap. He wanted to be served first and would push others out of his way. Just a bloody nuisance.'

Trevor continued to explain that George and others would tell him to calm down and wait his turn. Irrespective of the circumstances, Baz never took advice when angry and hungry. On one occasion he yelled loudly that if he wasn't served immediately, he would pull his chair up and sit at the bain-marie. No amount of advice could get him to temper his behaviour. His complaining constantly brought him under the attention of the corrections' staff.

On the night in question, Baz had really lost his temper and started to shove other prisoners around. They naturally moved to retaliate with the meal queue erupting into a wild unruly brawl. As Trevor recalled, 'George was trying to help a corrections' officer who had been hit from behind and had collapsed to the floor. While bending down, he was struck a strong punch to the back of the head. When the fight stopped, we all tried to assist George, but it was too late. He was gone.'

It was unclear who had struck George. There was no doubt that Baz had started the trouble and he was facing significant charges. Trevor, who had done his best to stop the fight, mourned the loss of his mate. He explained to the police about Will and Mary's recent visit and his conversations with George after they left. 'They visited a few months ago. I don't think the meeting went well and they left on poor terms. George said that they had cut him loose with no further contact. I suspect there's no other family.'

The police response to Trevor was largely non-committal, except to the extent that the visit had been properly recorded by the gaol authorities. When leaving the gaol, their brief advice to the officer-in-charge was, 'Thanks for the assistance with our investigation. We'll meet with the late prisoner's visitors. That'll most likely complete our report to the coroner. As at this stage it appears there is no outside connection. We have a prisoner in custody to face serious charges. A court will determine his future. We'll leave it there.'

The gaol authorities offered Trevor and Brian counselling support. After consideration they decided to remain in their room and support each other. They needed quiet time to reflect on the day's events. Although their only relationship to George had been as a fellow prisoner, they had spent enough time together to form some bonds. Trevor knew he would miss working and relaxing with George during the outside work detail. As they sat at the table in their unit, he said to Brian, 'George seemed a decent bloke who made mistakes along the way.'

'Yeah, well we all have, mate.'

'That's right. It wasn't clever to shoot through from his family. But things happen. He told me he wanted to put it right.'

'He would have done that. I reckon he was more good than bad.'

'I'm sure you're right, Brian. Will meant a lot to him. He wanted to go back home and try to mend bridges.'

'I agree. But he's gone now. He was a good friend to us during his time here. Should we seek permission to attend his funeral?'

'Not for me, Brian. I'm not sure the authorities would agree. I don't go well at funerals. I'll follow up when I'm able. I might write and try to visit Castle Hill.'

*

With Mary and Bob away in Melbourne, Will took the telephone call regarding George's passing. He was thankful that Rhon was at the farm to give him support by putting all her work to one side. Will's immediate reaction was shock and disbelief. How could his father be taken so quickly after their meeting?

'I know he abandoned us,' he said to Rhon, who sat opposite him at the kitchen table. 'But he was my father. I know mum would have struggled to meet him again, but I was open to a catch up when he was released from gaol.'

Will paused as he gathered his thoughts. 'He wouldn't have been welcome here at Roscommon Downs, but we might have been able to meet in Melbourne from time to time.'

During his discussion with Rhon, Jim arrived back at the house for lunch and was told the news. After a moment or two in quiet reflection, he said, 'I've been crooked on George for years over the way he shot through and left Mary for dead. Now he's been killed in gaol. Really not good enough. Do you know what happened?'

'The police said he got punched during a brawl. They said he was trying to protect a corrections' officer when he was king hit,' Will replied.

'King hit! I thought it was low security. How does that happen?'

'I don't know, Jim. We weren't close, but he deserved better than to end his life in that way. It's all a bit difficult to reconcile.'

'I can see your point, Will. It's a sad end. I only met George a couple of times when he came to help with the shearing and to do some odd jobs. I'm certain that Mary will be shocked and upset when she receives the news of his death.'

Will rose to his feet. 'I guess I should telephone Mum and break the news. I believe that her and Bob are staying at the Rex Hotel.'

*

Will's telephone call triggered mixed emotions in Mary. Having spent a pleasant day with Bob it was the last thing she expected to be confronted with on their return to the Rex Hotel. She was pleased to have Bob in support as she couldn't deny feeling some form of anguish over the news. The visit to meet George in goal had rekindled happy memories of their lives together, irrespective of her anger towards him. And while she would have been reluctant to reconcile with George, Mary recognised that they may have grown closer should Will have looked to strengthen his relationship with his father.

As they sat on the couch in their room, Mary admitted that she was sad that George's life had ended in this way. 'It was clear from what he said at our meeting Bob, that he wanted to make a fresh start.'

'I reckon he might have. We were workmates for a number of years. He'd always put in a good day's work. Just got mixed up with a bad lot which bought him undone,' Bob replied.

'Thankfully, Will's got things in hand at home. George deserves a proper funeral. He had plenty of friends in Castle Hill in his early days.'

'Yes, he'd have footy clubmates and the like. So, he'll get a proper send off.'

*

The next few days were a blur for Will as he worked through the arrangements for George's funeral. Delays occurred when waiting for the results of an autopsy, and the preparation of a coroner's report. Taking responsibility for funeral costs was a way to give his father a respectful end to his life. Detectives involved in finalizing matters met with everyone at Roscommon Downs.

Will received correspondence from a solicitor in Carravale informing him that George had left a will and he was the named executor. Advice from Paul Steele was clear. 'There's nothing to worry about, Will. I knew George quite well. We met a couple of times at footy club socials. I suspect the provisions contained in his will are not complicated. He had a couple of older sisters who left Castle Hill many years ago and may have passed away. I suspect if there's anything of value in his estate, it'll come to you.'

Will appreciated Paul's advice and the calm way in which he always conducted himself. To assist in his representation, Will relayed further information gathered in their gaol visit. 'I know there's a family home. He was keen for us to help him sell it. I got the address and went and had a look when we returned. It's rundown as you would expect. The proceeds were important in his hope for a fresh start. He wanted to financially aid the farmer who was injured in the robbery. Mum wasn't keen to get involved. I didn't go on with the sale at the time. We'll have to attend to that and finalize whatever else is discovered. I suspect George carried a few secrets with him. It might be quite an outcome before we're finished.'

Bob Murphy volunteered to say a few words at George's funeral. 'A few of his mates will come,' he said, 'I'll keep it light and tell a few stories about when we were young blokes.'

Will was unable to find any special provisions in George's papers regarding arrangements for his funeral. A discussion with the local minister determined that a simple church service would be organised with the minister, Bob and Will to deliver eulogies. Mary and Jim to attend in support.

Bob's contribution was well received by the many people in attendance at the service. Clearly there was a time when George was respected as an honest hardworker. Will followed these words with interest being sad to think they told of a father he never really knew.

'We met for the first time in prison,' Will sadly divulged when he began to speak. 'If he'd not been detained, we might never have met. But life is life. Despite the circumstances, I was pleased to meet my father. We might have reconciled after he was released. But it was not meant to be and now no one will ever know.'

The prison chaplain was an unexpected attendee at the funeral and requested an opportunity to speak. He had spent quiet time with George discussing his circumstances and his determination to reconcile with his family.

Despite the years that had passed since his disappearance, Mary felt a burst of emotion when the chaplain said, 'We had a couple of heart-to-heart conversations. George felt really lost in his life. He told me he loved Mary but panicked when he heard she was pregnant. He wished he'd stayed and accepted his responsibilities.'

The Castle Hill minister, in his final address, thanked the many community members who were in attendance. He added that he had serviced the area for many years and had known George and his mother very well.

Carried down the aisle by his mates as the bell tolled its sad tone, George was laid to rest alongside his mother in the church graveyard.

*

The days following the funeral were a quiet time at the farm. People reflected on the circumstances of George's death and coped in their own way. Mary was deeply affected, retaining her disappointment regarding George's actions. Despite what had occurred, she harboured a lingering affection for the man who may well have become her husband. She was thankful for the strengthening of her relationship with Bob Murphy which was working to assist her at a difficult time.

While wary at first, Mary was now comfortable that Bob's only motivation was a loving relationship, and he was not a gold-digger acting with an ulterior ambition to take over the farm. Marriage had not been dismissed, with recent conversations leading her to consider accepting Bob's longstanding proposal.

As they sat on the verandah, Mary said, 'It's times like these that show the value of a relationship. You've been a tower of strength and helped me through.'

'Well, Mary, we've been together for enough time for you to be in no doubt how I feel. I'm prepared to buy a wedding ring tomorrow.'

Following a thoughtful pause Mary replied, 'Okay Bob Murphy, I accept your proposal. When things settle, we'll have our wedding here at the farm.'

Mary could see tears developing in Bob's eyes which added to her own rush of emotion. 'Look at us, having a weep like a couple of teenagers.'

'Your acceptance means so much to me, Mary. You are my world.'

Comfortable that their future together had now been sealed, Mary said, 'I can't wait to tell Rhon to get ready to be my maid-of-honour. I know she'll be delighted for us.'

'You would be hardpressed to find a better friend. She's stuck with you through thick and thin.'

*

Paul Steele confirmed at a meeting in his office that there were no surprises in the provisions of George's will. The family home and contents, money and car had been left to Will. A minor problem being that the car and caravan were still in Tocumwal where George was arrested. 'There are no extra issues, Will. All of George's money and possessions are left to you.'

'I'm not sure what it amounts to, Paul. I've seen the house, it's not in great condition. Might be better to deal with that issue first and then have one of my mates drive me to collect the car and caravan.'

Paul passed some papers across his desk for Will to sign. 'Maybe you should prepare yourself for a surprise or two. There have been a few generations of Simpsons living there, and it has been locked up while George was away shearing and in gaol. You would expect it to be in a bit of a shabby state.'

'Thanks Paul. I'll take a look inside and work my way from there. I suspect that the antique shop might be in for a trailer load or two.'

Cleaning out the solidly built now run down three-bedroom timber house was not a task Will was approaching with any enthusiasm, his preference being to sell lock, stock and barrel. However, that was not going to be possible as the house clearly needed maintenance to prove fit for sale. There was also a curiosity as to what he might find pertaining to his father and grandparents.

He suspected there would be photograph albums and personal papers he could review and keep to pass onto any future family of his own. There might also be an item or two worth retaining, and he was hopeful of coaxing his mother to visit the home. She might identify something worth keeping which could help her bring closure to the relationship.

Will's entry to the house confirmed Paul Steele's view regarding its probable condition after twenty plus years without a good clean or a lick of paint. It was not fit to be lived in. Leading Will to decide the best way to approach the clean out would be to start by removing the kitchen table and chairs, beds and lounge suite.

He was certain that if these pieces of furniture could talk, they'd have some tales to tell. A large tallboy took up much of a wall in the lounge room. Probably purchased by Will's grandfather, it had seen better days. A search of the drawers revealed two photograph albums and a large wooden box containing receipts and letters. There were also pages torn from daily newspapers and a smaller box which contained many similar looking letters.

Will put the large box to one side for a later review of the contents. A quick shuffle through some envelopes in the small box revealed that they were addressed to George's mother care of the Castle Hill post office. Thinking that odd, he noted they had a return address in Queensland.

His curiosity led him to scan a couple of letters to find they were from Claude South. Will decided he would wait until he was able to devote more time to properly take everything in, perhaps when his mother was present. A small cabinet alongside the tallboy held a cake stand, a couple of dishes, and an old tea pot that Will suspected belonged to George's mother. Perhaps treasured wedding presents.

A search of the large shed behind the house convinced Will that his grandfather was a busy handyman as it held a good stock of useful tools, sheets of iron, and a large quantity of wood off cuts and some unfinished projects. The large spanner that Ted Simpson carried during his many years of walking the tracks to tighten the bolts on the rail fish plates hung from a wall. A well-worn pair of work boots that had carried him along the way rested in the corner.

Will documented the work that needed to be done to bring the house up to scratch. And as he was leaving, he noted a small jewellery box on the dressing table in the main bedroom. A closer inspection revealed some shirt studs and cuff links together with a watch that was inscribed on the back with the words, 'presented to George to mark his twenty-first birthday.'

Will was struck by a moment of emotion. He was aware his father, when receiving the watch, would have been full of hope for his future. Sadly, he had brought himself undone in so many ways.

When Will arrived home that day, he found his mother in tears. 'Gee, Mum, from the way you spoke about George, I really wasn't expecting his death to affect you to this extent.'

'No Will,' Mary said. 'Monica has passed away peacefully this afternoon.'

Chapter 26

The Marriage

The colours of autumn produced by the old trees planted by the farm's early owners reminded Mary of her first days at Roscommon Downs. She recalled that the Flanagans had followed their example by choosing to establish many deciduous trees to complement the original landscaping. The maturity of the elder and golden ash trees had this year, like every other, ensured a magnificent display of vibrant leaf colour. It was a joy to rise early and watch the day begin.

Jim had kept a stand of Australian trees that were regularly visited by a raucous group of colourful parrots and other native birds. Now a month after Monica's funeral, Mary's life had moved to a new phase and she was busy with arrangements for her wedding.

Mary had a chuckle to herself from time to time about Rhon, who had assumed a big sister role in her life. There wasn't much that got under Rhon's guard when it came to looking out for her friend's safety. Mary was also enjoying watching the courtship of Les and Rhon which had been developing since their first meeting. Now retired, Les had become a permanent resident of Castle Hill and his frequent visits to see Rhon had made him a regular at farm dinners.

Mary had taken the opportunity to gently tease her about her close relationship with Les. 'I didn't know you like blokes with red hair, Rhon. It didn't take you long to home in on Les,' Mary laughed.

'You can't fool me, Mary. I knew exactly what was going on in your mind when you started inviting him here. A little bit of the old matchmaking instinct coming to the fore do you reckon?'

Mary tried to look as innocent as possible. 'Matchmaking? Who, me? How could you think such a thing?'

'I know you Mary O'Rourke, I know you.'

*

Will had been urging his mother to get on with her marriage. He was looking forward to walking her down the aisle before he travelled to Ireland to visit some of the horse studs and attend a few regional race meetings with Sarah. The knowledge gathered during her earlier tour would greatly assist.

They had been engaged for three years, and much family pressure was emerging. The Quinns were determined to have a big day in Killarney. Mary was also contemplating her long-awaited trip to England and Ireland and not dismissing a joint trip with Will and Sarah. 'We could travel together, Will. Now that would be something different. Mother and son honeymooning together.'

As each day passed, Mary's pride in Will was growing as she witnessed his strong consideration for his family and the local community. The Castle Hill men's group had harboured a long-term ambition to establish a men's shed. Unable to take the first step without funds, Will had solved their problem by allowing the group to set up in the Simpson shed. He also donated all the tools and materials.

'Making the shed and tools available is just a small gesture,' Will told his mother. 'Now they have a venue, it'll help them get started. Sooner or later, after the necessary maintenance is completed, I'll have the house ready for sale. When we get to that point, they'll be well organised and able to stand on their own two feet.'

It was easy to see Will's enthusiasm for the project, and Mary was aware of the many hours he'd spent re-conditioning tools and equipment. He was firm in his view that 'Depending on what the house brings, I might be able to help with a donation towards a permanent shed, and some added equipment. There's the old cordial factory in town that has been closed for many years. With the right organising committee, we might get a council grant to establish a joint men's shed and youth club.'

Mary could imagine how excited Fred and Clarry, although now quite old men, would be to help organise the shed with an involvement on the foundation committee. It was difficult for her not to have recurring thoughts of George. At least Will was putting some of the circumstances to right. He was not trying to absolve George, but to turn some of the bad into good. Given the sensitivities concerning George, Will was careful to keep advising Mary of his work and activity at the house.

'I'm not trying to turn George into a white knight,' he said. 'There's a capacity to help. It'd be a wasted opportunity if we didn't use it. I hope that I can convince you to visit the Simpson home, Mum. I reckon it holds undiscovered secrets. I'll also pick-up George's car and caravan during the weekend as Sarah's agreed to drive me to Tocumwal to collect it.'

'That's fine, Will. I'm proud of what you're doing.'

'And while it's in my mind, when we get past all of this, you might like to reconsider your reluctance to nominate for a position on the local council. You'd receive plenty of support, and a sympathetic councillor would help develop community assets like the men's shed.'

While Mary could understand Will's reasoning, she said, 'I'm not sure if I'll take the step to seek a position. My first priority has always been the farm. Although it might be possible to nominate now that you're taking on more responsibilities.'

Recommitted to writing a memoir, Mary had started to review her diaries. She appreciated that Castle Hill historian, Cynthia Rogers, had volunteered to assist. Cynthia was aware of the disappointment Mary had suffered with the former writing group. And as Mary was to discover, Cynthia and other members of the community had had similar experiences as the Carravale group worked to exclude keen writers from their clique.

While enjoying a cup of tea at Manny's, Cynthia said, 'They just made it so difficult for us to attend the library, Mary. We all had a good laugh when they lost the use of the room to the shooters' group.'

*

Bob and Mary's wedding to be conducted by the Castle Hill, Anglican Priest, was arranged to be held during a community day at the farm. In memory of Monica, Mary decided to carry the lace horseshoes that Monica had carried on her own wedding day when she married Dan.

Working as a team, Sarah and Will, Rhon and Les, created an arch laced with flowers within a circle in the garden.

As they stood admiring their handiwork, Mary and Bob arrived to thank them for their efforts. Feeling the emotion of the day Bob said, 'What wonderful work you've done to make this special place. How lucky I am to be marrying a lovely lady and become part of the Roscommon family.'

Les said, 'Now steady on Bob. Just because Rhon hasn't left my side for the past however many months, doesn't mean I'm part of the family.'

'Well, I'm prepared to make this a double wedding with my brother,' Mary said.

Bob gave Les a pat on the back. 'There you are, mate. You couldn't ask for a much better offer than that. Mary's happy. All you need to do now is convince Rhon. How do you reckon you'll go there?'

'Hang on a minute you lot,' Rhon interrupted. 'Don't I get a say in all of this?'

'Yes, you do,' Mary said. 'All you need to do is say yes.'

'But he hasn't asked me yet.'

'Come on, Les. You're going to need to lift your game,' Mary said. 'It's time to make an honest woman out of her.'

'Steady on Mary. I can make Rhon my wife. But an honest woman is a bit of a stretch,' Les replied as the group laughed and enjoyed the moment.

*

As Mary prepared, with Rhon's assistance, for her afternoon wedding, she said, 'We decided to keep it simple. I have this pink outfit I bought for a day at the races.'

'You'll look stunning Mary. You always do.'

'And what about us,' Mary said jokingly. 'A year or so ago we were talking about the need to lift our game, otherwise we'd be the two old maids of Castle Hill. Here I am getting married and it seems as though Les could sweep you off your feet at any moment.'

'I'm not sure he's sweeping me off my feet, but I must admit I like the man.'

'Just think, you could become Rhonda O'Rourke.'

'I reckon there's enough O'Rourkes around here, but we'll see what happens. I'll say one thing in his favour, he stays close. It's a good feeling to walk around Castle Hill with a good-looking bloke holding your hand.'

*

In brilliant sunshine, Mary took Will's arm. She was surprised at how nervous and excited she felt as they walked the aisle between her friends. And when Mary met Bob under the floral arch she was caught with a rush of emotion. Although not a young man, Bob stood strong and proud as they exchanged their vows.

In the lead up to the wedding, Bob had his mother's wedding ring polished up like new to pass to Mary. It was the only thing of value that had been left to him by his parents, and he was very clear when he told Mary, 'I want you to have this ring as a symbol of my love for you.'

As Bob slipped the ring on her finger, Mary could see tears in his eyes that were about to match the flood of her own. Thankfully Rhon intervened with tissues. 'This is what a good maid-of-honour prepares for.'

At the conclusion of the service the large gathering of friends rose as one with loud applause and hearty congratulations.

Champagne corks popped and Mary clutched Bob's arm as they were swept along to a marquee for afternoon tea. She was surprised and delighted at the number of friends in attendance and hopeful that Will and Rhon were keeping a list to allow her to send them a note of thanks. Mary felt especially pleased to see her dear friends from Manny's bakery. Fred and Clarry were able to attend with some assistance, but sadly, Sid had passed away.

'We miss the old bugger, Mary. He was always the joker in the group. He had a good retirement, and a restful end to it all. Wherever he is, he'll be stirring up something or other. He was a good mate.'

'I could see you were all close friends, Clarry. I'm sorry for your loss. I really appreciate you and Fred making the effort to come to our wedding. You'll always be welcome at Roscommon Downs.'

With Bob at her side as she moved among the guests, one mystery was solved for Mary. Jim had unexpectedly added, Tess Lawrence, to the guest list. Rather than approach him for clarification, Mary decided to let the invitation stand.

Taking the opportunity during the afternoon to introduce herself, she said, 'Hello Tess, I've been looking forward to meeting you. Jim has kept you hidden away.'

'No nothing like that, Mary. We have one of those long-distance relationships.'

Tess explained that Jim had been a friend since their youth in Castle Hill. She was disappointed that their long friendship had never firmed to the position of permanence. As they spoke, it became clear to Mary that Tess was the woman she had seen Jim farewelling at the Castle Hill railway station on the day she arrived.

'Even though I was born in the country, I couldn't wait to leave and experience life in the city. So, I've been a teacher in South Australia for many years and come back home whenever I get time off during the school holidays to see my elderly mother and other family members. Jim loves it here, and unlike me was never keen on city life. He wants to stay at Roscommon Downs, and this is the dilemma. We write letters and catch up from time to time on my visits. Jim's a good man and I hope on retirement, he might hook up a caravan and come my way.'

'I wish you well with that, Tess. I suspect that Jim is not the retiring type. But you never know, we might be able to put some gentle pressure on him to visit for an extended period, and that might convince him to make the relationship permanent. I'll talk to Rhon as she is a bit of an expert in organising people.'

'I'd appreciate it if you would, Mary. Jim and I could then spend a few weeks together.'

'I'll get Rhon on the job. He'll be over before you know it.'

Bob, who had patiently stood back to allow Mary the chance to talk to Jim's friend, having overheard most of the conversation, said, 'Mind you, I reckon he'll get a bit edgy after a week or two away. He's a bit of a homebody.'

'Yes, Tess,' Mary agreed. 'He stays close to home, apart from the occasional trip to the pub or saleyards. But I'm pleased you're here as we're taking the opportunity to celebrate Jim's birthday. And as all his other friends are here as well, why not? There's a chance that Bob and I might travel to Ireland later in the year, so today's the day.'

Mary's agreement to have an open house with accommodation for her city friends, encouraged the dancers from Hawthorn to join the celebration. She was thrilled that Molly Smith, now retired from the Rex, had made the journey, and took even greater delight in introducing Bob to Agnes Wright who in turn introduced Mary to a tall balding man. 'Meet my husband Reg, Mary. He said it was time he visited Castle Hill given the time I've spent here.'

'I'm pleased to meet you Reg. As you know, Agnes has been a longstanding friend of mine. She's really helped me on many occasions. I would have been lost at the deb ball without her.'

'Yes, Agnes does talk about that time she spent here with you. It must have been quite a challenge.'

'But a lot of fun training the young people, Reg. All we oldies had a great night.'

As Reg and Bob wandered off to replenish their drinks, Mary quietly remarked to Agnes, 'Reg doesn't look at all like Gregory Peck, or William Holden for that matter.'

'Perhaps, Yul Brynner,' Agnes laughed. 'We had a lot of fun during those days at the pictures, Mary. Good memories. Reg did have a full head of hair when we married, although it would be a stretch to say he looked like Gregory Peck.'

Later in the day, Mary got quite a shock when answering a knock on the door to find a smiling and sprightly Glyn Harris. 'There you are Mary O'Rourke, or should I say Mrs Murphy, the lady of the house. You haven't aged a year since I last saw you.'

'Glyn Harris, well you are a long way from home. Still the charmer and ladies man I see.'

'Many ladies in fact; I've been dancing ladies around the world.'

Glyn explained that he'd answered an advertisement for mature-aged men of friendly disposition to be employed on cruise ships as dance partners for women travelling on their own.

'Talk about join the navy and see the world. No need for me, Mary. I've had a great time doing something I love and getting paid for it. Everyone is kind and polite. I've been able to travel to many parts of the world that I would never have otherwise been able to visit. it's been good fun.'

'I'm really pleased to see you, Glyn. I must say that we were all a bit concerned when you disappeared. It's a relief that you are safe and sound. I have fond memories of our days performing as exhibition dancers. It was an exciting time of my life. Those pivots and spins when we started the modern waltz during competitions were wonderful. I really felt like I was floating.'

When it came time for Mary and Bob to leave the party for a secret overnight destination, Mary positioned herself right in front of Rhon when about to throw the bouquet over her shoulder. Wanting to ensure that her friend had a fighting chance of catching the prize, Mary knew it really wouldn't have mattered if Rhon had been standing out in the paddock. She would have rushed forward and elbowed every eligible lady out of the way.

With flowers in hand, Rhon blew her friend a kiss as Mary turned to wave goodbye.

Chapter 27

Secrets Revealed

Prior to her death, Monica had made it clear to Mary that there was to be no fuss as she knew that her health was failing. She was feeling poorly and wanted the wedding to go ahead as planned should anything happen. Her wishes were for an intimate family service and private burial which had been carried out as she had instructed.

It was a period of contrasts, with moments of great loss and sorrow amid a promise of future happiness.

Mary felt it had now come time to think about Will's desire for her to visit the Simpson home. There were obvious challenges for her in doing so. Her mindset was quite firmly against this decision as she had wanted to put all matters concerning George behind her. However, Will was insistent that she accompany him for a last look before the clean out occurred and the house was sold.

The place had no meaning for Mary. She had only visited it with George on a couple of occasions. Bob, Jim and Rhon agreed to come along for support.

The caravan was completely foreign to Mary, as it had never – to her knowledge – been in Castle Hill. A search of the van revealed little of interest. The few items found consisted of some books, several cans of beer and a small amount of cash, confirming George's minimalist lifestyle.

Jim placed everything in a box. 'This humble abode was obviously no more than simple shelter to him, Will.'

'It seems so, Jim, but there was also this small folder with some letters and papers I found earlier today. They are mainly addressed to Mum and a couple to me. The essence of my letters is to apologise for being absent during my formative years. He addressed them all but never posted them. I suspect that the letters to you Mum, are in the same vein.'

'Thanks, Will. I think I'll put them away for another day.'

When entering the house, Will suggested that there was not much of value remaining. 'Obviously, the Simpsons were people who lived very simply and didn't accumulate many possessions. With George away working, I suppose he hardly ever stayed here. But there was something that I wanted your help to sort out.'

Will brought out the small box that he'd found on his first day at the house and placed it on the kitchen table. 'I haven't had a chance to read any of these letters. They were piled together in a separate place along with a notebook. It contains a very comprehensive record of names, dates and expenses. You might recognise some of the names, Jim.' Will said as he handed the notebook to Jim. 'The letters have been posted from Queensland to Wendy Simpson, care of the Castle Hill post office. Why would they be mailed to the post office, rather than straight to this address? Perhaps we should all read a couple, and the reason might become clearer.'

A quiet time fell over the group as they started to read the letters from Claude South to Wendy Simpson. After quickly scanning a couple it was Rhon who broke the silence. 'I don't want to speak ill of anyone, but it's my view that Claude was having an affair with Wendy. His transfer to Queensland was an initial move for them to set up house there together. I bet if we keep reading, we'll find why she got cold feet and decided to stay here.'

Mary nodded in agreement. 'This letter says that she can't move to be with him, as she has unexpectedly become pregnant to Ted.'

'I wonder if we're missing the point,' Rhon said when reading on further. 'I'm beginning to think that Wendy's two girls were conceived with Claude when George's father, Ted, was away working. The pregnancy was unexpected and occurred after Claude went to live in Queensland.' Rhon leaned back in the chair and stretched her arms. 'Now that I come to think of it. there was a bit of talk at the time. I have a memory of the sisters moving up north to live when they were old enough to travel. You would have heard something about that, Jim.'

'You're right, Rhon, there were plenty of rumours about why they were leaving. I didn't take much notice, thinking it was just small town stuff not worth worrying about.'

*

During the next hour, more letters were read, which confirmed their earlier views. Will asked them all to keep the information confidential.

'At least I know my lineage, and there will be photographs that I can save of my paternal grandparents, Ted and Wendy. George's two half-sisters, if they are still alive, are now old news, and we best let their memory be. There is nothing to be gained in seeking their whereabouts. I'm happy that we've taken the opportunity of a final look through. I'll have the house cleared and finalize arrangements with the estate agent to auction the property.'

During the conversation concerning the content of the letters, Jim had been idling through the notebook which contained a comprehensive history of Wendy's work as a midwife. It was evident that she had a long history of helping families whose unwed daughters fell pregnant. 'There are many Castle Hill family names here,' Jim said. 'Including women who must have wanted to keep a pregnancy secret. It doesn't record any details about where the births occurred, or if there was a termination.'

Jim passed the notebook to Rhonda, and it was her keen eye that spotted the name, Eunice O'Rourke, in an entry dated, May 1941. Never normally stuck for words, she was unable to speak when pointing out the entry to Mary. Choked with emotion, Rhon hesitantly gave voice to the obvious. 'That would be close to your date of birth, Mary.'

Also stumbling for words, Mary replied, 'That's certainly the month and year I was left at the orphanage. Surely it would be too much of a coincidence for Eunice to be my mother. It's a long way from here to St Kilda.'

'I'm not sure I would dismiss the possibility, Mary. Wendy has listed travel and accommodation costs for the families she assisted. In respect to Eunice, there is a trip to Melbourne recorded. But no record of father's names. Wendy must have restricted her activity to assisting the girls with their pregnancies and asked no further questions.'

The group were struggling to keep their emotions together, as each of them contemplated the information. Mary wondered if this was the breakthrough to establish her parentage. While thankful for the knowledge at hand she felt disappointment regarding Wendy's reluctance to record the father's details. Letting her mind run free, she guessed that might have been part of the value of Wendy's sought-after assistance. Families knew she would not pry or be judgemental.

As a respectful silence had fallen over the group, Mary felt the need to speak. 'How can I process this? On the face of it, Eunice may have been my mother. There does seem to be a link in respect to her name, and when I was born. I'm not sure how we can confirm anything. It's going to be difficult to find people who were in Castle Hill at the time.'

Will suggested a visit to the school. 'We might have a stroke of luck and find a yearbook. Hopefully, the principal has included student photographs. It's a bit of a longshot but we haven't got much else. I'll contact the principal and see if I can make arrangements for a visit to the school library.'

'Yes, please do that, Will,' Mary replied as she took Bob's arm to leave. Pausing in the street outside the house to process the information gained in the previous hour, Mary was staggered at the turn of events. If she was conceived in Castle Hill who was her father? What would a visit to the school reveal? Taking a stronger grip on Bob's arm, Mary knew that many emotional challenges lay ahead.

*

A mixture of nervousness and excitement welled in Mary during a sleepless night as she mulled over the unexpected information that was leading to her visit to the school. Many questions were asked as she contemplated what might be found in the records.

During her many years living in Castle Hill, she had not encountered any other O'Rourkes. Les was clearly not from the area. Her thinking, given the current information, was that Eunice and her family might have moved on to escape any community criticism. She wondered how she might verify any information gathered as many years had passed. Community members of the time would now be quite old.

But despite the possibility of disappointment, she decided that she would see the school appointment through. Will was keen to follow the trail. Perhaps some good would come from it. And in Mary's favour, was the diligence of former school principal, Cedric Newton, and those before him. History of the school was a priority, leading to a dedication to keeping school records.

Pride in their research had the principal very keen to assist. While ushering Mary and Will into the library he said, 'As you requested, I've gathered all of our information regarding 1940. The yearbook is on the table. You are welcome to spend as much time as you wish working through the contents.'

1940 final year students were a class of twenty, twelve boys and eight girls. Mary, for all her caution, could see a distinct resemblance of herself in Eunice's photograph. Although the image was slightly faded, a simple front-on group shot revealed a clear likeness in her eyes and hair supported by the way she held herself. Stunned into silence Mary pulled a magnifying glass from her handbag and continued to study the photo.

'Will leaned in closer and said, 'If that's not you all over, Mum, I'll be a monkey's uncle as Jim used to say. I realise it's circumstantial, but the photograph and contents of Wendy's notebook point very strongly to this schoolgirl in the photo being your mother.'

Nodding her head in agreement, Mary said, 'It's very difficult for me to come to terms with, as I did search for a long time and now we have come across all of this by accident.'

'I know, Mum. If we allow ourselves to think it through, the best assumption is that Eunice became pregnant here in Castle Hill. Yet it could be that the O'Rourke family may have kept to themselves and lived in some backwater out in the bush. Because it seems strange that Dan and Monica never mentioned them.'

'Yes, you have a point there, Will.'

'Her family probably sent her away to wait out her last weeks of confinement at a prearranged address in Melbourne. The parents could have approached Wendy, with an understanding that she would agree to travel there to deliver the baby when the due date was near.

'You know better than me what it was like in those days, Mum. Some parents disowned their daughters in these situations. And I'm sure the mothers had no say about what happened to the baby after giving birth.'

'It would seem on the face of it that you're right, Will. I'm disappointed that better records weren't kept by the sisters. We'll never know what happened when I was left at the orphanage.'

'That's right, Mum. It was 1941 and life was anything but normal.'

'I can accept that. While tossing and turning last night it occurred to me that we might be able to locate someone among the town's older group who knew the people and circumstances of the time.'

Will was confident that the loop had been closed. Despite his opinion, he arranged for Mary and himself to visit the Castle Hill retirement village. Some old memories might be stirred by their visit. He was pleased to be supported by Rhon who agreed with the need to follow it up. Mary, 'It's the best lead you've had regarding your mother. I go there occasionally to visit some of my parents' old friends. There are a couple of oldies in their nineties who have their wits about them. You never know they might remember something.'

'Thank you, Rhon, I've thought long and hard about it and I'm committed to do exactly that.'

The aged facility had been built as an addition to the bush hospital. Known in Castle Hill as God's waiting room it had many residents needing constant care to ensure a quality of life. Will accepted the limited possibility of a successful outcome. But he was committed to do everything he could to help his mother. Using the promise of a donation to the village Christmas fund would ensure them of a warm welcome during the morning tea break.

'I've retained your privacy, Mum. I'm not sure what additional benefit this might bring. We might be fortunate and find someone who knew Eunice. The suggestion is that a morning visit is best. That's when the residents are most alert.'

Will didn't have long to wait for confirmation during their visit a day or two later. On entering the day room with Mary, one of the older residents called out to her friend, 'Look its Eunice come to visit. I haven't seen her in years.'

As he took his mother by the arm, Will said, 'Well there you are, Mum. I think you can have no further doubt about Eunice being your mother.'

Mary broke down and cried right there on the spot. 'Don't cry Eunice the old lady said. We get treated well in here.'

Will hugged his mother and reached into his pocket for a tissue.

During the drive home, Mary found herself quietly weeping as a mixture of joy and sadness swirled around her. She realised she had long felt a closeness to the Western District and could never understand why. It was her home. Those feelings continued during the evening dinner. The day's activities and the preceding events were openly discussed by Mary's Roscommon Downs' family.

It was Jim who broached the delicate subject. 'Perhaps Dan and Monica were disappointed at the community treatment of Eunice and her family. When the opportunity presented, they set out to return Mary to her rightful place.'

Rhon was first to respond. 'I believe you're right, Jim. We know the Flanagans were good people. They may have been long-term friends of the O'Rourkes. It would have been difficult to keep secrets in the small community of the day.'

'We'll never truly know if that was the circumstance of my journey to Roscommon Downs.' Mary said. 'What I do know is that the people seated around this table are my family.' She raised her glass and said, 'Here's to each, and every one of you. I love you with all my heart.'

Mary got up and left the table. She walked to the window and looked out at the garden. It was dusk and the sun was going down – the colours were tinged with gold. Just like her life. She loved this place, and she loved the people.

At last, she was truly home.

Acknowledgements

This book would not have been completed without Colleen's encouragement and support. There were many occasions during the past couple of years when I might have given up and walked away.

But a gentle prod here and there along with a couple of vigorous writing workshops kept me focused.

I am grateful for the practical advice and efficient editing of Kara Bird.

My daughter Lisa and daughter-in-law Julie provided invaluable technical support.

Special thanks to Blaise and Kev at Busybird Publishing for their professional work in the design and development of my book.

About the Author

Bill Noonan OAM

Bill Noonan OAM

Bill was born in 1942 in Yarraville, Victoria.

He and his wife Colleen have lived in Briar Hill since 1969 and have two children and four grandchildren.

Bill spent most of his working life in the Trade Union movement with his final fifteen years as Branch Secretary of the Transport Workers Union for Victoria and Tasmania, before retiring in 2009.

Roscommon Downs, although a work of fiction, draws on many of Bill's life experiences and follows his previous book 'Retirement what retirement.'

www.ingramcontent.com/pod-product-compliance
Lightning Source LLC
Chambersburg PA
CBHW020753190726
48285CB00006B/2006